11/8/77   3 Fc

THE THREE WORLDS OF JOHNNY HANDSOME

When the door had closed, Jappy said conversationally, 'What did you say you were in Fredding for?'

'Felonious stupidity. I tried to crack a niggerhead safe.'

'I didn't know any of those bastards were still around.'

Mitchell told it easily, with just the right touch of ruefulness. 'It was a factor's office, an old-time firm, and they had an old-time safe. Breaking in was a breeze, but the lousy safe . . . I hit it with a fat charge of nitro. It must have blown the whole town awake, but it hardly dented the safe. Even so, I'd have gotten away, but I blew my cool. I was so goddamn mad at that safe, I went through the offices pinching coins, bus tokens, desk sets and clocks, even half-smoked packs of cigarettes. I walked out, finally, loaded down with all that junk, and right into the arms of a cop.'

'A niggerhead safe,' Jappy said. 'They should be outlawed.'

'Past history,' Mitchell said. He waved his hand to indicate the room, the alleys below. 'You own this whole setup?'

'Didn't Johnny Handsome tell you about it?'

'He never mentioned it.'

**Also by the same author,
and available in Coronet Books:**

The Taking Of Pelham 123

The Three Worlds of Johnny Handsome

John Godey

CORONET BOOKS
Hodder Paperbacks Ltd., London

Copyright © 1972 by John Godey
First published 1973 by Hodder and
Stoughton Ltd., London
Coronet edition 1975

For Lee Wright

---

*The characters and situations in this book are
entirely imaginary and bear no relation to any real
person or actual happening.*

This book is sold subject to the condition that
it shall not, by way of trade or otherwise, be
lent, re-sold, hired out or otherwise circulated
without the publisher's prior consent in any
form of binding or cover other than that in
which this is published and without a similar
condition including this condition being
imposed on the subsequent purchaser.

Printed and bound in Great Britain for
Coronet Books, Hodder Paperbacks Ltd,
St. Paul's House, Warwick Lane,
London, EC4P 4AH
by Hunt Barnard Printing Ltd,
Aylesbury, Bucks.

ISBN 0 340 18804 9

PART I
Free World

I

Mitchell opened the door into Little Georgie's Bar and Grill, and in his first glance, knew it was probably a waste of time. But he went on toward the bar, anyway. A dozen conversations stopped in their tracks, yielding the floor to the jukebox, blaring a funky blues that rattled the gaudy glass front of the machine. He ran a gauntlet of eye-whites emplaced like mortars in black faces.

At the bar two men grudgingly gave him standing room. The bartender squared toward him watchfully, with the inevitable cloth polishing the worn wood of the bar in smooth wide circles.

'Beer, please.'

He set his valise against the rail at his feet, and straightening up, caught a glimpse of himself in the back-bar mirror: a blurry moving impression of a pale face and thick, unexpectedly gray hair looping over his brow like the plume of a helmet.

'Beer.' The bartender's voice was a neutral statement, nothing more. In his working hours, a professional barman was a shade more tolerant than the rest of mankind. Mitchell's presence was an honest mistake, and the barman undoubtedly realised it. He was small and fat, and when he turned to draw the beer, rolls of flesh ridged up on his neck. He presented the glass and asked for forty cents in his neutral voice.

Wetting his lips in the soft coolness of the foam, Mitchell

7

taxed himself with having failed to draw an obvious conclusion from his short walk on Philbin Street. It was a street on its way down, waging a stubborn but doomed rearguard action against its certain fate. At this moment in its history it was perched on a rickety fence of racial balance, but in another six months, a year, it would tilt on its fulcrum, and there was only one way it could go. The remaining white faces would disappear, in a rush, as if someone had pulled a plug, and the street would resonate to a single solid color.

He had seen this, or sensed it, but been too preoccupied to realise that reflecting to population mix, the bars would have changed too, and some of them would be all black. Black and white might be able to live together in uneasy tension, at least temporarily, but not drink together, play together; tolerance drew a puritan line.

He drank half of his beer and set the glass down on the bar. The juke gave a low-register groan and expired. Behind him, at the tables, and down the wings of the bar, conversations had resumed again, but they were muted, guarded. He was spoiling the on-the-way-home stop for these people, and he was sorry. But still, hadn't there ever been a white man in the joint since it turned black? What was he – some kind of a devil? Well yes, maybe. Some kind of devil.

He drained his glass and nodded to the bartender, who came over promptly.

'Once more?'

Mitchell shook his head. 'I'm interested in locating a man named Jappy Schroeder.'

'Come again?'

'Jappy Schroeder. Know where I could find him?'

'Is this Mr. Schroeder supposed to be a patron of this bar? Or do you mean do I know him, anyway?'

'Well, either one.'

'I don't know that name,' the bartender said precisely. 'But nor do I know all my patrons by name. Is this Mr. Schroeder by any chance a white fellow?'

Mitchell scratched his head and said, 'Would you believe it, I never noticed?'

'That'll be the day,' the bartender said flatly, but tacked on a grin. He picked up the empty glass and made an automatic swipe at the bar with his cloth. 'I don't know where you can find this Mr. Schroeder, and I have never heard of him.'

He was probably telling the truth, at least about not knowing where Jappy Schroeder might be found, but even if he was lying, it didn't matter. It was no part of Mitchell's expectations to be directed to Jappy. Nobody who knew him would be likely to do that.

'You follow Philbin four, five blocks further on south,' the bartender said, 'you more likely to find a place where somebody help you.'

'Thanks.' He left a quarter on the bar and pocketed the rest of his change. 'Good night.'

The bartender pushed his cloth. 'Would you be a police officer?'

'In no way.'

He went to the door, running the battery of silence and sidelong eye-whites, and stepped out into the street. Even before the door shut, conversation surged up like an incoming tide. He shrugged, shifted his valise to his right hand, and continued south on Philbin Street. Another place came up almost immediately, at the next corner. While he was considering it, a short black man, holding his hat on his head with his hand against the wind, pushed by him and turned into the bar. It had green curtains over the windows, and it was called Mallon's Pub. Mitchell went on. The bartender would know what he was talking about. Four, five blocks, and he would find a bar where no black would go. Though, for all he knew, Jappy, moving along with the times, might have a token spade in his organisation.

In acknowledgment of his joke, he smiled secretly in the darkness. It was a stiff unused smile that touched his lips for a moment, then winked out abruptly without an lingering trace. It was the mechanical, compartmented way an infant smiled.

Four blocks south he walked into Chitty's and struck pay dirt. It was a workingman's bar, shabby and underlit, as if some social mechanic had sought to create an environment precisely attuned to the gloomy lives of its customers. Mitchell got a few looks – more curious than hostile – for his clothes, which were new and well tailored, though he had never before given a thought to the way he had dressed. Buying them, laying out two or three times as much money as he was accustomed to, he had tried to justify the expense by arguing that it was a form of disguise. But the truth was that he had bought them simply because he liked the set and feel of the fabric.

The conversational pitch, as he walked to the bar, was rumbling and joyless. The faces, like his own, were white. He ordered a beer from a bartender with a thin hatchet of a face, a knowing face with an underlying toughness, and he thought: He's been inside, he's an ex-con. So that when the bartender put the beer down, Mitchell spoke out of the corner of his mouth, as if to establish his credentials.

'Where do I find Jappy Schroeder?'

The sharply planed face showed nothing, the muddy brown eyes were opaque. But the rhythm of the bar cloth had become ragged.

'Never heard of him, mister.'

'Funny, I would have sworn you had.'

'What made you swear that?' There was a flicker of challenge in the sharp features.

'No particular reason, except that bartenders usually have a large acquaintance.'

'If I say I don't know somebody, I don't know them.'

'You work here a long time?'

Suddenly, as if some memory of caution had stirred in him, the bartender's tone became wary. 'Are you a cop?'

For no particular reason Mitchell said, 'And if I am?'

'So if you are, I still never heard of that name.' His voice rose, sharp and needling. 'Satisfied? Are you satisfied, mister?'

A man seated three places down the bar said, 'This character giving you any trouble, Joey?' His stare was truculent.

'Wait, I'll ask him.' The bartender's smile narrowed in malice. 'Are you giving me any trouble?'

Mitchell looked at the man who had spoken. He was glaring out of a heavy flushed face, leaning far forward on his stool, his weight threatening to carry him to his feet even if his anger didn't. A wrong move now, Mitchell thought, and he would have a meaningless fight on his hands. Expressionless, he turned back to the bartender.

'No problem,' he said.

He finished his beer and put some change on the bar. The bartender swept it up and moved away. The red-faced man on the stool was muttering. Beside him another man was attempting to quiet him down. Mitchell picked up his suitcase. As he went through the door, he looked back over his shoulder. The bartender was making a telephone call. Mitchell's smile made its fleeting appearance.

Two blocks farther on he discovered that he was being tailed. Since it was too soon to attribute it to the ex-con's phone call, he must have made a bad guess about the bartender in the spade bar. Well, that made the little fat black man a first-class dissembler – which was more than he could say for the tail. He was wrapped up in a large bulky coat and a Russian hat with earmuffs, making an ungainly package out of him, so that it was impossible to guess at his general size and shape. He was working too close, considering how few people were on the street, and his technique was laughable. At the moment, with Mitchell looking back, he was pretending a show of interest in a haberdashery window. The only trouble was, the store's windows were dark.

Mitchell walked on past dingy tenement stoops and dilapi-

11

dated storefronts set below the level of the pavement. Then, quite suddenly, the street changed its character. The houses began to be taller, brick rather than wood-fronted, less in need of repair. The occasional store was at street-level and togged out with neon signs. A corner drugstore, a Rexall, was large, clean, brightly lighted, and inside, two pharmacists wearing white coats and eye-glasses were visible behind a prescription counter. The black beachhead had reached just so far and met a holding action.

The street turned, jogged to the left, and then a sign leaped out at him: blue, white and green, with a series of intersecting red X's flashing on and off, and in tall white letters, atop all that electric splendor: BEEBEE'S. BAR. COCKTAIL LOUNGE. PIANIST. BEEBEE'S. He walked on into the rainbow glow of the sign, but before going in, looking behind him. The tail was half a block back and moving too quickly. He stopped abruptly and bent to the dark sidewalk, weaving from side to side as if searching for something he might have dropped. At this distance, there was something faintly familiar about him. Mitchell tried to place him, failed, and shrugged. Whoever he was, he was a dunce. He opened a paneled door and went into Beebee's.

It had nothing at all in common with the two previous joints. There was a lot of chrome, flash, dimmed lights, noise, figures moving anticly. The crowd was young and on the make and well dressed. Mitchell had no wories about fancy threads here. The men were a riot of double-breasted suits, bright wide ties, buckled and beribboned shoes, striped and colored shirts. And there were girls. He hadn't seen more than one or two women in the previous places. Here they were numerous and animated, elaborately dressed, fancily coiffed, with lots of leg and thigh on display, and soft young breasts flowing over the edges of low-cut gowns.

The bar was packed, but he found a few inches of space beside a boldly pretty dark-haired girl in a lime-green dress who was angrily trying to outshout her companion. Two men were working the bar, and they were moving fast to keep up with demand. If there was any beer being served, he didn't see it. Martini seemed to be the popular choice, with Scotch a lagging second. The younger of the two bartenders came over. He was prematurely bald but heavily sideburned, and he wore a glittering blue diamond ring on his left hand.

' 'll it be?'

'Scotch.' He named a brand and watched the young bartender whirl around and pluck the bottle from the back bar. 'And water.'

The bartender poured with style, from a height of a foot above the glass, finishing with a deft flip of the wrist that brought the flow to a stop. 'Dollarnaquarter.'

Mitchell took his time with his wallet, and the bartender drummed his fingers lightly on the wood. Mitchel held a five-dollar bill out, then pulled it back, leaving the bartender's fingers twitching on empty air.

'Where can I find Jappy Schroeder?'

'Jappy Schroeder? Well, he's – ' He cut himself off abruptly. 'I don't know. I mean, I don't know any Jappy Schroeder.'

'Not Schroeder, Jappy *Schreiber.*'

'No, *Schroed –* '

Mitchell laughed, and gave up the bill. The bartender went off in a half-run, bouncing on the slatted floorboards. He had six inches on the older bartender, and stooped awkwardly to whisper in his partner's ear. Listening, the older man glanced down the bar toward Mitchell, just once and then not again. He sent the young man off, out of sight, and then began to work his way down the bar, without hurry, moving solidly, not putting any strain on the boardwalk. The younger one, Mitchell thought, would already be making his phone call to Jappy. It would be the second, possibly the third, such call Jappy had received in the last half-hour, and he might be getting a little bored by now.

13

To Mitchell's left, the argument had escalated. The girl in the green dress and her friend, a broad-faced handsome young man wearing a pearl-gray suit and a hot pink shirt, were nose to nose, whispering insults at each other in hoarse passion. The girl's vocabulary was a fair match for the man's. As Mitchell watched, the man raised his hand, palm open, and started it toward the girl's face. She bobbed backward in reflex and jarred Mitchell's arm. A drop or two of his drink sloshed over the rim of his glass.

'Oh, excuse me.' She had violet eyes in a wide peasant face, a flushed complexion glowing with health or anger, and firm young breasts that billowed creamily over the cut of her dress. 'I hope I didn't make you wet?'

He shook his head and gave her his brief smile. She smiled back, and in the same instant forgot all about him, turning again to her companion, her soft neck flushing with a renewal of anger.

She said accusingly, 'You made me wet that feller, you shit-eating Polack.'

'Sooner or later I'm gonna *really* belt you, you lousy Polack tramp.'

The bartender stood in front of Mitchell. 'Want me to freshen that for you?' He had a lined face and squinted blue eyes, and he could have been an old sailor.

A little bored with the litany himself by now, Mitchell said, 'I'm trying to locate Jappy Schroeder.'

'You a friend of his?'

'Friend of a friend.'

At the far end of the bar the young bartender had re-appeared and was making a self-conscious show of avoiding looking in their direction.

The bar cloth was moving in a slow circle. 'You wouldn't happen to be a police officer?'

'Would a friend of Jappy's have a friend who was a cop?'

'What's this friend of Jappy's name?' the bartender said.

'I forget,' Mitchell said. 'Look, let's stop making such a

14

big deal out of it. Can you put me in touch with him or not?'

'It's possible,' the bartender said calmly. 'Only I don't know how to reach him this very minute.' He took a pad and a stub of pencil from his apron pocket. 'In case I hear from him, leave your name and where he can get hold of you. Okay?'

'Okay.' He pulled the pad to him and wrote *J. Mitchell* and then paused. 'What's a decent hotel in town?'

'Depends on what you call decent. Philbin Arms ain't bad. Three blocks straight ahead south.'

Mitchell nodded and wrote *Philbin Arms Hotel. Urgent.*

While the bartender studied the message, Mitchell looked at the quarreling couple. They had made up or something, and were exchanging tiny hard kisses, pecking at each other like snappish chickens.

'Okay,' the bartender said, slipping the pad back in his apron pocket. 'I'll pass the word along.'

'Your partner forgot to bring back the change from a five-dollar bill in his excitement,' Mitchell said. 'Take it away from him and keep it.'

'I'll do that,' the bartender said. 'See you.'

Mitchell picked up his valise and went out. The street seemed unnaturally quiet after the tensed-up boozy din of Beebee's, until the sudden machine-gun splat of a revved-up motorcycle redressed the balance. He paused to light a cigarette – with that guilty twinge about smoking tailor-mades that he still hadn't shaken off completely – turning his back to the stiff wind blowing from the south and peering over the flaring match in his cupped hands. The tail was parked in the black shadow cast by a high stoop, so still that he might have been asleep. Mitchell considered walking back to him and nudging him awake, just for laughs. But it would have been a pointless grandstand play. He picked up his bag and moved on.

The street darkened again beyond Beebee's fling of neon

brightness. Just ahead, a building was missing, like a gap in an unattractive but nevertheless serviceable set of teeth. The wreckers had been and gone, and a bulldozer had come in after them and leveled the remains after a fashion, creating a flat rubble that was more desolate and dehumanised than the discarded bathtubs, wrecked picture frames and sagging burnt-out chairs it had replaced. The blankness stretched out in brooding darkness, like the landscape of a bad dream. He stood looking at it for a long time, trying to place what it reminded him of. It came to him. It reminded him of his life.

He heard footsteps and turned. Someone was running toward him. The tail discreetly pulled to one side to give him room as he went by.

The runner raised his arm and shouted. 'Hey, I wanta see you.'

Mitchell waited. The runner slowed to a walk and approached warily. It was the young man in the pearl-gray suit, the one who had been fighting with the girl in the green dress. He had dark brown hair covering half his forehead in bangs and carefully designed sideburns that came down an inch below his earlobes.

'I wanta see you,' he said again.

'Okay.'

'I hear you been . . . ' He stopped and took a gulp of air. 'You been asking certain questions about Jappy Schroeder.' His tone was meant to be forceful, but his hard breathing chopped it up and the effect failed.

'Not questions, just where he can be found. You're out of condition.'

The young man suddenly became aware of the chill wind. He turned the collar of his jacket up and hunched his shoulders. 'Let me give you some advice, buddy. It's unhealthy going around asking questions about certain people.'

Mitchell studied the young man's face. It was youthful and handsome but lumpy, tough. Under close scrutiny, the in-

16

nocence the bangs conferred upon it vanished. It was a
face that went with his bulk — a heavy chest and powerful
arms and shoulders.

'I take it you know Jappy?' Mitchell said mildly. 'Then
maybe you can tell me where he is.'

'I ain't telling you *nothing*. You want to be smart? Just
take off and stop asking questions about Jappy Shroeder.'

The young man poked him in the chest with his finger
for emphasis, and the touch unaccountably enraged him.
He balled his free hand into a fist, but opened it again at
once. He was getting edgy. Bad. He took a deep drag at his
cigarette and simmered down. He spoke quietly.

'You didn't talk to Jappy. The bartender passed the word
along that I was asking for him.'

'Don't be so smart. Don't try to tell me who told me something.'

'Because if Jappy spoke to you, he would want to know
who I was and what I wanted, and he wouldn't have instructed you to tell me to take off.'

The young man's eyes narrowed. 'You some kind of a cop?
Because fuzz don't scare me. I tell you to your face, I hate
their guts and they don't mean nothing to me.'

'Would a cop go around openly, asking where he could
locate Jappy? Especially in a neighborhood where he knew
the bars were filled with characters who would get the word
to Jappy quick?'

'How do I know what a cop would do? I hate their rotten
guts.'

The young man was stupid, and Mitchell was suddenly
weary of him. 'You and your buddy there.' He hitched his
head in a gesture beyond the young man's head. 'Some tail.
Jappy must be hard up for hired help. Between you and that
one, he's scraping the bottom of the barrel.'

'What kind of tail — ' He started to turn, then stiffened,
and his pudgy cheeks bunched up around his narrowed eyes.

'You trying to get me to look behind so you can jump me? You don't sucker *me,* Jack.'

Over the young man's shoulder the street was empty. Either the tail had learned how to conceal himself or he had given up the whole thing as a bad job.

'What's this bottom-of-the-barrel crack?' The young man's face darkened. 'I'll tell you something, Jack, I don't know who you are, but you better get a civil tongue on you.' His finger extended again, reaching for Mitchell's chest.

Mitchell moved back, just enough so that the finger pointed at air. He was trembling. 'Look,' he said. 'Look. Have you got a gun on you?'

'What's it to you, have I got a gun? What kind of weirdo question is that?'

'Because if you haven't got a gun, and can't get it out fast, and aren't sure you'll use it . . . then you better not touch me again. Because the next time you touch me, I'm going to bust you up.'

The finger quivered in the air, but it didn't move forward. The young man tried a smile. 'I mean, you're sure you can do that? I mean, you're some kind of a terrific muscle?'

'I mean bust you up so that you have to go to a hospital. For about two or three weeks, and eat out of a straw and shit in a pan.'

'I mean,' the young man said, 'I mean you are very tough, and I'm scared shitless.'

'You want to try me?'

He spoke very quietly, but it was a quietness just barely this side of blind rage. The young man sensed it. Sensed it and judged it and let his finger make the decision. Slowly, as if counterweighted, it lowered to his side.

'Some other time,' the young man said stiffly. 'I happen to have a young lady waiting inside for me.'

'Okay.' Mitchell was still trembling, but the fire was damping down now and he began to be angry with himself. 'Okay. Okay.'

Over the young man's shoulder he saw the door of Beebee's open up a square of light and admit a man, who went inside, hurrying.

He shifted his grip on his suitcase. 'Don't keep your girl waiting.'

The young man looked baffled. 'I ain't through talking to you yet.'

'You haven't got anything to say to me.'

The door to Beebee's opened, and a man came out. Mitchell recognised him as the man who had hurried in a moment ago. He started toward them, walking purposefully.

Mitchell said, 'That makes four of you. The first one began to tail me when the spade made his phone call. There'll be one waiting for me in the lobby of the Philbin Arms, after the sailor phoned my address in – '

'How did you know his name was Sailor?'

'And there's you, but you just happened to be in Beebee's, and now there's this one, who got the call from the ex-con in Chitty's, and just checked in with Sailor . . . ' A shape loomed up behind the young man. 'And I think he'll be taking over from here on in.'

He was wearing an open topcoat that sailed out to the wind, and a Tyrolean hat with a small brush growing out of the band. He was about the same height as the young man but wider across the shoulders and heavier through the trunk. Mitchell guessed that the newcomer was probably as tough as the young man thought himself to be and tried to be.

'Is this the fella, Tully?'

The young man was surprised. 'Battler? How'd *you* get here?'

Battler looked past him at Mitchell. His gazed contained no hostility or even curiosity, it was simply appraising, and even that in a very limited sense. He was assessing the man he looked at as a possible opponent and figuring on how to take him – not whether or not he *could*, but *how*, a matter

19

of technique. His skin was thick and coarse, and his eyes were black beneath seamed, papery lids. His nose was flat, tipped to the left from a battered bridge.

'I hear you want to meet Jappy Schroeder, mister?' His voice was muffled, hoarse, but not to much so; just enough, Mitchell thought, to put the clincher to the fact that he was an old fighter.

Mitchell nodded, and Tully jumped in. 'He got himself made as a very tough feller, Battler. Maybe we could show him who's tough?'

Battler ignored him. 'You wanta tell me what you wanta see Jappy about?'

Mitchell shook his head. 'It's a private matter.' He picked up his suitcase. 'Okay? Do we go?'

Battler nodded. 'I got my car parked down the street.' He turned to Tully. 'You wanta come along?'

'Sure, I like to come. I'll have to pick up Sunny in the bar.'

'Okay. We'll stop off at the Philbin Arms and pick up Bobby.'

'Bobby,' Tully said. 'He *said* there would be somebody at the hotel. Who told him?'

Battler said, 'Listen, mister, I got to do something.' He made a gun out of his hand and waggled his forefinger. 'You know? Just to make sure?'

'Sure.' Mitchell put the suitcase down and held his hands out at shoulder height.

Battler patted him expertly and quickly. 'Clean,' he said. As if to cancel out the indignity of the frisking, he picked up the suitcase and handed it to Mitchell. 'Let's go to Jappy.'

'How about the tail?' Mitchell said. 'Aren't you going to take along the tail?'

Battler looked blank. 'Nobody was tailing you. There's just me here, and Bobby at the hotel.' He turned to Tully. 'Was you tailing him?'

'No. I told you, I was in Beebee's, and Sailor passed the

word somebody was asking for Jappy, so I came out to see.'

'There wasn't nobody tailing you,' Battler said. Then suspicion narrowed his eyes. 'Listen – are you hot?'

Mitchell shook his head. 'Maybe I was mistaken.'

'He tried to *show* me the tail,' Tully said.

'Did you see one?'

'I didn't look. I thought he was trying to sucker me.'

'Maybe I just imagined it,' Mitchell said. 'It might have just been some bum trying to get up nerve to brace me for a handout.'

'Jappy got nobody who looks like a bum,' Battler said.

As they walked back toward Beebee's the door opened and the girl in the green dress came out.

'You got a hell of a lot of nerve, you bastard,' she said to Tully. 'Leaving me sitting there alone at the bar.'

'Shut up,' Tully said. 'Go inside and get our coats, we're going to Jappy.'

'Jappy! You promised we would go out on the town, you cheap bum –' She flinched as Tully raised his fist. 'Go ahead, hit me, you lousy shit!'

Battler stepped between them. 'We ain't got all night. Go inside and get your coats, the both of you. We'll meet you at the car.'

He nodded to Mitchell and they walked half a block to the car. It was a big Chrysler sedan, and it was parked beside a fire hydrant. They stood beside it silently and waited. The door to Beebee's opened and Tully and the girl came out, shrugging into their coats.

'I wish they would stop pissing on each other,' Battler said. 'It's boring. You know what I mean?'

They came up, not speaking but glaring at each other. Battler opened the rear door and the girl ducked in. But when Tully started to follow she put her hand out and pushed him back. He swore at her.

'Now what?' Battler said.

'I rather have the other guy sitting next to me than that

freaked-out chiseler.' She patted the seat beside her. 'Come on, honey, sit next to Sunny.'

'You bitch,' Tully said, lunging at her.

Battler pulled him back. 'It don't make any difference. Stop pissing on each other, chrissake.' He nodded to Mitchell. 'You get in, mister.'

Mitchell shrugged. The girl shifted to the far end of the seat and he got in beside her. Battler pushed Tully in and shut the door, then went around to the front seat. The car started with a powerful purr and shot away from the curb. The interior of the car was flooded with the overpowering fragrance of the girl's perfume.

She pressed her thigh against Mitchell's. 'What's your name, honey?'

'Shut up,' Mitchell said.

2

The Philbin Arms was a relict of another time. It was a small city hotel of quality that had remained in place after the city grew and shifted its social center elsewhere. It was well kept, by someone whose pride was probably ancestral, and certainly without economic justification. So, although all around it the city had surrendered to deep-running tides, or moved away, the Philbin Hotel had held its ground. No well-to-do visitor – excepting a few sentimental commercial travelers – would stop there now. But the hotel maintained itself serene and little changed: a quaint ten-story building faced with stone, its steps and sidewalks scrubbed down every morning, the fluted pillars of its entry chipped but invincibly clean, the graffiti patiently washed away with caustic cleanser.

The stop at the hotel took less than a minute. Battler sent Tully inside. The boy bounded up the graceful steps between the large, bright globes set on scrollwork posts, and disappeared into the marble-floored lobby. The man who came out with him a moment later was wearing a wraparound coat of some synthetic fur, and his thick, carefully combed hair glistened in the spread of light from the globes. He got into the front seat, and the car pulled away.

'Hello, Bobby,' Mitchell said. 'How come you have more hair than you had six years ago?'

Bobby turned in the seat and looked back, blinking. 'You know my name?'

'He heard us say it,' Battler said. Then his head turned briefly to Bobby. 'What's this six years ago? You know this feller?'

Bobby peered into the back of the car. 'Never saw him.'

Mitchell flashed his sudden smile. 'Six years ago you weren't wearing a rug.'

'It's my own hair,' Bobby said. Tully guffawed. Bobby said, 'You want to lose some teeth, Tully?' But puzzlement diluted his anger, and he turned to Battler. 'Who is this wise-ass feller?'

Battler shrugged, and whipped the wheel effortlessly, sweeping by a green bus with a horizontal stripe listing a series of suburban towns. Further on, he eased into a four-lane highway. It had a center mall and was lined with gas stations, ice cream stands, and an apparently limitless number of discount furniture stores.

'Maybe he saw your picture someplace,' Sunny said. She giggled. 'Maybe in a post office, an old picture like, without the rug?'

'Nobody asked *you* to open your mouth,' Bobby said.

'Frig yourself,' Sunny said.

Tully snapped at her and she snapped back, and they started to shout at each other, leaning forward to by-pass Mitchell. Battler showed his profile, knotted grimly. 'Knock it off!'

They exchanged parting insults, then subsided, glaring. Satisfied, Battler gave full attention to his driving. He edged into the left lane, and accelerating smoothly, slid by three cars in the right lane, rode up to the bumper of a fourth car, and stayed there until it got the message and edged over to the right. It was very competent driving, Mitchell thought – no, better than that; it was professional driving.

Bobby was still troubled. Addressing Battler's profile, he said, 'You know this joker?'

'We're going to find out. All I know is he was asking around about Jappy.'

24

'I never saw him before.' He faced the rear, his dark face lowering with suspicion. 'Did somebody tell him I was wearing a hairpiece?'

'Nobody told him,' Battler said.

'Then how did he know?'

Battler shrugged. 'Ask him.'

'You know me, wise-ass?' Bobby said.

'Sure,' Mitchell said. 'Your name is Roberto Mendoza, you're of Portuguese descent, you were born back East in Providence, Rhode Island, your old man disappeared before you were born, your old lady got stoned and drowned in a ditch one rainy night when you were fourteen, you were a shoeshine boy around the courthouse in Providence, you got caught boosting radio sets when you were fifteen, you got sent to the work farm –'

'Jesus!' Bobby said breathily.

'You want me to continue?'

'You already said too much. I like to know how you know that stuff. I really like to know.'

'He's a stinking cop,' Tully said.

'No gun,' Battler said. 'No gun, no cop. Anyway, he takes chances no cop with all his marbles would take.'

'Even if he is a cop, he got nothing on me,' Bobby said. 'I'm clean, straight as an arrow.'

He had pulled a grandstand play, after all, Mitchell thought, and all it had accomplished was the creation of another element of tension. It had been unnecessary, pointless. Still, he thought dryly, taking note of the air of bafflement in the car, everybody loves a mystery, don't they?

Battler said patiently, 'Also, a cop wouldn't have to go around to joints trying to locate Jappy. The cops know where he lives. Here we are.'

He moved over to the right lane and continued his glide at a softly braked angle into a large parking area. Several dozen cars were clustered in front of a long low building, brightly spotlighted. On the roof, running almost the entire length, a glowing blue neon sign read. PIN 'N WHISTLE. BOWLING COCKTAIL LOUNGE DINING; and beneath, in red letters: *A Rendezvous for the Entire Family.* The building was new, finished in an imitation knotty pine, and the rustic design was reinforced by a post-and-rail fence, a deep overhang of the roof, and black false shutters beside the windows. The entrance was decorated with a plaster adaptation of the American flag curved over the doorway, ruffled and ruched so that the stars bunched up on each other, the stripes ran in hilly bulges. It all struck Mitchell as highly respectable and equally highly predictable; you could find the same thing repeated, give or take a detail, a thousand times or more, over the whole country.

Battler pulled the car around to the right side of the building. He stopped for a link chain drawn across the road, with a sign hanging from it: NO ADMITTANCE, EMPLOYEES ONLY. Bobby got out and unhooked the chain, and after Battler drove through, hooked it again and got back in the car. Battler went around to the back of the building and parked beside a small rectangular stockade of factory-weathered paling. The headlights picked out neatly covered garbage cans and an assortment of mops and brooms. Deeper in, there was a kitchen, brightly lit. When they got out of the car they could hear the rattle of crockery, and a ventilator fan blew out a pervasive smell of fry cookery. To the left of the stockade an exterior staircase of black metal climbed upward to a wooden door.

They went up the steps in pairs, with Battler bringing up the rear, whether by coincidence or as a precaution, Mitchell couldn't tell. Bobby knocked at the door with three sharp, deliberate raps of his knuckles. An automatic release buzzed. Bobby opened the door and they filed in. The room was large, and furnished inexpensively as an office with a large desk, a chrome sofa and chairs, a small safe, a filing cabinet. There were no windows to the outside, but on the far wall a shoulder-high pane ran the width of the room, looking down on the alleys below.

As Mitchell took a step toward the man who was sitting on the edge of the desk, it occurred to him that any stranger, given his nickname, would have no difficulty picking Jappy Schroeder out of a crowd. He studied him briefly and dispassionately: the broad bland face, the upward fold of the eyelids, the dark almond eyes, the yellowish tone of the skin. Above all, the air of something withheld or concealed, the classic poker face, which was never so inscrutable as when it put its smile on display.

Mitchell said, 'Hello, Jappy, nice to see you,' and found that he was listening critically to the sound of his own voice. It was all right. At least he thought it was all right, that it was technically perfect, that it didn't seem to be concealing something.

Jappy said. 'We ever met?'

'Not until a half-minute ago.'

Jappy said, 'Ah-hah,' and stared at him.

He stared back, forcing himself to challenge Jappy's stare, to dare it to do its worst. Jappy broke the deadlock; his eyes wandered. Mitchell relaxed. He felt fine. His panic was over.

He said, 'You sent the whole army out after me, and they surrounded me and brought me in.'

'Stop standin around, ferchrissake,' Jappy said. 'Everybody sit down.'

He waited until they all took seats, his foot swinging slightly, thumping the desk each time it rebounded from its outward kick. Mitchell remained standing, a distance of six feet from Jappy, keeping his gaze fixed on those long, slightly veiled eyes.

'Okay,' Jappy's foot became motionless. 'What's the story, mister?'

Mitchell became aware of a rumbling sound vaguely sourced in the floor beneath his feet. He listened, and heard a muffled clatter followed by what might have been a distant chorus of human voices. The glass window vibrated to the sound.

Tully tilted his chin to the invisible alleys below. 'Some dumb broad must of lucked a strike.'

'I wanted to meet you,' Mitchell said.

'Why all the fancy footwork? Why not look me up in the book and use the telephone?'

'You'd have turned me down. This way, I was sure of getting to see you.'

'Okay,' Jappy said. 'You see me.'

Tully said, 'He's a cop, Jappy.'

'He's got a whole goddamn dosser on me,' Bobby said. He was half out of his seat, in a guarded crouch. 'Stuff you wouldn't imagine – like how my old lady died.'

'A cop wouldn't have no old information like that,' Battler said. 'Besides, he got no gun.'

'Maybe it's in his suitcase,' Tully said.

Battler laughed hoarsely. 'The day I have to worry about somebody beating me by pulling a gun out of a suitcase, that's the day I retire.'

Jappy watched each speaker from under the black wings of his brows, his head immobile, his narrow eyes moving in quick sidelong glances.

Bobby began to subside into his seat, then jumped up again. 'A cop might not know about my old lady, but a parole officer sure as hell might.'

Jappy smiled, large teeth cramping the space between his lips. 'You been cozy with Bobby's parole officer, mister?'

'On which fall?'

'It's no goddamn joke,' Bobby said. 'He knew about my rug, too, and nobody has ever seen me without it in six years. Not even a chick.'

Sunny said, 'I'll bet *I'd* get you to show me your bare scalp.' Her voice was bantering, but with an undertone of sexuality.

'*I'll* show you something,' Tully said. 'I'll show you a set

28

of knuckles if you don't close your goddamn mouth.'

Jappy kicked his heel sharply against the desk. He said to Mitchell, 'You went to a lot of trouble to get yourself brought here, mister. Are you going to start telling us why?'

'Sure,' Mitchell said. 'It's just that I'm still trying to get used to the fact that you've got a whole new bunch here — with the exception of Bobby Mendoza.'

Jappy gave his cramped Japanese smile. 'This is interesting. Now you know exactly how long I know my friends? Go ahead. Be interesting some more.'

'Well,' Mitchell said, 'I guess I should have figured that there would be some attrition. For example, Harry Jackson is gone — probably racked himself up in a car one night when he was shooting speed. Eddie Murry? I don't know . . . Maybe some trouble with a woman, and her husband cut his throat?'

'Shot the hell out of him,' Bobby said. 'Jesus, this joker knows all the answers.'

Jappy's foot was frozen stiffly in mid-swing. 'That's enough laughs, mister. What's on your mind?'

'Sorry,' Mitchell said. 'Just a little fun. Okay. I happened to get to know one of your guys, and he did some talking.'

Jappy said cautiously, 'One of my guys? Is that right? Well, how come he talked so much?'

'He liked talking, I guess.'

'Where did you know this so-called friend of mine?'

'Fredding.'

'The state pen? What would one of my friends be in the state pen for?'

'For being a thief,' Mitchell said.

'How about you? Were you up there on a social visit or something?'

'I was an inmate,' Mitchell said. 'I'm a thief, too.'

Tully said, 'Jappy, it goes against my grain to even be in the same room with a thief. Can I leave?'

Battler said thoughtfully, 'But I wouldn't put it past a

29

character with a record to pack his gun in a suitcase. Especially if he expected to get frisked.'

'Don't buy it,' Tully said with sudden urgency. 'He could be an undercover cop trying to infiltrate –'

'Undercover cop,' Jappy said. 'Shit. You're reading too many dumb paper books. They don't waste undercover cops on small-time crooks, they can't afford it.' His voice became bitter. 'You have to be real important to rate a spy cop, like a gang of revolutionary kids, say. For small-time crooks they just use small-time cops. You better give up those lousy books.'

Mitchell listened to the rumble and muted clatter of ball and pins.

'What's your name?' Jappy said.

'Mitchell.'

'That's the whole thing?'

'John. But they call me Mitchell.'

'Okay, Mitchell. Do you happen to remember the name of this friend of mine you knew at the state prison?'

'Johnny Handsome.'

Whatever the reaction of the others might have been, Mitchell was interested only in Jappy's. But Jappy's face was expressionless, as he had guessed it would be. Nothing would deepen Jappy's impassivity as much as a surprise. It was a carefully prepared defense, and it would toughen in proportion to the strength of what it must defend against. So that when, finally, he allowed a look of mild surprise to arch his black eyebrows, Mitchell knew that it was an act, that Jappy had already absorbed the shock and was putting on a performance. But he couldn't or didn't bother to carry it over into his voice, which, when he spoke, was as flat and uninfected as always.

'Johnny Handsome. How about that? It's a small world. But I never knew Johnny Handsome was such a talkative fellow. Right, Bobby?'

'Telling about my old lady,' Bobby said, agrieved. 'That's really talking out of turn about something sacred.'

'She's dead, and it can't hurt her,' Jappy said. 'Keep quiet about your old lady already.'

'As long as he was respectful,' Mitchell said gravely. 'He was very respectful even when he was talking about the ditch she drowned in.'

'Did he bad-mouth us?' Bobby said. 'You know, he was sore – '

'He was too nice a fellow to bad-mouth anybody,' Jappy said, his gravity matching Mitchell's. 'But the gabbiness, that's a new wrinkle.'

'We were cell partners,' Mitchell said. 'So is was a natural enough thing to do. If you get along with your cell partner, you usually unload. I did the same with him, after all.'

Jappy was looking over him carefully, critically, and Mitchell met his eye unconcernedly. 'I wouldn't have taken you for an ex-convict,' Jappy said. 'You don't have the look. You know what I mean by the look?'

'Thanks. I did just short of five. I've been out in the free world a little over a year. They're never going to get me back in there again, either.'

'I heard the that same thing before,' Jappy said, grunting. 'On parole?'

'Finished. I'm a free man.'

'Have a job inside?'

'I was a dentist.'

'You're a goddamn dentist?' Tully said.

'Helped the prison dentist,' Jappy said. 'You got to forgive the boy. He hasn't done time – yet.'

'That'll be the day,' Tully said. 'You'll never see *me* in a jail.'

Jappy said to Mitchell, 'What were you in for?'

'Robbery,' Mitchell said, and added dryly, 'I was framed.'

'Naturally. I never knew anybody who wasn't. Johnny Handsome, too? I imagine he told a thing or two?'

31

'Johnny Handsome,' Jappy said dreamily. Then he frowned. 'I hear tell he's doing bad time.'

'No. He's doing good time. The very best.'

Bobby started to say something, but Jappy cut him short with an abrupt downward slash of his palm. 'I'm glad to hear that,' he said to Mitchell. 'When is he coming out?'

'He's out.'

'You don't say?' Jappy's eyes were fixed on his swinging foot. 'When did that happen?'

'Couple of months ago. Feet first.'

'I'm sure as hell sorry to hear about that.' The room was tense with the silence of held breath. 'He get beat up in a prison fight?'

'Cancer,' Mitchell said. 'He got out of prison a while back, and went out to the Coast. I hear he died in a city hospital out there.' His smile winked on and off. 'But you knew all that, right?'

'The old cankro,' Jappy said. 'Well, he'll be the homeliest man in the graveyard.' He paid no attention to Tully's raucous laughter. 'Still, you didn't come all the way here just to tell me Johnnie Handsome copped it with a case of the old cankro?'

Mitchell shook his head. 'I'm interested in doing a little work with you.'

'All full up.' Jappy permitted his features to express regret. 'I'm sorry, there's nothing open.'

'I can see you're already staffed, and with some wonderful people. But I wasn't exactly looking for a job. Actually, what I want to do is bring in a new account.'

'I certainly hope you aren't suggesting work of a criminal nature,' Jappy said. 'I don't deal in that kind of work any more.' He considered is words. 'In fact, I never did.'

'As one honest man to another, I assure you the account I have in mind is perfectly respectable.'

'Still, you did do time in penitentiary.'

'I've paid my debt to society,' Mitchell said. 'Besides, I was framed.'

Jappy tired of the game. 'All right, soldier, what's on your mind?'

'Can we talk in private?'

Jappy seemed to weight the question, then nodded and said, 'Why not?'

3

Mitchell watched them file out through the door at the left, and caught a glimpse of a standardly furnished living room, including the great blank face of a television set.

When the door had closed, Jappy said conversationally, 'What did you say you were in Fredding for?'

'Felonious stupidity. I tried to crack a niggerhead safe.'

'I didn't know any of those bastards were still around.'

Mitchell told it easily, with just the right touch of ruefulness 'It was a factor's office, an old-time firm, and they had an old-time safe. Breaking in was a breeze, but the lousy safe . . . I hit it with a fat charge of nitro. It must have blown the whole town awake, but it hardly dented the safe. Even so, I'd have gotten away, but I blew my cool. I was so goddamn mad at that safe, I went through the offices pinching coins, bus tokens, desk sets and clocks, even half-smoked packs of cigarettes. I walked out, finally, loaded down with all that junk, and right into the arms of a cop.'

'A niggerhead safe,' Jappy said. 'They should be outlawed.'

'Past history,' Mitchell said. He waved his hand to indicate the room, the alleys below. 'You own this whole setup?'

'Didn't Johnny Handsome tell you about it?'

'He never mentioned it.'

Jappy grinned sourly. 'He didn't know. It was long after his time.'

'You're testing me again?'

'You dropped in from the sky. Am I supposed to buy the whole bag without a word?'

'What could I be – a cop? We checked that bit out already.'

'Sure. I'm a small-timer. Let's don't go over it again. You don't get into trouble by being suspicious. I did a piece in the peniteniary once, and I didn't like it much.'

'I can tell you a sure way of staying out of prison.'

'That right?'

'Turn straight and stay that way.'

'Thanks,' Jappy said. 'I'm grateful for the tip.'

Mitchell showed his instant smile. 'I want you to listen to a proposition, Jappy.'

'No dice. Not interested.'

'It's sweet, Jappy.'

'They're all sweet, until they turn sour. I don't even want to hear about it.' He paused, and listened to the rumble and clatter below. Then he got up and went to the window overlooking the alleys. 'It's beginning to get active. By eight o'clock all the alleys will be busy, and people waiting for their turn. I'll sell some booze, a lot of beer, and enough food. At the end of the week I'll clear a profit.'

'It's so exciting it sends shivers down my spine.'

Jappy turned. 'You're forty? I'm forty-five. I don't need so much excitement any more. And what I especially don't need is another prison sentence. So you can shove the excitement.'

'You're straight? I don't believe it.' Mitchell pointed to the door of the adjoining room. 'Or those characters wouldn't be hanging around.'

'I do a little bit of numbers business, and a little loan-sharking, and I run a few girls. No burglary. No theft. Just nice easy stuff where I can buy protection. Nobody sells protection for robbery, so I don't rob anything.'

'According to Johnny Handsome you were a real smart thief.'

Jappy seemed not to have heard him. 'I have a partner, a brother-in-law. He's straight, and he knows this business. I never let him come up here, so he stays straight. When the cash comes in, we put it back into the business. We just got finished renovating the kitchen, it cost better than twenty thousand.'

'You must be getting rich, Jappy,' Mitchell said softly.

Jappy came back to the desk. 'Don't ride me. You know goddamn well who's getting rich. The cops. From the chief on down to a couple of chiseling harness bulls. I'm taking the business risk and they're getting rich, without no invest-ment.'

'If you don't take risks, you don't get rich.'

'Thanks again,' Jappy said. 'I certainly appreciate all this wonderful advice you're handing out.'

Mitchell exchanged a neutral look with Jappy, a kind of pause, he thought, while they regrouped for some war of attrition. Jappy bent toward a drawer of his desk, then arrested the movement and converted it awkwardly into a scratching of his shin. But Mitchell knew that he had been reaching for a bottle, and that his cheapness had short-circuited the impulse. He would deny his own thirst rather than share with someone else. In a tortuous way, in a very roundabout way, Mitchell thought, it was Jappy's tightness that would bring him down.

'Risk,' Mitchell said. 'I would like to interest you in taking one.'

'Just a little risk, and it can't miss – right?'

'Anything can miss,' Mitchell said, 'including this one. But I don't think it will.'

'If it's that good, why don't you keep it all for yourself?'

'You know the answer to that. It's a four- or five-man job. You've got the horses.'

Jappy said, 'You make me keep repeating myself. I'm finished with the life. I'm satisfied. I had it once, and it cost me a jog in the penitentiary, and now I'm through. I'm satisfied.'

'Bullshit,' Mitchell said evenly. 'You're not satisfied and you never will be, because you never made the big score.'

'That's more inside dope from Johnny Handsome?' Jappy looked around as if for a place to spit.

'Maybe. But you've already told me as much yourself. You're nothing but a small-time hustler, and it burns your ass because you've got a lot of brains and they're going to waste. You book numbers, you lend a little money. It's all crap, the leavings that the syndicate can't be bothered with. They let you handle the garbage –'

'You got a very big mouth on you, mister.'

'A police spy?' Mitchell laughed. 'Even in this lousy town there must be twenty bums in line before they ever get around to you. Who are you? You're forty-five and sweating out dimes, and paying off a lot of fat-ass cops for your living. Maybe it's a funny way to put it, but you're a failure, Jappy.'

Jappy's smile was bitter but calm. If there was a fury underneath, Mitchell thought, he was containing it beautifully. 'But my life would be redeemed if I made a big score?'

'The score I'm talking about,' Mitchell said, 'is one million dollars.'

At once, as if some sudden profound change in his metabolism had taken place, Jappy's face became covered with a slick of sweat, and his eyes turned murky. He wet his lips carefully, as if their parchedness could rasp his tongue. His hand edged downward to the desk drawer, stopped, quivered, as if parsimony fought need in that battleground. Then he groaned and jerked open the drawer and brought out a bottle and two shot glasses. Mitchell read the label as Jappy poured, his hand trembling. Cheap booze, a rye blend with a liquor store's brand name. Jappy pushed one of the glasses toward Mitchell and quickly picked up the other and drained it.

37

Mitchell picked up his glass, sniffed the grainy new alcohol, then put it down and looked steadily at Jappy.

'What's your proposition?' Jappy's voice was bitter with the despair of self-knowledge.

Easy, now, Mitchell cautioned himself. The fish had bitten. Easy, now. He picked up his glass and tossed it back, feeling the green whiskey burn its way down. He smacked his lips, revolved the glass against the light, and slowly put it down.

'It ain't that good,' Jappy said. 'Save the cornball craperoo and get to the point. What's the deal?'

'It's a bank hit,' Mitchell said. 'And did I mention the score before? It's a million. One million dollars.'

Jappy tipped whiskey into his glass and threw it back. He looked at Mitchell broodingly. 'There's a lot more than that in the mint, but I'm not crazy. I'm not about to crack a bank, either. I like the free world too much.'

'Figure three hundred thousand, maybe more, for your end,' Mitchell said calmly. 'And not a penny to pay off. Put half of it in securities, invest the rest in real estate. Even with inflation, that's retirement money.'

'Take it to somebody else,' Jappy said. 'I don't want it.'

But he sounded plaintive, defensive. The hook was firmly set, Mitchell thought. 'I brought it to you because I want to cut the risks all the way down. The word is that you're brainy and a careful organiser and dependable.'

'Johnny Handsome said I was dependable?'

'He said that you had one serious weakness, that you were the chintziest man he ever knew. He said you screwed him because of that. But he didn't deny your good points.'

'I'm conservative about money. I don't like to throw it around like a lot of other characters.'

'Johnny claimed you let him go to prison because you were so goddamn tight. He claimed you could have bought his freedom with a couple or three thousand, but wouldn't spend the money. I'm quoting Johnny Handsome, you understand.'

Jappy said earnestly, 'There was no way I could have made a deal. If there was, I would have done it. Johnny never believed me. I couldn't convince him.'

'No, you didn't convince him. It burned him up. He hated your guts. Maybe he was right, maybe not. I couldn't say. As far as I'm concerned, you get the benefit of the doubt. But even when Johnny was bad-mouthing you at his worst, he never denied that you were smart, that you knew how to run a job. In fact, a few times, after he began to cool down about you, I heard him say that he wouldn't mind coming back to you.'

'I wouldn't have taken him back. Once a man has a grudge against you, he's unreliable. I don't mean he would necessarily deliberately foul up – though he might do that, too – but sooner or later he would screw you, maybe without even knowing he was doing it. The unconscious – you know what I mean?'

Mitchell nodded.

'So what's in *your* unconscious?'

Jappy's voice was so uninflected, so subtly insinuating, that Mitchell was almost surprised into protesting his innocence. But he said lightly, 'I try to be conscious at all times. I look out for *numero uno*. I don't bleed for anybody else, and besides, Johnny Handsome is dead. If you screwed Johnny, too bad – for Johnny. I'll try to watch out that you don't screw *me*.'

'I want to remind you,' Jappy said, 'that you don't have any deal yet. What you're saying, so far, it's strictly talk. Academic – you know what I mean?'

Jappy's face was closed up, unreadable. His forehead was still damp with sweat, but he was calm, his fever had subsided. It might be time to tug at the hook as a reminder, Mitchell thought. He said, 'It's a matter of indifference to you? You wouldn't care if I didn't say another word about it?'

'A man wants to talk, I'll listen.' Jappy shrugged. 'It's all up to you.'

'No,' Mitchell said coldly. 'It's your move. Yes or no.'

Jappy reached for the whiskey bottle, tilted it over his glass, then changed his mind and slammed it down on the table. 'Tell it,' he said. 'Tell the fucking thing.'

The hook was still secure, Mitchell thought, and he could take his time. He cleared his throat and said patiently, 'As I told you before, it's a million-dollar score. And it's a bank job.'

'I got the price before,' Jappy said. 'And also that it's a bank. That's what bothers me. Everybody wants to knock over a bank, because that's where the big score is, and where the glory is. Hitting a guy on the head and snitching his wallet – any dunce with muscle and a lead pipe can do it. But cracking a bank, that's the big leagues, that's the thief's wet dream.'

'I couldn't care less about glory. I'm in business for money.'

'And everybody knows it,' Jappy said, as if Mitchell had not spoken. 'The banks know it, the thieves know it, the cops know it. Banks don't give their money away, they make it rough to steal from them. I'll bet more thieves fall in bank robberies – by percentage – than any other kind. It stands to reason – if the stakes are high, the odds have to match them.'

'As you say,' Mitchell said, 'muscle is easy. But the take for hitting a guy on the head or rolling a lush is probably less than ten dollars a time. Well, you can make a million that way if you hit a hundred thousand guys on the head. I don't say you can't do it if you work all around the clock, but I don't recommend it. A bank – you get it all at once, in one operation.'

'If you get it at all.'

'There are more risks in being a thief than being straight.

If you don't believe in taking a risk, you would be straight. The whole idea is not to avoid taking any risks, but to minimise them.'

'Okay,' Jappy said, 'now that I know your philosophy, let's hear a few of the details.'

'Sure. You know the town of Amesville?'

'Downstate somewhere, I think.'

'In the southwest corner. Home of the Munchmore Biscuit plant.'

Jappy nodded. 'That's the connection I probably heard about it.'

'A small town of about eight thousand people. The Peoples Bank of Amesville – that's our score.'

Jappy snorted. 'You're crazy. The Peoples Bank in Amesville hasn't got no one million dollars in stealable liquid assets.'

'Most of the time, no. Every other Wednesday, yes.'

Jappy looked up sharply. 'They handle the Munchmore payroll?'

'Right. You would expect that Munchmore would use one of the banks in the city, in Melton, which is only about ten miles away from the plant. But the president of the biscuit plant is an old buddy of the president of the Peoples Bank of Amesville, so the little bank handles the big payroll.'

'Keep going,' Jappy said.

'But it's still a little bank. The whole staff, including the president and the janitor, is about seven or eight people.'

'But a little bank can still have a big vault with a time lock, and I haven't heard any sure way yet of licking one of those.'

'Yes,' Mitchell said, 'the Amesville Peoples has such a vault.'

'So?'

'So a bank is as vulnerable as a supermarket when the vault is open.'

'I'll keep that piece of information in mind,' Jappy said. 'It's something every thief should know.'

'On every other Tuesday afternoon, after regular banking hours,' Mitchell said with deliberation, 'an armored car drives to Amesville with approximately a million dollars in cash – in small bills and silver. It comes from the Federal Reserve, which does *not* record serial numbers.'

'Wait a minute. Are you saying that the biscuit plant doesn't pay by check, that they still fill up pay envelopes with cash?'

'Checks. The bank is tied in to a computer system that makes up the payroll. It prints out everything – names, amounts, deductions for social security, pension, insurance, federal and state taxes, hospitalisation, all of it cumulative.'

'That's fascinating stuff,' Jappy said. 'I'll have to keep it in mind whenever I rob a bank.'

'They get paid a fee for the service, which for a bank the size of the Peoples is meaningful. But the real profit for the bank – '

Jappy interrupted. 'It gets more interesting by the minute.' He cocked his head to the door of the adjoining room. 'I got four people stashed in there, and they don't like the idea. They're probably needling each other by now. Next step they'll start pulling hair. You think you can get to the point?'

Mitchell went on calmly. 'The easiest place to cash a pay check is at the bank that issues it. So, on payday, practically everybody on the payroll drives in to town to turn their checks into cash. Most of them at lunch hour, but a lot of them after work, too. The bank stays open late for them. Altogether, better than ninety percent do it. That means that the bank must have the cash to handle it, and that's why they have a million dollars every odd Wednesday in the month.'

'What's in it for the bank? It's just a nuisance, isn't it?'

'That's where their big profit is. They induce the plant

42

workers to open up accounts there, and a lot of them do, since it's convenient for them. One-stop banking, like the ads say. So the Peoples Bank of Amesville gets a hell of a lot of customers, and that's how they make their money.'

Jappy drummed his fingers impatiently on the desk.

'On Tuesday evenings, before the odd Wednesdays, the armored car unloads the million in cash, and it's stowed away in the vault with the time lock set for the next morning.'

'Knocking over an armored car is a great way to get killed, unless you've got an arrangement with one of the guards. And even then – ' Jappy shook his head. 'Even then, a lot can go wrong.'

'Right,' Mitchell said. 'That's why we don't try to boost the armored car.'

'And we don't try to crack the vault. That means we have to wait until the plant people start coming in, at lunchtime, and they open the vault. But by then you've got a crowd of thousands. You like working with a big audience?'

Mitchell said, 'The vault opens up first thing in the morning.'

Jappy sat up straight. 'That's crazy. Why not wait until they need the money?'

'Because there are a lot of other things in the vault besides the million in cash, and they need them to carry on their routine business.'

'Then that's the weakness of the whole thing,' Jappy said, and took a deep breath.

'That's the weakness. And that's when we make our hit.'

And now, Mitchell thought, Jappy would do the rest. The fish would boat itself.

Jappy's eyes were more than half shut, as if in concealment. But his hand, lying on the table, betrayed him. The fingers were twitching. Mitchell got up and walked to the window. Below, almost all the alleys were in use now, and there was a brisk business at the bar and the restaurant adjoining it, as well as at the soft drink and sandwich fountain. The crowd was made up of young boys and girls – almost identical in long hair, bright shirts and slacks – and young married couples, whose children sat restlessly on the bright blue plastic banquettes behind the starting line.

Behind him, Mitchell heard the soft clunk of the bottle on the desk. Jappy had sneaked another drink. He flashed his fleeting smile and started to turn, then froze.

He was standing, or slouching, at the bar, a strange, misshapen figure in the oversize coat and scarecrow fur hat. Again something about him tugged at Mitchell's memory, but again it eluded him. If he would turn, show his face . . .

He said over his shoulder, 'Come over here a minute. I want you to take a look at somebody.'

Jappy got up and joined him at the window. Mitchell pointed at the shadow, and Jappy sighted down the length of his finger.

'The sloppy one,' Jappy said. 'I see him. What about it?'

'He tailed us from town. Know who it is?'

'No,' Jappy said. 'Let's find out.'

4

They might have been spectators in a loge, watching a theatrical performance, with the window a proscenium arch framing in the action below. There was a constant turnover of people at the bar, but the man in the shabby coat had scarcely seemed to move, his back as stolid and anonymous as a stage prop. When Tully and Bobby appeared, there was a slight stir of recognition at the window, as an audience might stir, Mitchell thought, at the entrance of a familiar actor. Bobby lingered in the entrance, lighting a cigarette, and Tully moved to his right, strolling casually. Neither of them looked toward the bar.

Mitchell was standing behind and slightly to the side of Jappy. Sunny, to his right, kept swaying, touching him softly at intervals. But it was probably innocent, he thought, because she was all revved up, obliged to be in motion even when she was technically at rest. Battler was further to his right, breathing with audible difficulty through his battered nose. Below, everything seemed suspended, frozen, even though the bowlers were in constant antic motion and the glass window kept quivering with the rumble and clatter of the balls and pins.

Bobby started out of the doorway, edging slowly toward the bar, patting his hair gently as if to assure himself that it was properly anchored. A second later Tully came into view, swaggering. Both men converged on the bar, closing in but not quite touching the shadow. When he became aware of them, they pressed against him, not with the full force of their weight, but just enough to let him know that he couldn't break away. Bobby bent toward him and said something close to his ear, and he responded with a gesture that even at that distance could be read as part protest, part denial. Bobby spoke to him again. It occurred to Mitchell that it was like watching a television set with the sound turned off, comic and yet disturbing, as if some basic rule of nature were being violated.

Tully began to use his weight, and the whole group – the *gestalt*, Mitchell thought, remembering a word Katsouras had used a few times – moved as a single unit to the door. The shadow clutched at the bar, slowing them up for a moment, but Tully applied pressure and the man's hand slid off the wooden surface. Although he was now half turned toward them, he kept his head lowered, and his features were obscured. But in a flashing instant Mitchell knew who he was. His blood turned cold with disbelief and anger and dismay.

'Know him?' Jappy said.

He forced his voice to firmness, disinterest. 'No. He looks like an old bum, that's all. How would I know him? It's your town, not mine.'

'He could come from *out* of town,' Jappy said. 'Like you.'

Now, below, they were close to the door, moving more quickly. The old man tried to hold back, but he was helpless. He seemed to be talking, and his hemmed-in arms were attempting to free themselves, as if to reinforce what he was saying. Bobby appeared to be listening politely, his head bent toward the old man, but Tully was unyielding.

They went through the door and out of sight, and in the room there was a concerted exhalation of held breath. Jappy went back to his desk. Mitchell remained at the window, staring out at the busy alleys, trying to tell himself that he might have been wrong about the old man. But it was a forlorn hope.

46

Jappy said, 'Real smooth work. They cut that guy out of there and nobody knew it, not even the bartender.'

'What's so wonderful?' Sunny said. 'Two strong studs handling one old creep.'

'Keep quiet,' Jappy said.

'Why should I keep quiet? Why shouldn't I talk if I got an opinion?'

'Because all your opinions are between your legs, and talking ain't your best way of expressing yourself. So button up.'

Sunny opened her mouth, outraged, but Battler interrupted. 'You heard him.'

'You heard him,' Sunny mimicked. 'You sound like one of those creepy old movies on the TV. Edgar or whatever-his-name-is Robinson says something, and his faithful pal says, "You heard him." I mean, come *on*.'

Jappy was looking at Mitchel. 'You never saw him before? You're sure?'

'Never,' Mitchell said, and thought bitterly, 'What's the point of it? If I had any sense I'd cut and run right this second, while I can.

'Who would tail any of us unless he was a cop?' Jappy sounded puzzled. 'And that character is one hell of a crummy-looking cop.'

'You heard him,' Sunny said.

Battler said to her, 'Are you looking for a crack in the mouth?'

'Do me a favor,' Jappy said wearily. 'Everybody just calm down and keep quiet and stop bickering.'

'You heard him,' Sunny said softly.

Bassler said, 'Here they come.'

The metal steps outside were singing. Mitchell stiffened but didn't move. His mind seemed to have quit working. Jappy held his finger poised over the door release button. He waited for the knocks, and then pressed the buzzer. The door opened, and Bobby came in. He was breathing hard

47

and his face was white. He shut the door and stood against it for a moment, as if to collect himself. There was a small tear and a smear of mud on the knee of his trousers.

Jappy said, 'Where the hell is Tully and –'

Bobby raised his hand, cutting him off. 'Get the woman out of here, Jappy.'

Jappy responded at once to the urgency in Bobby's voice. He nodded to Sunny and pointed his finger at the door to the adjoining room.

Sunny broke toward Bobby. 'Where's Tully? What happened to him?'

'He's okay. Will you go in next door, ferchrissake!'

She glared at him, then turned abruptly and stomped angrily toward the door. 'You heard him!' she said vindictively.

Bobby waited until the door shut firmly behind her, and then he said, 'He's dead, Jappy.'

'Tully?' Jappy's voice skittered upward on a note of querulous disbelief.

'The old guy,' Bobby said. 'He's dead.'

Mitchell's legs trembled. He shifted his feet wider to steady himself.

Jappy's complexion, which had bleached white, darkened to a dull, heavy red. 'What do you mean dead? You mean he had a heart attack or something?'

'Tully hit him. Jesus, he –'

'Hit him! I didn't tell anybody to hit anybody!'

A portion of Mitchell's mind began to function, and he realised that, astonishingly, he had been delivered. But he was still numb.

'He made a break for it,' Bobby said. 'He ran around the back and headed for the field. Tully caught him and pushed him down. The old guy jumped up and came through with a punch, and Tully got sore and knocked him down with a punch, and the old guy got up, and damn if he didn't belt Tully again and take off across the field. So this time Tully chased him again, and when he caught him he pulled out his sap and cold-cocked the old guy. He hit him a couple of more times while he was lying on the ground, before I could get there – '

'Where the hell *were* you all of this time?'

Bobby flushed. 'The old bugger tripped me up when he broke away, and the rest of it happened so fast . . . ' He touched the muddy rip in the knee of his trousers with solicitous fingers. 'It sounds like a long time when I tell about it, but it was just a few seconds. Besides, I didn't think there was any hurry, I thought Tully could handle him easy. By the time I saw he was having some trouble, with the old guy punching him and all, and I started to run over, by the time I got there – '

'Jesus,' Jappy said. 'Jesus Christ.'

'I didn't think Tully hit him that hard. But you know, he's a powerful kid, like an ox, he split his goddamn skull open like it was paper.'

Jappy said, 'Are you *sure* he's dead?'

'I checked him over careful. No pulse. No heartbeat, either.'

What do I do, Mitchell thought, send up a prayer of thanks?

'If there's one thing I hate,' Jappy said, 'it's something that's pointless. Especially pointless killing.'

It was time to say something, Mitchell thought. 'Also,' he said, 'you probably feel rotten about the old guy.'

'I don't give a damn about the old guy. He was asking for trouble. But it was *pointless* to kill him.'

'Tully, he's like an ox,' Bobby said. 'He don't know how to hit somebody with science, he just uses his power. Nobody saw a thing, Jappy. It was out in back, out in the woods, and nobody was anywhere near. They was all alone.'

'Where is he now? And where's that shithead Tully?'

'He's out in back, staying with the stiff. They're in those tall weeds, and you can't see them. They're well hid.'

Battler spoke for the first time. 'We better get moving.'

'What do we do, Jappy?' Bobby said.

'Get rid of him.'

'Where?'

'Who cares? Throw him on the garbage dump. Put him in the goddamn river, maybe the current will carry him down into the next county. But get rid of him. Right away.'

Bobby looked at Battler. 'Can I borrow your car?'

'You better go along and supervise,' Jappy said to Battler. 'Find out who he is. The papers on him.'

'Bring his stuff back here?'

'Don't bring *anything* back here. See what's on him and then get rid of it someplace. Toss it on the garbage dump.' Jappy wheeled suddenly toward Mitchell. 'You brought us bad luck.'

'Shit,' Mitchell said. 'Don't blame it on bad luck, it's plain stupidity. In your place, I'd ship that kid far away from me.'

Battler was shrugging into his coat. 'Any blood?' he said to Bobby. 'I got a tarp in the car.'

'Sure there's blood. He smashed his whole goddamn head in.'

Battler and Bobby went to the door.

'Take him along with you to look at the stiff.' Jappy gestured to Mitchell. 'You got any objections?'

Mitchell shrugged and followed Battler and Bobby out onto the metal landing. He looked out over the field, straining through the darkness. He could see only an unbroken line of tall weeds, running back into deeper darkness toward the black border where the woods began.

'The weeds hide them pretty good, don't they?' Bobby said.

They went quickly down the elastic steps. A half dozen cars, belonging to Pin 'N Whistle employees, were parked, front-end out, against a berm, beyond which the weeds began, three or four feet high, rustling reedily in the wind. A hundred feet in, midway between the parking lot and the

woods, they found Tully, sitting on the ground with his legs stretched out in front of him. He didn't look up. The body was five feet further in, face down, the legs drawn up as if in some final spasm of pain.

'Better keep low,' Battler said. He and Bobby were already squatting, their heads several inches below the top of the weeds.

Mitchell dropped down and duck-walked to the body. The back of the head was misshapen, and there was a black liquid gap in the skull. There was no need for him to look at the face, but it had to be done. Slowly, almost gently, he rolled the body over on its back. The bony emanciated face was streaked with blood, and it looked very old. The red-rimmed eyes were open, staring at the distant sky. Mitchell backed off and crawled over to where Battler and Bobby waited.

'Never saw him before,' he whispered.

'Okay,' Battler said. He nudged Tully. 'Let's go, shithead, lend a hand.'

Mitchell didn't wait. He waded back through the weeds and climbed the spidery metal steps. He knocked three times, and Jappy let him in.

'Well?'

'I don't make him,' Mitchell said. 'Some old bum. His eyes are open.'

'What do you want me to do? Kiss them to sleep?' Jappy lit a cigar. Like his whiskey, it was a cheap off-brand, and it stank. 'I'll tell you something, Mitchel, I think you're hot. I'm having second thoughts.'

'I'm clean,' Mitchell said. 'Nobody even knows I'm in town.'

'The shadow knows,' Jappy said in a sepulchral voice.

'The shadow is dead. Remember?'

'But he was tailing you. Remember?'

'He was tailing *somebody*. Maybe one of your boys.

Maybe me. It's possible he saw me flash a roll in one of those joints.'

'And followed you all the way out here? Some ambitious jack-roller. You talk to anyone about the bank job in the pen?'

'I didn't know about the Amesville Peoples until I was *out*.'

'Let's wait and see what we can find out about the stiff,' Jappy said. 'Something is unkosher. After we check the stiff out, I'll give you my decision about the bank.'

'You'll give me your decision?' Mitchell said. 'Well, you can kiss my ass, sweetheart.' He picked up his suitcase. 'I'll find another connection. Maybe not as smart as you, but someone who makes up his mind and sticks with it.'

'Go ahead,' Jappy said. 'You want to walk out, nobody's stopping you.'

'Nice to have met you,' Mitchell said.

He went out, slamming the door behind him. He was half-way down the metal stairs when the fling of light from the open door swept past him. He kept on going, and had almost reached the bottom step when Jappy spoke.

'Keep your drawers on. What are you so sensitive for?'

Mitchell's smile winked on and off. His face was solemn as he started back up the steps.

Jappy opened the door for Sunny, and she bounded out like an animal released from a cage. 'What am I,' she said indignantly, 'like your Turkish harem slave, getting pushed around like cattle? Go in the room, go out of the room . . . Like it was the nineteenth century. I don't have to stand for that kind of crap.'

'Don't make so much noise,' Jappy said. 'Keep it down.'

'Like a Turkish slave,' Sunny said. 'You don't give any-body a freedom of choice.'

'You can have all the freedom of choice you want. Just say the word and you can go back to being a cocktail waitress and getting goosed by hosiery salesmen and turning five-dollar tricks.'

'I never turned a five-dollar trick in my life. I may have given it away, freedom of choice, but I never turned a friggin' five-dollar trick in my whole life. Never!'

'Okay,' Jappy said wearily, 'so you get prosperity prices.'

'I got beauty and youth, I got real good market value.'

Jappy said to Mitchell, 'Christ, what a bunch. The only one who got any sense is Battler, and even he ain't got any brains, just good judgment. I wouldn't blame you if you ran scared and wanted to take your little proposition someplace else.'

'As long as there's brains at the top,' Mitchell said, 'and the rest of them follow orders, that's all I ask.'

'Where did you make Tully go?' Sunny said. 'Something is going on that stinks. We were supposed to be partying tonight. Christ, we just had time to get settled at Beebee's and before we know it we end up at this dump, and now Tully disappears. Where the hell is he?'

'He went to a funeral,' Jappy said. 'Now are you happy?'

'Shit,' Sunny said.

Mitchell went to the window overlooking the alleys. It was nine o'clock, and most of the families had departed, leaving the alleys to the young people. The bar was busier than it had been earlier, and the restaurant adjoining it was well patronised, with two waitresses in red miniskirts moving about briskly between the tables with their trays. To divert himself, he watched a young baldish bowler in a sweatsuit who seemed to be on his way to a fine score. When he heard the door release buzz, he didn't turn at once, but watched the bowler throw another ball.

Battler was standing beside Jappy's desk, Bobby and Tully were near the door. Tully was holding a handkerchief to his cheek, and above its whiteness his eyes were sullen. Jappy was on his feet, gesturing Sunny into the adjoining room. She glared at him mutinously.

He raised his voice. 'And no goddamn arguments. Either get into that room or I'll kick your ass down the stairs. Move!'

Sunny looked broodingly at Tully. He averted his eyes. She turned abruptly and stormed into the other room, shutting the door with a bang. Tully brought the handkerchief down, revealing an angry red welt on his jaw. He scrutinised his handkerchief closely, then returned it to his face.

Jappy said, 'What happened to you?' When Tully didn't answer, Jappy turned to Battler. 'What's with him?'

'He got smart. I had to give him a shot. I didn't hurt him.'

'Knocked him clean on his ass,' Bobby said. 'A beautiful shot.'

'You should have knocked a couple of his teeth out,' Jappy said. He made a gesture of dismissal. 'What about the stiff?'

'His name is Morris Laplace,' Battler said. 'Don't know where he's from. But there was a letter in his pocket from a con in Fredding. He was an inmate there himself.'

Jappy turned to Mitchell. 'Morris Laplace. Ever heard the name?'

Mitchell shook his head.

'You didn't know him at Fredding?'

'There's over four thousand inmates at Fredding. I never heard of him.'

Jappy eyed him speculatively for a moment, then said to Battler, 'Get rid of him?'

'The town dump. There's a big fire going. We threw him on it. Burned up his papers, too.'

'It's hard to burn up a body completely,' Mitchell said. 'Suppose they find some remains tomorrow?'

'If they do,' Jappy said, 'we'll sing. We'll tell the cops who knocked him off. Right, Tully? Right, shithead?'

He moved awkwardly but with surprising speed, so that Tully had no time to defend himself or even to dodge, and Jappy's fist caught him on his left temple. His head struck and bounced off the plywood wall, and his eyes dulled. But

54

he got his hands up in front of his face instinctively, and shied away as Jappy drew back his fist again. Jappy feinted, looking for an opening, and Tully kept moving his head. Finally, with a snort of disgust, Jappy drove a short hard blow to the ribs that made Tully wince.

Jappy dropped his hands and turned away from Tully. He said to Mitchell, 'You want to go back to your hotel?'

Mitchell nodded. 'Can you call me a cab?'

'I'm embarrassed you saw all this,' Jappy said. 'If I thought it would help anything, I would kill that greaseball with my own hands.' He shrugged, and almost smiled. 'Maybe the cops will get him.'

'Let's hope so,' Mitchell said. 'It might teach him a good lesson to be executed.'

'Come down ten, eleven tomorrow morning,' Jappy said, 'and we'll go for a little auto ride. Okay?'

'Sure,' Mitchell said. 'I'd like that.'

Mitchell registered at the Philbin Arms and was taken upstairs in an open-cage elevator. At the door, he dismissed the bellhop with a dollar tip and opened the door himself. The room was high-ceilinged, spacious, with graceless turn-of-the-century furniture, heavy maroon drapes drawn over the tall windows, and a pervasive smell of furniture polish. He checked the bathroom: white tiles, a large old-fashioned sink, a massive tub set on scrolled legs. He went back into the room and sat down on the bed beside the telephone.

He gave the switchboard operator a number and waited, his mind blank, listening to the sound of dialing, and then the mechanical burring ring. The ringing stopped and a voice said hello.

He said, 'I think he's in.'

The voice said, 'What?'

He spoke slowly and deliberately, and with a trace of impatience. 'I said I think he's in. I'll know for sure tomorrow.'

The voice grunted noncommittally.

'Another thing. Did you put Morris Laplace on me?'

'Did I . . . Who? Morris Laplace? Oh. The old con who was a ward boy at Fredding? Did I put him on you? Why would I do that?'

'I'm asking *you*. Did you put him on my tail?'

'Shit. If I wanted you tailed, would I put somebody like Morris Laplace on the job?'

'Well, if it's of any interest to you, he met with an accident.'

'What kind of an accident? Are you trying to tell me that you – '

'I didn't lay a hand on him. I just happen to know about it.'

A pause. 'How serious was the accident?'

'Very serious. He's dead.'

'You sonofabitch.' The voice rose at once, without gradation, to a pitch of absolute fury. 'If you think I'll stand for murder – '

His lip curling, Mitchell slammed the phone down on the shouting voice.

5

The Chrysler sped smoothly through the flat countryside, always a little under the authorised speed limit, always strictly obedient to road signs and warnings. As he had the night before, Mitchell observed Battler's driving with approval. He was a first-class wheelman.

In the intervals between a succession of drab interchangeable towns, the fields lay still and empty, resting, recuperating for the spring five months hence when they would be put to work – turned over, fed, seeded, spurred into life so that they could once again bring forth provender . . .

Jappy sat upright, his position unchanged from the moment when, as if it were some place of special pride or privilege, he had taken his place beside Battler, leaving the entire back of the car to Mitchell. Earlier, Tully and Bobby had objected vigorously to being left behind, but Mitchell had insisted on their exclusion and Jappy had backed him up.

'Who the hell is this cat supposed to be, giving orders?' Tully was loud and angry. 'Less than twenty-four hours around here, and he's took to running things.'

'Shut up,' Jappy said. 'You're on the shit list as it is, after last night, without making it any worse.'

'*I* ain't on the shit list,' Bobby said.

'You should have stopped him from bashing that old guy's head in.'

'I'm not a mind reader,' Bobby said earnestly. 'If I had *knew* what he was going to do –'

57

'The point is,' Mitchell said, 'that you don't take the whole army along when you reconnoiter.'

'And you're the general, right?' Tully said. 'So what does that leave Jappy, a second lieutenant or something.'

From his place at the window, Mitchell had a view of the deserted alley floor. A crew of two men and a woman, identically dressed in blue denims, with white scarves covering their heads, were cleaning up – sweeping the alleys, vacuuming the carpets, sponging down the plasticene banquettes, checking the equipment for damage . . .

'If it's his show, say so,' Tully said, 'and we'll know who to take our orders from.'

'It's *nobody's* show yet,' Jappy said. 'That's what we're trying to decide today. Whether or not there's going to *be* a show.'

'That's still no reason why I shouldn't go.'

Mitchell said coldly, 'We won't have any use for your specialty. When we need an old man killed, we'll be sure to call on your services.'

Tully charged toward him with clenched fist, but Battler intervened, planting himself squarely in Tully's path.

'I'm going to pound on that sonofabitch,' Tully said. His flushed face was barely visible over Battler's shoulder.

'Go sit down,' Jappy said.

'I'll kill him,' Tully said.

'Listen to me, dummy,' Jappy said conversationally. 'You haven't got any permanent position here. It's like any other job. I can discharge you, kick you the hell out, and that's what I'll do if you don't stop being an asshole. Go sit down.'

Tully made a token surge against Battler's immobility, then turned away and flung himself into a chair.

Jappy spoke to Bobby. 'Like Mitchell said, you don't take the whole army on patrol. You don't want everybody in town to see an army mooching around a bank.'

Sitting forward in his seat, and raising his voice over the

rush of wind from the vent window at Jappy's right, Mitchell said, 'The idea of Tully in this operation doesn't grab me. It's going to need plenty of cool.'

'I can control him,' Jappy said. 'He's a punk and too full of piss, but he's got nerve, he don't scare. I can handle him.'

'I hope so. It's about time he started acting like a grown-up thief instead of a spoiled kid.'

'I can handle him. I know him inside out. I can handle Bobby, too, I know *him*. In fact, the only one I don't know is you.'

'Fair enough. If you see something you don't like, speak up. There's still time. We haven't got a deal yet.'

'It's a matter of personalities with Tully. Stop riding him. Try to like him a little.'

'You don't have to like the people you work with, just be able to depend on them.'

'Just don't be so feisty. Meet him halfway and things will go easier.'

'Okay,' Mitchell said. 'But I'd hate to see a million dollars go out the window because of a hot-headed punk.'

'He gets out of line,' Battler said, speaking for the first time, 'I know how to straighten him out. Like last night. Belt him one. He don't like to be hit, I guess it's his looks.'

Jappy nodded. 'Battler makes sense.'

'I've been noticing that,' Mitchell said.

'When he was in the ring, he got his brains jolted up pretty good, but it didn't affect his judgment.'

They stopped fifty miles northeast of Amesville for coffee at a roadside diner, then went on again. When a billboard advertising the Amesville Motel (AAA-Approved, Heated Swimming Pool) appeared, Mitchell tapped Battler on the shoulder.

'Take a left at the traffic signal coming up. It's another way into town, and it passes by the biscuit factory. We ought to see it.'

'Does it figure in robbing the bank?' Jappy said.

59

'Only the payroll figures. But it won't hurt you to look at it. Right here, Battler.'

Battler turned onto a three-lane concrete road. A billboard, duplicating the design and colors of the nationally famous label on the Munchmore Biscuit box, announced that the plant was four miles straight ahead.

'You'll begin to smell it in about five minutes,' Mitchell said. 'Less, if the wind is right.'

'I don't see the point of seeing it.' Jappy said. 'I can live without smelling it, too.'

'It's a stimulating sight.' Mitchell said. 'It has the look of money.'

Traffic increased, and they began to see small scruffy businesses along the sides of the road, fronted by small bare patches of blacktop that passed as parking lots: package stores, roadside food stands, a rundown frozen-custard stand, a 'factory seconds' sweater store, a 'factory outlet' furniture 'warehouse' – traps for the loose money of the biscuit plant workers.

Mitchell inhaled deeply. 'There's the smell now.'

Battler sniffed the air. 'It's not too bad. Sweet.'

'Sweet and warm,' Mitchell said. 'You can imagine what its like inside. More sweet and more warm. You bring that smell home with you in your nostrils and clothes and hair. It stays with you. After a while you hate it, and it even touts you off eating anything sweet again.'

'I like it,' Battler said.

'Just smelling it puts me right back into the plant again,' Mitchell said.

'You *wanted* to come this way,' Jappy said.

'I once worked in a prison bakery,' Battler said. 'I liked the smell.'

'I didn't know it would hit me this hard,' Mitchell said. 'You'll see it in a second – right around this curve.'

The sun struck blindingly off the field of cars in the parking lots around the buildings, endless ordered rows of painted cars – maroon, black, gray, salmon, yellow, green. The two-storied buildings were like a toy construction on a giant scale, orderly, identical, studded with windows brilliantly lit by the sun. Battler slowed down, and they eased past a wide pillared entrance, guarded by a booth manned by two special cops in blue-gray uniforms. Farther on, another wing of the plant had its own toy buildings, its own densely packed parking lot.

Jappy said, 'Now we can go take a look at the bank?'

'The bank is much smaller,' Mitchell said. 'You might not be impressed.'

'I'm impressed by money,' Jappy said. 'Size is no object.'

'It's got the money all right. Every other Wednesday.'

The parking lot was crowded near the entrance to the supermarket, but almost empty near the road. Battler parked in the last aisle of chalk-marked stalls. The Peoples Bank of Amesville was directly in front of them, across a sloping single-lane service road that led behind the supermarket. The bank occupied a neatly landscaped plot. It was a small, attractive Colonial building, red brick with white wooden facing, one story high and running about ninety feet deep. It was ringed with parking stalls.

Jappy said. 'It's a little bank. Just three cars parked. It don't look like any million dollars' worth.'

'Mornings, it's a little busier. Usually storekeepers, putting in last night's proceeds if they didn't drop it in the night depository, or picking up small bills and coins for change, an occasional housewife getting some cash for early-morning shopping, and so forth.'

'I wouldn't mind six or seven people around. It gives a normal look to the place from the outside.'

'Later in the day, on payday, it's a mob scene at lunch-time, and then it starts again in the evening when the plant lets out. But by then we'll be long gone.'

'Or dead.'

Mitchell went on. 'Battler can park here. In this same spot, if he wants to, right next to the road. It'll be empty. Everybody likes to get as close to the store as possible. When we come out of the bank we have about twenty-five feet or so to run from the bank to the car –'

'Which we can't make very fast. Not if we're loaded down with all that money.'

'Nothing is perfect,' Mitchell said. 'We'd be a lot faster without the money, but where's the fun?'

Battler said, 'I don't like the exit. It's too narrow. All it needs while we're trying to get out is one car coming in a little over the middle line and we're in trouble.'

'You don't have to use the exit. Just turn out here. The berm is only a few inches high. Bump over it, cross the sidewalk, and then swing into the road.'

'Okay,' Battler said. 'You rob the bank, you run across the service road with the money, you jump in the car and we take off. Then what? How do we get away and drive a hundred and sixty-five miles back home without getting caught?'

'It's a problem,' Mitchell said. 'I'm counting on Jappy to solve it. To think it out and organise it.'

'Don't go so fast,' Jappy said. 'First I have to be convinced that we can take the bank.'

'Go inside and look around. I told you about the layout, now see for yourself.'

Jappy opened the car door. 'I'll open an account. That'll give me time to hang around and take everything in.' He got out of the car. 'You have any idea what interest rate they pay?'

Mitchell snorted. 'Suppose they don't pay a satisfactory interest – will you get mad and blow the whole job?'

Jappy stood outside the car, straightening his jacket. 'If I don't like their interest payments I'll only put twenty-five dollars in the account. I'll use a fake name. Give me a street in town.'

'Twenty-nine Cross Street. It's a boarding house.'

He watched Jappy walk into the bank, cool and self-contained. In the front seat, Battler seemed made of granite – head, neck, shoulders, all making a solid and impervious unit. Battler knew how to wait. In fact, waiting was one of the basic requirements of his vocation. Imaginative people were bad waiters; they consumed themselves with fantasies. Battler would not invest his energy in chimeras.

Jappy came out of the bank twenty minutes later. Mitchell watched him as he stopped on the service road, took out his wallet, and carefully stowed away a piece of paper he had been holding. Then, unhurriedly, he continued to the car and got in beside Battler. There was an unlit cigar in his mouth.

'I'm a depositor in the Peoples Bank of Amesville,' Jappy said. He put a match to his cigar and puffed clouds of sour smoke against the windshield. 'They pay a straight five percent from day of deposit to day of withdrawal, compounded quarterly. It's better than I can get at home.'

'Congratulations,' Mitchell said, 'you're going to be independently wealthy. Incidentally, what did you think of the setup?'

Jappy puffed three times on his cigar before answering. 'It could work, but then again, there's no guarantee.'

'If they gave guarantees,' Mitchell said, 'it would take all the romance out of being a thief.'

'Yeah. I took a good look at the vault. It's a monster. I'd sure as hell hate to try cracking it.'

'There's no question of cracking it. It'll be open.'

'If it's *not* open, we're up the creek. You can't stop halfway through a robbery and say "Excuse me, I thought your safe would be open." No rainchecks in a robbery.'

'Say something helpful,' Mitchell said.

'I don't like the vault being all the way at the back of the bank. Further to go when we make the getaway.'

'But it has an advantage, too. It's harder for anyone outside to see what's going on.'

'Could be. But I like to see all the possible booby traps in advance, so I can plan for them. I never want to be surprised. What kind of protection have they got?'

'On payday, beginning at noon, they've got practically the whole police force, not so much to guard the money as to keep the lines orderly and moving along. In the morning there's just one town cop beside the bank dick.'

'He helped me find a place in line,' Jappy said. 'And he called me sir. Big old boy, fat belly. Retired cop?'

'A Dutchman. He was a harness bull on the Melton force until he retired about three, four years ago.'

'You figure him to be a ball of fire?'

'I doubt it. He doesn't move too well. Arthritis or something. He wasn't famous for bravery when he was a cop, so I don't think he'll start going for medals now, especially with a few guns aimed at him.'

'You can't always be sure of Dutchmen. They're stubborn and thickheaded. I'm one myself, so I know. What about the town cop?'

'It varies, but it's usually one of the younger ones. A small-town cop, you should know the type.'

Battler stirred. 'A big-city cop is more dependable. He knows the odds and he won't try to be a hero if he can help it. Small-town cops are dumb, they can't read the odds.'

'Well?' Jappy said. 'Can we expect trouble from the local lawman?'

Mitchell shrugged. 'All I can tell you is that I don't *think* so.'

'Yes,' Jappy said. 'But what if we do?'

Mitchell shrugged again. 'Then we'll kill him.'

Jappy made a wry face. 'That's what I thought you'd say.'

'Do you know another way?'

'No,' Jappy said. 'I don't know any other way.'

6

A waitress from the Pin 'N Whistle kitchen brought sandwiches and coffee up to the office and collected a dollar apiece from everyone.

Mitchell complained. 'On the brink of a million dollars, you'd think somebody would pay for my lunch. A finder's fee.'

'The business is a separate entity,' Jappy said. 'I have to pay, too.'

The return trip from Amesville had taken three and a half hours. Tully and Bobby were waiting in the office, sulking. When the waitress had gone, Jappy had taken his usual place behind the desk. The others sat facing him. Mitchell took his sandwich and coffee mug and went to the window.

Tully was still smoldering at his exclusion from the morning's exploration. 'You want me to stick my fingers in my ears when you talk, so that I won't hear your secrets?'

Speaking through a mouthful of hamburger, Jappy said, 'We looked into Mitchell's proposition this morning. It's a bank hit. There are a few tough angles that have to be solved, but it looks like a big score. We're going to get into it. Now here's the setup . . .'

Calm and lucid, Jappy spelling out the main facts. Mitchell listened for a moment, then faced about to the window. The alleys lay still and deserted, limitless, but there was a figure at the far end, and it established a spatial relationship, the way a landscape aquired scale by the insertion of a person or an animal. It was Sunny. She was leaning against the padded back of one of the booth railings, but even in repose she seemed restless.

Jappy was finished. 'And that's the main outline. That's the way it stands right now.'

'Where is it?' Bobby said. 'What's the name of the bank?'

'I'll tell you when it's the right time to tell you.'

'Why tell us at all, ever,' Tully said. 'When the time comes to hit the bank, just point us at it and we'll go in and rob it, and with a little luck we'll *never* know the name of it.'

'Right now,' Jappy said, 'the less people who know the details, the better.'

'Battler knows,' Tully said. 'And you can hear his brains rattle around when he shakes his head.'

'If yours rattled,' Jappy said, 'at least we would know you had some.'

Mitchell tuned out the bickering voices and turned back to the window. Sunny was no longer alone. She was talking to, almost hidden by, a man who stood with his back to Mitchell, a big man in a black raincoat and a gray snap-brim hat. Mitchell stared at him, and felt himself become rigid with anger. He pinched his nostrils comically, and thought. Even at this distance, you can smell cop.

Mitchell saw him stride off, lumbering and brutal. Sunny watched him go, then walked to the bar and picked up a telephone. She dialed quickly, glancing up at the window between each spin.

The phone rang on Jappy's desk. He picked it up and grunted into it guardedly. He listened, then said, 'What the hell does he want? It's a week until payday.'

Mitchell saw the girl speak. Then her mouth stopped moving and he heard Jappy again.

'Did he give you any clue what he wanted to see me about?'

She spoke, and shrugged her shoulders. Jappy swore. She hung up.

66

Jappy slammed the receiver down. 'Shannon. The sonofabitch. He's coming up here.'

'So what are you panicking for?' Tully said. 'He's on the payroll, ain't he?'

'In his language *see you* is translation for he wants money. The sonofabitch.'

Battler said, 'You want us to blow?'

'What's the difference? It won't be telling him any secrets to see you here.'

'Shannon is a cop?' Mitchell said.

'Lieutenant in charge of detectives. The ace bloodsucker of the force.'

'You think he has something to sell?' Mitchell said.

'*He* may think so, but I know he hasn't got a goddam thing – ' A heavy, demanding knocking at the door cut him off. 'He even knocks on the door like a cop.'

He pressed the buzzer and the door pushed open, the fading daylight all but blocked out by Shannon's bulk. He closed the door and looked around him with smiling contempt.

Jappy said, 'Tully, get up and give Mr. Shannon your seat.'

Shannon said, 'I'll stand. I'm here on business.'

'You're a week early for business.'

'This is new business.' Shannon's eyes roamed the room, arrogant and challenging, and settled on Mitchell. 'Who's this joker?'

Mitchell stared back unblinkingly, but he was stiff with tension.

'A friend,' Jappy said.

'Is that what you are?' Shannon said.

Deliberately, Mitchell turned back to the window.

'Your friend ain't very polite,' Shannon said. Mitchell didn't turn. 'Ain't you going to introduce him?'

'What for?' Jappy said. 'He's met a cop before.'

'You're not just kidding,' Shannon said. 'I know a bum when I see one.'

'You want a drink?'

'That ant piss you call whiskey? No, thanks, I never drink ant piss while on duty.' He redirected his voice to Mitchell. 'My name is Lieutenant Joe Shannon, mister.'

Mitchell faced about and looked at him – the high-flushed skin, the broken nose, the bulging pale blue eyes. It was a face to remember, he thought, a face to stoke old memories. 'I'm thrilled,' he said.

'Ah,' Shannon said. 'A joker. You know, Jappy, I don't think I like your friend.'

'He's crazy about *you*,' Jappy said.

'What's your name, mister?' Shannon said. Mitchell looked at him without expression. 'I said what's your name, mister?'

'Tell him your name, forchrissake,' Jappy said. 'What's the difference?'

Mitchell said, 'John Smith.'

'Thanks. Maybe some day we can be properly introduced. You know what I mean?'

'Now that you got him properly scared,' Jappy said, 'maybe we can get down to business?'

'Sure,' Shannon said. 'What do you know about how Morris Laplace got killed?'

His voice was casual, even bored, and the surprise was well executed, Mitchell thought. Nevertheless, Shannon had made a tactical error: he kept his pale eyes fixed on Jappy, and Jappy wouldn't show any reaction. But, Mitchell thought, Shannon was smart enough to know that, too. It didn't matter to him. He wasn't here to uncover a murderer but to be bought off.

'Who is this Morris you're talking about?' Jappy said.

'Morris Laplace is a stiff we picked up on the garbage dump. His head was smashed in and a lot of him was burned up, but we got enough off his prints to make an identification.'

Jappy said, 'I draw a blank, Lieutenant, a perfect blank.'

'He was seen here.'

'Here?' Jappy was emphatic, pointing specifically at the top of his desk. 'Somebody told you he was seen *here?* You been misinformed, Lieutenant.'

'By here I mean the alleys. He was placed here at the alleys last night.'

'He was? Oh well, I draw three, four hundred people a night, so it's possible he *was* here. But not that I *know* of.'

'Maybe some of your boys know of?' His eyes ticked off each in rapid succession. He got four headshakes. 'They say no. How about that?'

Jappy said, 'Nobody here knows anything about this Morris, dead or alive. You're not just fishing here and there around the town?'

'Would I do a thing like that?' His voice was mocking. 'I'm acting on solid information.'

'I hope it didn't cost you anything, because it stinks. What's the chances of your stoolies maybe feeding you bad info because they're hard up for a five or a ten?'

'Five or ten – you're living in the past. Didn't you ever hear of inflation?'

Jappy yawned. 'Will I see you around in a week, Lieutenant?'

'You'll see me right now,' Shannon said. 'I'm making an official investigation of the death of Morris Laplace at the request of the police in his hometown. I promised them some results – by this afternoon.'

'I never saw this man,' Jappy said, 'and neither did any of my guys. I don't know any cops in his hometown. I don't even know where his hometown is. There's no witnesses and no evidence. And how come the lieutenant of detectives handles a routine request like this in person, and doesn't just send one of his bulls?'

'Tell me how to run my bureau, I appreciate it,' Shannon said. 'I'll level with you. Maybe there's evidence or eye-witnesses, and maybe not. But this is what's important – the police in Laplace's town will act or will not act on my recommendation.'

'It can't be that hot, then, or they'd send one of their own guys to look into it. If they had a real lead, they wouldn't just make a routine request like this.'

'So you got a logical mind. But the question is – do you want some trouble or don't you?'

'Trouble,' Jappy said. 'It's a goddamn shakedown.'

In the sudden silence, Shannon began to quiver, and his eyes lightened until they were almost colorless in the deepening pink of his face. He seemed on the verge of exploding with rage and violence, and Mitchell thought, Beautiful, there's nothing so righteous as a crooked cop being accused of being crooked. Then the tension drained out of Shannon and he managed a rigid smile.

'Let's keep something in mind.' He continued to smile but his voice was icy. 'We do business, you and me, but that don't put us on any equal footing. I'm still a police officer and you're still a bum, and your friends along with you. If I made the money I deserved to make I wouldn't be on the take. So the point is – there's still that difference between us, and don't you ever go beyond the boundaries. Don't you ever do it, you hear?'

Tully said loudly, 'Shit.'

Shannon faced to Tully. 'The next time I see you downtown, the very next time, I'm going to find some excuse to pull you in, and then I'm going to give you one beautiful working-over. That's a solemn promise, punk.'

Tully leaped to his feet, but froze when Jappy said sharply, 'Don't you open your goddamn mouth.' Pale, furious, Tully gasped for air like a beached fish, then shot across the room. Shannon tensed, but Tully went right by him, jerked the door of the adjoining room open and disappeared behind it.

'Okay,' Shannon said, 'let's start the business discussion.'

'And if I don't think there's any business to discuss?' Jappy said.

'Then I'll give you the hardest time you've ever had in this town.'

Jappy nodded with resignation. 'So what must I do before it turns out that I'm clean?'

'Now you're making sense,' Shannon said. 'Now you're being practical and worldly.'

'But I want you to know one thing personally – I *am* clean. Somebody – not you, Lieutenant, naturally not you – somebody is trying to frame me. I'm innocent.'

'Oh, you're innocent all right,' Shannon said. 'But what's the difference?'

'I thought it might make some difference in the negotiations.'

'Oh, it does, it does. If I thought you had something to do with killing Morris Laplace, I'd really put it to you. But since you're innocent, I'm cutting away back to fifteen hundred dollars.'

Jappy let out a muffled moan of agony.

After Shannon left, while his weight could still be heard vibrating the outside staircase, Jappy put his face into his hands and rocked back and forth in his chair, emitting squealing sounds of pain. He was like a man bereaved, a mourner. Mitchell thought; he loved money dearly, and each time he parted with some it, was like enduring a death in the family. Bobby and Battler were staring at the floor, embarrassed. Jappy's attitude was thoroughly alien to them. For them, money that was hazardously earned was freely spent: on clothing, luxuries, above all, on partying, as though to put in a supply of happy memories they could draw on if and when they fell. And who was to say they were wrong? Where was the pleasure in sitting in prison and dreaming of a big bank account? Memories were made of good booze, fast cars, willing broads.

71

Jappy uncovered his face and looked up suddenly at Mitchell. 'How come Shannon didn't know you?'

'Why should he know me?'

'Before he came to Philbin he was a prison lieutenant in Fredding.'

'I know that.'

'Well?'

'I knew who Shannon was, but there's over four thousand –'

' – prisoners in Fredding. Yeah, I know. You said the same thing before when I asked you about this Laplace. You sure you were *in* Fredding?'

'Who makes up a thing like that?'

Jappy gave him a suspicious look, then went back to grieving again. 'The waste, the goddamn unnecessary*waste of all that money!'

Mitchell said, 'Stop crying. You got off cheaply.'

'Fifteen hundred dollars. Is that your idea of cheap? Fifteen hundred dollars tossed away on a chiseling, blackmailing cop?'

'To square a murder rap, it's not high.'

'How did he know?' Jappy said in anguish. 'How did the sonofabitch know?'

'He bluffed you out. The cop in this Laplace's town might have sent through a request for a routine inquiry after he was informed of Laplace's death, but he damn well didn't send Shannon up here. Shannon came on his own, looking for money.'

'He claimed he had a lead to me. After all, Laplace *was* here.'

Mitchell shook his head. 'He told the truth about the half-burned stiff turning up and making an identification through the fingerprints, but the rest was crap. They found a burned body on the garbage dump, and Shannon wasn't about to waste the opportunity to make a dollar. So he hit you up, you're one of his clients. I'll bet he's going to use

72

the same story and collect in two or three places around town. He'll get good mileage out of the stiff, and then he'll take a verdict of person or persons unknown. He doesn't give a damn who killed Laplace, and neither do the cops in Laplace's hometown.'

Jappy sighed. 'I know all that myself. He faked me out. But I couldn't even take a *chance* on being held as a suspect, even if there's no evidence, even if there's never any indictment. I couldn't afford to call his bluff.' He turned to Battler. 'Tell Tully to come in here.'

He reached into his drawer and took out a roll of coins in a bank wrapper, and he was on his feet when Tully came in, whistling and combing his bangs. He saw Jappy clench his right fist around the roll of coins.

'Hold him,' Jappy said.

Battler pinned Tully's arms behind his back. Jappy planted his feet and swung. His fist connected with a meaty thud and Tully staggered back against Battler, blood oozing from his nose and forming a Hitler mustache on his upper lip. His expression altered from surprise to fury, and he struggled against Battler's grip. With a controlled violence of his own, Battler lifted him off the floor and then dropped him back with a jolt. Tully continued to struggle, but not too convincingly, as though he was more afraid of Battler's potential power than Jappy's actual. He snorted, and Jappy jumped back fastidiously from a thin spray of pink.

Battler wrenched on Tully's arms, straightening him out. 'Hold still so he can hit you.'

Jappy said in disgust, 'That's enough. Let him go. I could keep hitting him every day for a month, and it wouldn't do any good.'

'I ain't gonna let you get away with belting me,' Tully said, but he didn't move, and he watched Battler warily.

'So you got a fat nose,' Jappy said. 'It's cheap enough for fifteen hundred.' He turned away. 'You and Bobby get out of here, we got work to do.'

73

Tully took out his handkerchief and dabbed at his nose. Battler moved away and sat down. Bobby opened the door, one hand on his head, as if to anchor his hair against the possibility of a surge of wind. He held the door until Tully went out, head down, shuffling, and then followed.

'The fifteen bills is going to come off the top of his end of the score,' Jappy said. 'Okay. Let's study the road map.

Mitchell ate dinner alone in the three-quarters-empty dining room of the Philbin Arms. The food was plain and indifferently prepared, but the service – in terms of both the table-setting and the ancient, sad-faced waiter – was excellent. Halfway through, he stopped looking at the waiter because he reminded him of Morris Laplace. Poor Morris Laplace, poor stupid old lag, who in his ignorant greediness to be a part of something had followed him from Amesville to Philbin – and had the bad luck to end up in a funeral pyre atop a garbage heap.

Bad luck. Morris Laplace's bad luck, Mitchell thought, was my good luck. The old fool could have ruined everything, and would have, if not through malice then by inadvertence. But Tully was all muscle and no skill with a sap, and he had crushed Morris Laplace's skull. If he hadn't, it would have been all over before it had fairly begun. My good luck, Mitchell thought, and Morris Laplace's bad. Maybe luck was a limited rotating pool, and you drew on it against somebody else's account, so that the balance was always maintained . . .

By hindsight, it wasn't too hard to figure out. Morris Laplace had worked at the Munchmore Biscuit plant, and on every occasion, when Mitchell ran into him, slyly suggested that he would like to be included whenever Mitchell got tired of the straight life and decided to pull a job. Poor Morris Laplace; he was yearning for the inside of a prison again, and didn't know it. Each time Mitchell had told him that he was straight, but Laplace had taken it with a wink.

Laplace knew better. Well, Mitchell thought, he *had* known better. And so, when he had taken the bus from Amesville yesterday, Morris Laplace had followed in his beat-up old car.

One point bothered him. How had Laplace *known* he had quit his job at the plant? It puzzled him until he remembered Laplace's job. He was a messenger, he picked up and delivered internal mail, pushing a small-wheeled cart from department to department. Through accident or by design, through curiosity, he had read the interoffice memo from Mitchell's supervisor to the effect that he was leaving the plant, and giving the effective date of the resignation. So sly, stupid Morris Laplace had tailed him from Amesville to Philbin Street, and from Philbin Street to the Pin 'N Whistle...

The favorite reading of thieves, those who read anything but comics, is paperback books about crimes and criminals, and they devour them uncritically even though the authors innocently fill them with mistakes and implausibilities that even the dumbest thief could pick out. Mitchell was a devotee; he had read enough of them himself. But now, at the hotel newsstand, he passed by the book rack and bought two weekly news magazines.

He went up to his room in the slow open-cage elevator, and father chaining the door, took off his jacket, tie and shoes and lay down on the bed to read. He went carefully through the first of his magazines, and rapidly through the second, which covered the same ground in much the same way. When he found himself yawning he threw the magazine down. He got out of bed and had begun to unbutton his shirt when someone knocked at the door.

He didn't move for a moment, except to turn his head toward the door. The knock came again, sharp, impatient. He buttoned up his shirt and walked slowly to the door. He opened it without unlatching the chain, and peered through.

He hesitated for an instant, then, frowning, slid the chain free and opened the door. Shannon came in.

'What do you want?' Mitchell said.

'Hey, try to sound a little hospitable.' Shannon was jovial. He went over to the bed and sat down on it. 'Say, "Good evening, Lieutenant Shannon, how wonderful that you dropped in".'

'What do you want?'

'That was pretty funny this afternoon in Schoeder's office. I thought I was very funny in there this afternoon.'

'I haven't got any sense of humor.'

'When I said "Who's your friend there, Jappy?" *That* was pretty funny. I thought you would piss your pants.'

'I thought putting the arm on Jappy for fifteen hundred dollars was pretty funny, too.'

'*Pretty* funny?' Shannon grinned. 'That was the *best* part of the whole thing. That was the *cream*.'

'You're a lousy cheap chisler.' Mitchell's voice was level, without heat.

'Oh. Oho. You're getting tough. You're getting mean. Oho.'

For the third time Mitchell said, 'What do you want?'

'I want to find out about a few things. That's okay, isn't it? That's in the contract, isn't it?'

Mitchell nodded. 'What's wrong with the telephone? It's safer.'

'And also, you don't have to look at me on the telephone. Right?' Shannon was still smiling, but his eyes were bleak. 'That's not a very friendly attitude. You know what I mean? I'd like you to be a lot friendlier.'

'Let's get to the point,' Mitchell said.

'I can *make* you be friendly. I have a way. You know that? It'll blow everything, but I can do it. You know that?'

Mitchell was silent.

'I can get you killed,' Shannon said. 'It's easy. Just tip you off to Schroeder. Just tell Schroeder that you're Johnny Handsome.'

PART II
Inside World

7

The visiting specialists' consultation room was an oasis of individuality in the desert of institutional sameness. Not that it could even compare with the warden's office, which was carpeted and wallpapered, and sported such personal touches as an elephant's-foot ashtray, a tear-gas canister autographed by John Dillinger (but it was a fake; the warden had never met Dillinger), a few inches of rope purporting to have been cut from the noose around the neck of the last man to be hanged in the state, and a snapshot of the warden as a young, smiling World War II M.P. lieutenant riding a jeep through the Ginza.

The doctor's desk was an aged but well-preserved rosewood, conspicuously free of the scars and nicks and gouges that prison furniture seemed to be born with. The chairs were leather-covered, the seats rounded and comfortable, of an entirely different family than the inhospitable straight-backed wooden chairs that were prevalent everywhere else. The walls were painted a pale green, but the color was concealed, neutralised by a scattering of diplomas and certificates, and by a series of engravings of medical subjects, mostly of people in various stages of comical or even grotesque distress.

The man behind the desk wore a white coat with short sleeves that showed powerful forearms forested by a dense growth of black curly hair. He was olive-skinned and he wore a thick black mustache flecked with gray. His face was round, and his brown eyes were warm and alert.

He consulted a folder on the desk and said, 'You're John M. Sedley. Correct?'

'Correct.'

'What do they call you?'

'John M. Sedley.'

'Joker. Come on, man, what do they call you?'

'Johnny Handsome.'

'Phooey. How about when you were a kid? Did they call you John? Or Johnny? Jack?'

'I was called Mitchell.' He paused, then decided to satisfy the doctor's unspoken curiosity. 'My middle name. Three of us were named John among the kids I grew up with. We called one John, and one Johnny, so I became Mitchell.'

'I'll call you that, if you don't mind. I'm Douglas Katsouras.'

Dr. Katsouras stretched across the desk, grunting, and extended his hand. Mitchell hesitated, then took it, and later was to remember the moment because Katsouras didn't smile. Prison officials always sent a wintry little smile along as an outrider with their handshake. For sincerity, Mitchell preferred a snarl.

'I'm a plastic surgeon,' Katsouras said. 'We're initiating a program of surgical rehabilitation at Fredding. I'd like to tell you about it.'

'Needle tracks,' Mitchell said. 'I'm not an addict.'

'I know you're not. I've decided not to work with any addicts. You seem to know something about this kind of program.'

Mitchell shrugged. 'A junkie I met in here had the tracks removed. He told me about it. You understand anything I'm saying?'

'Every word. I've done a lot of work with cleft-palate cases, I'm tuned in to the sound. Where did the addict you're talking about have his surgery done?'

'Some pen or other.' Mitchell shrugged again. 'This character told me about it. You remove the scars – '

'We can't remove them, actually. We change them. I suppose you know what needle-track is. Scars on the forearm of heroin addicts that come from prolonged injection with contaminated needles. Or – and sometimes *also* – little depressed pockmarks from skin-popping. Well, we disguise the tracks, we revise them so that they look like some kind of surgical scar.'

Mitchell said, 'Don't you know why the addict submits to it?'

'*Our* idea was to eliminate a stigma, and provide a better climate for rehabilitation. The junkie submits so that when he's picked up by the police he hasn't got needle tracks to identify him as an addict. Look, we're trusting, but we're not stupid.'

'Surgery or no surgery, the addict gets out of jail, races right back to his hometown, makes a connection, and starts shooting again. You can't win.'

For the first time Katsouras spoke stiffly. 'The rate of recidivism with addicts has shown negligible decline thus far. We admit it.' Then he brightened. 'But with non-addicts we've been able to show some good results. I've got some figures – '

'No, thanks. I'll take your word for it.'

'Okay. No statistics. But I'd like to explain the hypothesis behind the use of surgical intervention as a deterrent to recidivism.'

'I don't understand all your big words,' Mitchell said.

'Don't try to put *me* on.' Katsouras opened the folder on his desk, found a place in it, and speared it with his finger. 'Your I.Q. is more than twenty points higher than mine.'

'I cheated,' Mitchell said. 'I had the answers written on my shirt cuffs.'

Katsouras said, 'You know, there's no rule that says you *have* to give me a hard time. Relax, forchrissake, and spare a few minutes of your valuable time to listen to what I have to say.'

'Every second I'm gone, some whiskery old lag is tearing pages out of dirty books. There'll be nothing left but Dickens and Frances Parkinson Keyes.' He paused. 'Okay, Doc, I'll listen.'

'Thanks,' Katsouras said, and there was no sarcasm in his tone. 'To begin with, the hypothesis isn't new. It's been a long-standing assumption that physical defects, disfigurement, can be a powerful contributing factor in anti-social behavior.'

Mitchell snorted. 'It's also a short-standing assumption that social behavior, as you define it, isn't all that wonderful. At least us anti-socials aren't going to blow the world up.'

'It goes back before there was a bomb, and I can cite you examples – at least, literary ones. Quasimodo, the hunchback of Notre Dame, moved by hatred for his appearance into a life of crime. Richard III. Allowed his deformities to become a motivating factor in his life. Mr. Hyde –'

'No,' Mitchell said. 'Not the same thing at all. The stuff he drank turned him bad inside *as well* as outside.'

'I won't argue. Just grant me my central point.'

'That ugly is as ugly does? If you say so.' Mitchell smiled. 'I never identified myself with any of those cats. My boy was Caliban. You know? He looked in the mirror and raged.'

'So? I was a fat kid, a big tub of schmaltz. My alter ego was Humpty Dumpty. How do you like that? I was afraid to climb, because I thought that if I fell I might crack open.'

'You lost weight,' Mitchell said flatly. His hand lightly touched the crushed indentation of his nose, a scarred eyebrow. 'I picked up a few extras.'

'Lombroso,' Katsouras said. 'You've heard of Lombroso?' He paused for Mitchell's slow nod. 'Lombroso postulated the theory that there were congenital criminals who – in his words – "had the ferocious instincts of primitive humanity". And that these people were genetic throwbacks to earlier stages in the development of man. From this, he formed the theory that the facial appearance of criminals is distinctive, that certain physiognomic features are telltale signs of the criminal. It has absolutely no basis in scientific fact, though in a more ignorant age it was accepted as being true.'

'Yet, in a way, that's exactly what you're saying.'

'Use your head, man! What *is* true is that certain deformities are the *result* of a life of crime, which is to say, a life of violence or a life spent among violent people. But these are *traumatic* deformities – broken noses, knocked-out teeth, lacerated ears or eyebrows, scars of all kinds from wounds inflicted by knives, blunt instruments, other weapons.'

Katsouras was leaning across the desk, sweating, intense, eager, and Mitchell thought, I envy him; he believes in something.

'Lambroso is utterly without validity,' Katsouras said. 'Our theory is not that criminals are born, and bear the stigmata of criminals, but that stigmata can *make* criminals.'

'And what kind of theory do you have to explain unmarked, undisfigured, even good-looking criminals?'

'Goddamnit, you know I'm not claiming that only disfigured people are criminals, or that *all* disfigured people are. All our theory claims is that disfigurement *can* lead to deviant psychological behavior. Most disfigured individuals see themselves as they think others see them, only their imagination makes it a little *worse* than it really is. Disfigurement cuts down on social acceptance, and that in turn can push people into deviant behavior.'

'Wait a minute,' Mitchell said. 'If a disfigured person becomes an outcast in straight society because of his appearance, why isn't he just as much an outcast in criminal society?'

'Because criminals, who by performing unlawful acts repudiate middle-class *behavior*, repudiate middle-class *standards*, and so they're willing to accept disfigurement. In that sense, criminal society is more democratic, more tolerant than straight society.'

'Careful, Doc. So far, criminals are coming off pretty well.'

Katsouras allowed himself a grin before going on. 'Disfigured people are limited so far as equal economic opportunities go, too. So there's another inducement to drift off into a society where disfigurement *isn't* a drawback to earning money.'

Mitchell looked skeptical. 'So if you pretty people up, they leave prison and go straight and become taxpaying middle-class squares, a credit to society – right?'

'Don't put words in my mouth. We're still groping. We don't deny that the root causes of criminal behavior, even with disfigured people, are deeply buried, and often surgery doesn't help at all. And as I said before, we're almost a total washout with addicts.'

'You're wasting your time giving an addict a straight nose or nice ears. All he cares about is his fix, and he doesn't give a damn if his nose is straight – or if he hasn't *got* a nose – as long as he can warp that needle into his vein.'

'Everybody strikes out with the addict. Not only us, but Lexington, psychiatrists, groups like Synanon . . . '

Mitchell was sweating, and his denims were beginning to stick to his body. He squirmed, and Katsouras looked at him questioningly. 'The chair is too comfortable,' Mitchell said. 'You, too. You're treating me exactly like a human being, and the mixture is too rich for my blood. You must be trying to con me, somehow.'

'Jesus, you're a suspicious character. Jesus, it would be hell if you turned out to be a goddamn paranoiac.'

'Still, remember the old joke: Just because I'm a paranoiac doesn't mean that somebody *isn't* shoooting electric flashes through my head.'

'Give me a break. Nobody's going to force you to become my patient. In fact, *I* may not accept *you*.'

Mitchell laughed. 'In the business world, that technique is known as the negative sell.'

'Let me explain how we operate. In the first place, it's standard procedure to ask for volunteers.'

'A screw instructed me to come here. You call that voluntary?'

'The others *are* volunteers. I asked specifically for you. Two reasons: your intelligence and . . . ' His pause was barely perceptible. 'And your problem.'

'Something to get your teeth into?'

'Yes. We find that it doesn't pay to deal with minimal problems, because you can't judge results on just a minor change in appearance.'

'And you don't want to louse up your statistics.'

'Don't knock statistics. We're scientists –'

'And we're guinea pigs?'

'You're patients,' Katsouras said. 'And I'm a surgeon. I believe I can help some of you stay out of jail.'

'You believe that about me? That if you fixed up my appearance I would stay out of prison?'

'Statistically, the chances of your recidivating would be lessened. We don't give guarantees. And we don't ask our patients for them.'

'It's just as well you don't. I've known guys who tried to make it straight. With all the best will in the world, they're not equipped for the free world. All their abilities are criminal. And the benefits of going straight aren't so wonderful. Who wants a sixty-dollar-a-week job?'

Katsouras brushed by the question. 'Let me go on. I told you we asked for volunteers, but we don't accept those we feel are poorly motivated. Naturally, to begin with, we rule out psychopaths.'

'They don't give you significant statistics?'

'Try not to interrupt me. We also try to eliminate the *focusing* individual, the person who attributes all his problems to his deformity and uses it as a crutch to relieve his sense of failure. Finally, we eliminate the person whose *ideas*, like the operations, are cosmetic, who thinks that having his acne scar removed, for example, automatically makes everything rosy for him.'

85

'How long have you been doing this work, Doc?'

'Fifteen years ago, during my residency, I was part of a program at Sing Sing. Not since then. But I've kept up with the literature.'

'Gee,' Mitchell said, 'that's great. It's terrific that you've kept up with the literature.'

'Smart-ass. Tell me. Has the thought of having plastic surgery ever crossed your mind?'

'What has crossed my mind is that I am extremely ugly, and that it would be nice not to be. And that's about it. You learn to accept the fact that you were born to hard luck, you learn to adjust.'

'You weren't born with all of it. The ears, the palate, the chin, yes. But the nose and eyebrows were traumatic.'

'If you subtracted the busted nose and the eyebrows, I'd be pretty?'

'No, I just mentioned it.' He was silent for a long moment, and then he said casually, 'You know something, Mitchell? I could operate on you so that your own mother wouldn't know you.'

'No great improvement. Most of the time she was so bombed out on booze she wouldn't know me if I sat in her lap.'

'I may look like a linebacker,' Katsouras said, 'but I'm a real surgeon and I took the usual oaths. I meant exactly what I said. Change you so your own mother wouldn't know you.' He leaned across the desk earnestly. 'You may turn out to be a terrible pain in the ass, but I would like you to become my patient.'

Unbidden, Mitchell's childhood dream re-created itself: of the benign magician who would come one night and transform him with a single pass of his wand. But he had stopped dreaming that dream – and a lot of others – a long time ago.

He said, 'Suppose I said no. Would I get tossed in the hole or something?'

'Come on, Mitchell. Yes or no. And if it's no, you go back

to your library, and we had a pleasant ten-minute chat and that's the end of it.'

'It's sudden. I'm confused. You've thrown a big idea at me. I need time to think it over.'

Katsouras looked pleased, and Mitchell realised that he had been tested; and that his reaction had won him a passing grade. 'By all means. You want me to give you something to read on plastic surgery?' Mitchell shook his head. 'Whatever you say.' Katsouras stood up, a stocky, powerful man running to fat. 'So – think it over. I'll be here again next week.'

Mitchell got out of the embrace of the soft comfortable chair. 'Metamorphosis. You know Kafka's story? This is Kafka in reverse – cockroach into man.'

'It's stupid to think of yourself as a cockroach.'

He shook Katsouras' hand, and when he opened the door Katsouras called another name. A con got up from the waiting bench. He was blond and stringy, and his harelip pulled up away on the right side of his face, showing six white moist teeth in a permanent grimace.

8

In a week Mitchell had examined so many possibilities and fantasies, peered into so many dark places of his mind, that seeing Dr Katsouras was almost an anticlimax. And so he sat on the wooden bench and looked at the closed door of the consulting room with indifference. Another inmate occupied the far end of the bench, his head lowered into a magazine as if in an attempt at conscious concealment of a rough thick skin pitted and furrowed with acne scars. The disfigurement could be fixed up, Mitchell thought, with a faint smiles for his self-conscious knowledgeability, by a procedure called dermabrasion – a patient planing down of the outer skin with a small abrasive wheel, electrically driven, like a dentist's drill, until the scars disappeared, or, at least, were dramatically reduced.

He had spent a few hours reading up on plastic surgery in whatever books and periodicals he had managed to dredge up in the library, that dumping place of highly random reading matter from people who purchased a tenuous foothold in heaven by contributing their unwanted books. He had read, or skimmed, three books – a novel and two medical textbooks, both published decades ago, and, therefore, probably behind the times. Most up-to-date was an article in an elegant fashion magazine that had somehow descended into these inappropriate surroundings. It was about a fashionable European doctor who specialised in cosmetic surgery for chic, well-heeled ladies who sought to eliminate the inevitable disfigurement of aging.

The surgery was remarkable, and it actually did restore (at least on a temporary basis) youthfulness to flaccid tits and asses, jawlines, eyes, mouths, skin. The story of the magazine, breathless and fatuous, made plastic surgery seem frivolous and trivial, though it did treat briefly with the more serious side of cosmetic surgery – salvaging the wrecks of human beings after awesome auto accidents, repairing some of the obscene wounds of war . . .

The consulting-room door opened, and the harelipped con Mitchell had seen the week before came out. His lip looked worse than ever, livid, tortured, as if it were curling back in revulsion from its own ugliness. Mitchell knew what the man's speech would sound like – muffled, nasal, snorted, an idiot's voice even worse than his own. What would it be like to have a harelip *and* a cleft palate? But he remembered from his reading that the odds were fairly high against occurrence of such a hopelessly complicated affliction. Small blessing.

'Moretti.'

The acne-scarred man put down his magazines and went into the consulting room. Would Katsouras rub and scrape his face until it was as smooth as a bady's ass? And would Moretti then go out into the free world and become a model citizen, a square john with a nine-to-five job and life insurance and the same woman in bed every night for the rest of his life? Or would he recidivate like the hardened criminal he undoubtedly was? Would the cop's shibboleth hold – once a bum (to use their favorite term of endearment of their natural enemy), always a bum?

He shifted his position and looked through the waiting-room door to a segment of the prison ward – flaked dun bedsteads, coarse muslin sheets, gray blankets, and patients in various stages of convalescence or decline, much like any other overcrowded hospital ward, except that the windows were barred. A ward boy crossed the path of his vision, wheeling a medicine cart. Some boy: an old lag, an habitual con who must have been pushing seventy . . .

What was happening to Moretti behind the closed door? Had Moretti, too, spent an agonising week? Or had it been an easy decision for him: a few scrapes, the unmourned loss of some skin, and, presto, no need to duck his face behind magazines. What had Moretti's mirror, consulted by seeking eyes, said back to him? As for himself, for the first time in many years he had looked in a mirror neither in disgust nor bitter acceptance, but in wonder. This was *himself*, this broken-nosed, lop-eared, chinless, broken-browed horror was John Mitchell Sedley, also known as Johnny Handsome. If these things were taken from him, these possessions, these individual markings, who then would be left, who then would be the substance that cast the new image? If his speech became limpid, instead of a huffing imbecilic sound, whose speech would it be? In place of Caliban, who?

Doc had a point; not the whole bundle, maybe, but a point. His face had made him a criminal; or, at the very least, made it difficult not to become one. His face (and cleft palate) had been a barrier between him and a normal relationship with girls, kept him sequestered with books all through high school, barred him from the silly college fraternity he had so desperately wanted to belong to in a last-ditch effort to breach the wall of separateness, led him to drop out of college in his first semester, and pushed him, literally, to the brink of self-destruction. Finally, it had brought him to the commission of his first crime, the first of many, in many places.

Moretti came out of the consulting room, his eroded face impassive.

'John Mitchell Sedley.'

He went in. Katsouras stood up behind his desk and shook his hand, then waved him to the soft leather seat. He was wearing a dark blue shirt, open at the throat as before, showing sprigs of dark curling hair.

'Cicles under the eyes,' Katsouras said. 'Have a rough week?'

'You going to do a dermabrasion job on Moretti?'

'Well, well.' Katsouras' black eyebrows winged upward. 'I haven't made a decision on Moretti yet.'

'What are you – a teaser? Getting him all steamed up and then letting him down?'

'What the hell business is it of yours? So you did a little reading. Does that make you an all-round expert? I'm sending Moretti to see the psychologist.'

'Good. Pass the buck.'

'Jesus, you're feisty. I'm turning him over to the psychologist because he's better qualified to make a decision than I am. What I sense with Moretti is that he thinks the whole world is going to be beautiful once we scrape him clean. It doesn't work that way. Surgery is just the beginning.'

'What happens to Moretti if he's turned down? He puts his dreams away and returns docilely to being ugly again?'

'Do me a favor. Stop helping me run the show.'

Mitchell said mildly, 'I just thought you might have an answer.'

'I haven't got all the answers. I haven't got all day, either. What about *you*? What's your decision?'

'One thing bothers me – if I say yes. I'll be trading a certainty, no matter how crappy it may be, for an unknown. And people, even convicts, hate and fear what they don't know.'

Katsouras nodded eagerly, and Mitchell thought, I'm not like Moretti. I know how to sell him. But do I want to sell him?

'Can I give you some advice?'

Mitchell shook his head. 'We don't look at things the same way, though eventually our interests might come together. Basically, what you care about is my staying out of jail. What I care about is: What do I become, who will I be?'

'You – the *essential* you, whatever the hell that might be –

won't really change. What *will* change is the environment of the world you live in. It will become more hospitable, less suspicious, no longer repelled.'

'Maybe.' He studied the ceiling for a moment. 'Okay. I'll take a chance. Let's try it, Doc.'

'Good,' Katsouras said. 'I'll enjoy working with you.' He stood up, smiling, and put out his hand.

Taking it, Mitchell said, 'Do I have to shake your hand coming and going *every* time I see you?'

'Start learning to be more respectful to your surgeon. Otherwise, you could end up with your nose grafted to the back of your head.'

He lay stretched out on the white table while Katsouras, pushing, probing, pummeling, presented him with an under-view of batches of black hair growing a quarter-inch outside his nostrils. Katsouras ran a fingernail down the soles of his feet, and his toes curled.

'Sit up, please.'

He levered himself upright, dangling his legs over the end of the table. The whiteness of his body was startling, and he was aware of the folds in his belly, the slackness of his muscles. The prison fare of starchy food and minimal exercise didn't make for sound bodies. Or minds.

Katsouras said, 'You're in good shape considering how you spend your time. No reason why we can't proceed.'

'Would you do me a favor?'

Katsouras nodded, and ran his finger firmly, lightly probing, down the length of Mitchell's spine.

'Stop saying *we*. If you mean *you*, say so.'

'It's the way doctors talk. I think it's meant to be modest.'

'Or royal.'

Katsouras was rapping Mitchell's spine gently, almost absently, with his knuckles. 'Okay. You can get dressed.' He watched Mitchell slide off the table. 'There's nothing wrong with your back that I can detect. No curvature of the spine, no inherent weakness. You don't have to stoop the way you do. It's just rotten posture.'

'So?'

'So I'm making a cosmetic suggestion. Stand up straight. There's no reason for you to slump.'

'Isn't there?'

'You mean you're hiding, making yourself less conspicuous. I know that. When I'm finished operating on you, you won't *want* to hide. Why not look ahead and start improving your posture now?'

Mitchell braced his shoulders back and stood up straight. It involved a certain strain, but there was also a sense of pleasure and he felt taller.

'Just keep practicing it, and before long it'll became natural. Work at it. Come back to the office when you're finished dressing.'

When Mitchell took his seat across the desk again, Katsouras said, 'I've got enough patients lined up to get the program started next week. On my own. No team. No panel of surgeons and no gaggle of social workers. Oh, maybe a resident in plastic surgery once in a while, to gasp at my brilliance, and an anesthetist when I need one, and a competent nurse, but that's it. No team. No mass program. A maximum of ten or twelve patients. Sound good to you?'

'I'm gasping at your brilliance.'

'Okay. Unless you have any objection, we'll get you started next week.'

'How long will the whole thing take?'

'About a year – at least.'

'That's a lot of time.'

'You going someplace? Look, you're practically a compendium of cosmic surgery, so a year would mean moving along at a pretty fast clip. It assumes that we'll *do* everything that's indicated. You might want to cop out. It's painful and uncomfortable – not too dreadful as surgery goes, but no pleasure.'

'Can you handle so many different kinds of operations yourself?'

'Yes, but only because I'm fantastically talented.'

'And humble, too.'

Katsouras took a sheet of blank paper. 'Let's take inventory.' He began to jot down notes. 'Nose. Chin. Palate. Ears – '

'What's so bad about my ears?'

'They're shapely enough, but they're what we call Dumbo, or radar, ears. People rarely think of their ears as being particularly disfiguring, maybe because they're at the side of the head, out of the way. But you'd be surprised to see what a difference it makes when we pin the ears back close to the head. Okay, ears. Eyebrows . . . ' He glanced up quickly, as if to anticipate a question. 'Yes. We can remove the scars and make the broken brows whole again, hair and all.'

Mitchell touched his face gently with his fingers. 'It's quite a list. Can you fix all of that?'

'We've got the techniques for all of it – and more.'

'What about scars?'

'What do you take us for – shoemakers? None. Not a single visible scar.' Katsouras put down his pencil. 'We'll start with the cleft palate. Now. How much do you want to know about the procedure. I can tell you nothing, a little, or a great deal. Which do you think will make you happiest?'

'Who's the doctor here?'

Katsouras studied him thoughtfully. 'I've found that with imaginative people it's a good idea to give them a blow-by-blow description of what will take place, because nothing I'm going to do is as bad as what they speculate. You get the point?'

'I get the point. You're a terrific psychologist.'

'Well?' Katsouras said.

'Tell all.'

'Okay. In the simplest terms, cleft palate is exactly what it sounds like – a palate that's split, or cleft. The palate is the vault or roof of the oral cavity –'

'What's an oral cavity?' Mitchell said innocently.

'Okay, the mouth. The palate divides the mouth from the nasal cavity and nasopharynx. The anterior half of the vault is the hard palate, the posterior half is the soft palate, or velum. It's the velum that is most important to speech and deglutition.'

'Does that word have anything to do with swallowing?'

Katsouras gave him a look. 'The soft palate is easier than the other to work with, which makes you lucky. By the way, was there any cleft palate in your family?'

'Yes,' Mitchell said in surprise. 'My father.'

'It's normally hereditary. It occurs in embryo, and incidence is about one in five thousand.'

'I'm lucky, making it against those odds.'

'You're lucky because your hearing is good. Frequently a cleft velum impairs hearing. Also, you might as well know that the optimum age for cleft-palate surgery is about eighteen months. How old are you?'

'Eighteen months plus. Anyway, cleft-palate surgery probably wasn't even invented when I was eighteen months old.'

Katsouras smiled. 'The first successful cleft-palate surgery was performed in France by a dentist named Le Monnier – in 1776.' Katsouras rubbed his chin. 'After the operation you'll need speech therapy; you have to be taught how to use your new palate. I can arrange for a therapist to come to the penitentiary.'

'And after that?'

'After that Caliban should sing like Ariel.'

'Jesus,' Mitchell said in a whisper. 'Jesus, that would be fine.'

'Jesus,' Katsouras said mockingly, 'it's human.'

The night before the operation he lay awake on the hospital

bed, his head cradled in his hands, his thoughts fragmented, undisciplined, using memory as a whip to punish him. Katsouras had offered him a pill to assure a good night's rest, but he had refused it. Why? Some dumb idea of showing his toughness or pride, like the man before a firing squad waiving a blindfold. In the convict's world you had to be tough, or pretend to be tough, which sometimes came to the same thing. Your survival depended on it.

In the course of his life, it had taken him a long time to develop toughness, though he had been given more opportunities to learn than most, beginning early in childhood. At first it had nothing to do with his looks. His father had been a seaman, and although he remembered him without affection, there was no denying that he had been, for what he was, an interesting man. His strongest impression – although he couldn't recall a specific word or phrase – was of the quality of his father's rhetoric (and never mind that it was snuffling cleft-palate speech) in his fights with his mother. When he wasn't locked in furious domestic argument, he was sullen, silent, withdrawn. Strife seemed to bring him out, as if only then was his attention fully engaged by life.

On the visits home between voyages, or in the rare times when he found himself on the beach, his father and mother drank, had sex and fought, sometimes all three at once. As time went on, and her husband's absences became more protracted, his mother started to take lovers, first as one-night stands, then on a semi-permanent basis. Once his father had come home unexpectedly (*whenever* he came home, by that time, it was unexpected), and found his mother and her lover, both naked, sipping booze at the kitchen table. Curiously, there was no explosion. Instead there was a great deal of noisy convivial drinking, then all three went to bed together. This was the last time he had seen his father. He never returned. Nor did his mother care, although she missed his money, those remittances that used to arrive with surprising regularity from this or that foreign port.

What had become of his father? Years later, more out of curiosity than real interest, he had made an effort to trace him through his union, but he had let his membership lapse and was no longer carried on their books. So he was either dead or at sea under a foreign flag, and it didn't really matter which. All he had even gotten from his father was the dubious gift of life and a few books he had left behind, a bequest by default, but a precious and enduring one . . .

He had been ugly in the cradle – so awesomely ugly that the more impressionable of his mother's friends considered it a punishment of God. It didn't take long for his own innocence of his looks to be disabused. His mother, in a triumph of maternal blindness, had cooed over him, making much of the delicate transparency of his skin, which was the entire catalogue of his good points, and others had restrained their comments in her presence. But once he was out on the streets, he learned quickly, not only from his playmates, but even from the gratuitous comments of insensitive adults. His friends ragged him mercilessly at first, but not for long, because such things didn't count for much in the community of small boys.

But as he grew into adolescence he was suddenly set apart again. One's looks became obsessively important, and he became agonisingly aware of his own. Once, in high school, he had withdrawn totally rather than expose his face to his classmates, and had simply stayed home for several weeks. Eventually, a truant officer fetched him back, and a psychologist, after a brief interview, had advised him, as if he didn't know it, that he carried a burden his contemporaries were spared, and that he must learn to compensate for it in some – unnamed – way. They were to have pursued the matter on another day, but the psychologist, through oversight or indifference, had never gotten in touch with him again.

It was at this time, seeking acceptance of some kind, any kind, that he began a slow drift toward the shape of his future. He tried sports for a while, but he was only a fair athlete, and the meaningless intensity of the competition bored him; and, anyway, after the game, after the shower, when social life resumed, he was once again excluded. So he gravitated to the company of the outcasts, the social misfits – the academic boobs, the disciplinary problems, the abnormally shy. Like him, they bore stigmata, and among them he found a precarious community of aggrieved apartness.

It was dangerous company. Not only were they developing a posture that sought to be self-sustaining outside of society, but they began to take pride in their differentness, to nurture themselves upon it. And so it wasn't long before they began to commit 'anti-social' acts: mindless vandalism, intimidating or even beating up other kids, giving teachers a hard time, stealing cars as a prank. The turning point from delinquency to purposefulness came when they began to steal for profit. The hardening process was under way.

Mitchell stole on several occasions, because it was necessary to show his toughness. But he was uneasy about it. His reading, if nothing else, had given him a decent sense of moral values. And unlike most of his companions, he was a bright student. A teacher almost saved him, one of those marvelous spinsters with selfless dedication to her profession and, possibly, a stifled maternal instinct. She pulled all sorts of strings to get him a one-year scholarship to a small college. He had hopeful visions, then, of a new life, but they were not to last, and he must have suspected it himself, because of the two valises he had arrived with on campus, he never unpacked one at all.

The incident that pushed him over the brink, finally, was so outrageously stupid that it should have been part of a bad movie rather than life. There were fraternities on campus, and through the efforts of a boy in his English class, with whom he shared a community of interest in books, he was pledged to one of them. He was aware that fraternities were trivial and anachronistic, but hungering for acceptance, he

98

cheerfully endured the mindless trials of a pledgee. Then, at the end of that silly season, he was blackballed. The fraternity, with idiot insensitivity, instead of assigning his sponsor to break the bad news, dispatched the very man who had instigated the blackballing. This manly dunce had said, 'It's nothing to do with you personally, it's just that we have to protect the frat. With your, well, with your looks, you wouldn't add anything to the credit of the fraternity, or help in getting the pretty girls; in fact, some of the brothers felt you might hurt our standing on campus . . . '

The encounter took place on a campus parking lot, at night, and Mitchell had turned without a word and walked away, too desperately miserable even to be angry, wanting only to hide, or kill himself. He never knew whether he would or could have taken his life, because just before leaving the parking lot, some instinct of self-preservation saved him. Red rage came, unbidden, heedless. He went back, intercepted the blackballer as he was getting into his car, smashed him to the pavement, and was well on the way to beating him senseless before a campus guard interceded.

The next morning he packed, left the campus without word or note, and returned to his home, or what was left of it: a mother now in the final stages of acute alcoholism. That night he looked up his old friends, the outcasts. Two nights later he walked into a liquor store and emptied the cash register while one of his companions was enthusiastically gun-whipping a clerk who hadn't gotten his hands in the air quickly enough to please him.

In less than a month he suffered his first arrest.

The superannuated ward boy, Morris Laplace, waked him early in the morning, presenting a gray, furtive, and at the same time innocent, face: the face of a habituated con who had spent the greater part of his life inside, and who, when released, would contrive to return again, and, eventually, die in prison, his only real home. Laplace told him that he could wash up, but that there would be no breakfast for him this morning.

Mitchell went to the john, and then lay down again on his high hospital cot. He shut his eyes and listened to the sound of the waking ward, men slowly coming back to life, or some semblance of it, with a medley of groans, farts, curses, phlegmy throat-clearings, incoherent protests, as if to re-assure themselves with the noises of life that they had not died sometime in the long bleak night. He heard feet shuf-fling to the john, and once, in a far corner of the ward, a scream that contained pure terror.

'Calm as a clam. You wouldn't think he was about to get butchered.'

Mitchell opened his eyes to an underside view of Dr. Katsouras, swarthy, neatly shaven, jowly. He was wearing a white shirt, with the sleeves rolled up over the hairy muscu-lar forearms that tapered down to strong wrists and efficient blunt fingers. A taller, younger man stood behind him, dressed in a dark business suit.

'Are we ready?' Mitchell said, and for the first time felt a dark thrill of apprehension.

'Not yet. Got to do an otoplasty first, radar ears, worse than yours, if you can imagine it. This is Dr. Wilson.' The tall man nodded. 'He's a first-year resident in anesthesiology. We let him practice his craft on people like you. It's cheaper than buying white mice.'

Dr. Wilson blushed and murmured a protest. Mitchell returned his nod.

'We're using a general anesthetic, and with Dr. Wilson putting you out, you have only one thing to fear – not wak-ing up again.'

Wilson, trying to match the bantering tone, said, 'Anyway, I guarantee you won't wake up *during* the operation,' but gave Mitchell an apologetic look.

'If you'll be so kind as to turn over,' Katsouras said, 'Dr. Wilson will give you a shot in the ass.'

Laplace stepped forward with a tray. Mitchell rolled over and tugged his pajamas down. He felt the cold refreshing wetness of alcohol and then a sharp jab.

Katsouras said, 'That'll make you drowsy and relaxed, so that when we roll you in for general anethesia –'

'Scopolamine,' Dr. Wilson said, 'inducing a dreamless sleep.'

'I like that,' Mitchell said. 'I'd like it every night, in fact.'

He felt relaxed, whether because the medication had already begun to work or because he imagined it had. Katsouras and Wilson moved off, and he shut his eyes on a pleasant, uninflected timelessness. Later he was aware of being lifted onto a table, and of the ceiling moving above him. When he bent his head far back, in a form of wrestler's bridge, he saw Morris Laplace's wrinkled face above him.

In an all-white room, Katsouras was standing with Wilson and a female figure in white – a nurse, middle-aged, gray-haired, solid. Katsouras was holding something up for Wilson's inspection and saying, 'This is a Dott, double-T, mouth gag. The blade holds the endotracheal tube securely on top of the tongue, and improves the operative exposures.'

Katsouras' fastidiousness about the double-T struck Mitchell unaccountably as being one of the funniest things he had ever heard, so that he was grinning broadly when Katsouras bent over him, his face dark and serious above a pale blue surgical gown. Then Katsouras withdrew, and Dr Wilson was telling him to breathe naturally, and something shadowy edged toward his face and then covered it . . .

. . . But he had dreamed it all. He had never left his bed in the prison ward. He felt pleasantly drowsy, and the noises of the ward seemed muted. His throat felt scratchy and warm. He raised himself on an elbow to ask someone for a drink of water, and saw Katsouras come into the ward. He was dressed in a business suit, not the surgical blue Mitchell had seen him wear in his dream. He started to speak, but was waved to silence.

'No talking. You won't want to, anyway, you'll start to hurt in a short while. I'll leave a pad for you. Write on it if you have anything to say.'

Mitchell stared at him in bewilderment.

'The operation is over. Took a little under an hour. That's the virtue of scopolamine – you don't know nothing.'

Then it was over. He hadn't dreamed the whole thing. He became suddenly conscious that his lips and tongue felt sore. Probably because of the Dott blade (double-T). The operation was over, and his palate was no longer cleft. In time, if Katsouras had not been putting him on, he would stop snuffling like a rooting pig when he spoke, and would sound like everyone else. Could he believe Katsouras?

'I'm putting you on a liquid diet for a day or two. I'll look in tomorrow, and probably get you out of bed. If the pain gets too bad, ask the ward man for relief. He's instructed to give you Demerol if you require it. The operation, as we say, was a success.'

He watched Katsouras leave, and as if his departure took with it some form of sustenance, at once began to feel pain. Its intensity took him by surprise and he rose up compulsively on his elbows, then lay down again. Most pain was not unbearable, unless you let it become so. He knew that from harsh experience: he had had to bear enough of it in his lifetime. But it didn't work. The pain became increasingly severe, and he knew he would need relief.

Laplace was across the ward, sitting on the edge of a bed and talking to a patient. Mitchell gestured to him. Laplace continued his conversation. Mitchell waited for a minute, two minutes, with the pain rising like a flame in his mouth. He reached for the pad Katsouras had left him, and printed on it in large block letters: PAINKILLER! Bracing himself on his elbow, he scaled the pad across the room. It fluttered in midflight, but held its course and struck Laplace lightly on the chest.

Laplace picked up the pad and scurried over. 'You bastard!' He had a high-pitched, quavery old-man's voice. The finger he pointed was gnarled and shaking with anger or age. 'Where you come off –'

Mitchell reached out and captured the finger. He bent it back toward the wrist, and Laplace bent to ease the pressure until his grimacing seamed face was an inch from Mitchell's.

'Painkiller,' Mitchell said. *'Now.'*

In consternation, he heard the sound of his voice – the same nasality, the same huffing congestion. It hadn't changed. He released Laplace's finger with a backward shove and fell back on the bed. Laplace went off, muttering. He was still muttering when he returned with his cart.

'Bastard, throwing a pad at me in my own ward.'

But he administered the drug, and presently Mitchell felt the pain slipping away, taking his consciousness with it. In his last waking instant he heard a replay of his voice, and thought, That Greek sonofabitch, he failed me . . .

9

The speech therapist arrived a week after Mitchell had been allowed back on solid foods. He had dropped ten pounds on the diet of liquids, baby foods, and semi-solids. But he told Katsouras the weight loss came from worry over his speech.

'You cut me up for laughs. The operation was a success, but the patient still sounds like a retard.'

'In a few months, if you want to badly enough, if you use your intelligence, and if you really sweat it, you'll be speaking as well as I do.'

'Jesus, who wants to sound like a Greek short-order cook?'

The therapist was a black girl in her early twenties, with a master's degree and a very serious view of her profession and its responsibilities. She was tall and stringy and intense, and Mitchell learned after her second or third visit that it was easy to make her cry. He had come close to crying himself during their first meeting.

They sat in a pink-walled room that was used for group therapy sessions, and she looked at him nervously and told him stiffly what was on her mind.

'We have to begin by determining our main line of attack. We must move along the lines of least resistance by deciding what is most easily learned by the patient, what will make the greatest difference to him, and what he wants to learn.'

Mitchell said, 'I'm your first patient, right?'

'You are not my first patient. You are my first *adult* patient.'

'Are you nervous about being inside a prison?'

'I think I'm safe here. We're wasting time. It's your hour, you know, and if you want to waste it –'

'Okay. I'm sorry, sister.'

'Very well. We start by teaching you how to swallow correctly and how to control the air stream. Directing the air stream from the nose to the mouth – once you learn to do that consistently, it's half the battle, and then we can move on to voice quality.'

'How long will it all take, sister?'

'My name is Miss Carter. We don't feel it advisable to make predictions about the length of treatment. Too much depends on the attitude and motivation of the patient –'

'Still. Make a guess.'

'Four months. Or six.' She paused. 'Or possibly three. Shall we begin?'

'Let us begin, Miss Carter.'

'You may call me Erna if you wish.'

Katsouras bent Mitchell's head back, focused a bright light on his open mouth, and peered inside, his attention concentrated, his breathing loud and regular. He switched off the light and went back to his desk.

'It's pretty,' Katsouras said. 'How's the therapy going?'

'How do I sound to you?' Mitchell was challenging, almost belligerent.

'Up to now, very well. But your last speech was poor. You got tense, and regressed. I've known it to happen on occasion as much as a dozen years later. How do you like the therapist?'

'The spade? I like her.'

'Do you have to call her that?'

'Shouldn't we call a spade a spade, Doctor?' He noted Katsouras' annoyance. 'Sorry. A joke. I like Erna. She's very serious and she works very hard. She regards me as a big challenge and she wants to win. So do I, so we make a good team.'

'Okay. Let's do another operation.' Katsouras looked at him over appraisingly, his eyes touching each feature, as if taking an inventory. 'What about those ears?'

'You're the doctor.'

'Keep that in mind, joker.' He reached into a drawer for a large metal-backed mirror with a handle. He handed the mirror to Mitchell, then got up and stood behind him. 'What do you see in there?'

Mitchell took a sidelong, furtive glance at himself. 'I see Caliban in there.'

Using both forefingers, Katsouras gently pressed Mitchell's ears close to his head. 'Now what do you see?'

'Caliban with his ears close to his head.'

Katsouras sighed and went back to his desk. 'Ears. Ear operations. Called otoplasty. Ears. Even at their prettiest they don't win a beauty contest, but they're interesting. Did you know that the configuration of the external ear is so individually distinctive that some European police bureaus use them for identification, like fingerprints?'

'Trust a cop. They'd print appendixes if they could.'

'The operation takes about an hour. It consists of making an incision behind your ears, reconstructing them by remodeling the cartilage, then stitching them down snug to the head in mastoid region. Presto, no more taxi-door ears.'

'Scars?'

'They don't show, because they fall in the natural lines of the ear crease.' Katsouras reached under his desk and brought out a camera in a leather case. 'I'm going to shoot a few pictures.'

'Mug shots?'

'It's standard procedure in plastic surgery to take before-and-after shots.' Katsouras took the camera out of the case and adjusted the settings. 'Before you go, I'll give you a

106

bottle of Phisohex. It's an antibacterial agent. Wash your face with it for the next few days, especially around the ears. Get your hair cut short. Use the Phisohex through the weekend and we'll operate you on Monday morning.'

'I'm going away for the weekend.'

'Smart-ass.' Katsouras brought the camera close to Mitchell's left ear, squinting through the viewfinder. 'Smile.'

The huffer-puffer was an ingeniously simple and effective device to aid a patient in directing the air stream correctly. It consisted of a piece of cardboard or stiff paper folded so that it presented two parallel surfaces about an inch apart. The patient placed it with the upper plane resting on his upper lip, directly under his nose. This naturally brought the lower plane against his lower lip, just underneath his mouth. A fluff of cleansing tissue was placed on each surface, and when the patient began to speak, the action of the tissue told him whether or not he was speaking properly. If the top piece of tissue moved across the surface of the cardboard, he was directing the air stream improperly through his nose; if the bottom, correctly through his mouth.

Erna Carter had introduced the huffer-puffer early in the game, and Mitchell had practiced with it endlessly. Now, at a stage where he hardly needed such a primer device, Erna nevertheless insisted that he use it to make sure he didn't regress unconsciously. Actually, he had learned quickly to direct the air stream through his mouth, and it was only occasionally, when he was fatigued or under stress, that he resorted to the old snuffling nasal mode.

Erna was very pleased with his progress. 'I'm going to leave a tape recorder with you so you can work on voice quality yourself between my visits.'

She had pointed out to him that the patient had difficulty judging his own voice quality as he spoke, but that if he *listened*, if he played his voice back, he was capable of making an impartial judgment.

Mitchell said, 'Tell me, Erna, are you happy with your pupil?'

'Oh, yes – ' She cut herself off and blushed, embarrassed by her unprofessional burst of enthusiasm. 'Compared with the children, you're doing quite well. But you should, shouldn't you?'

Mitchell grinned at her, and read from the card in his hand, 'When in the course of human events it becomes necessary . . . Come on, Erna, giving me stuff like this to read. It's all a crock of fit.'

'Crock of what?'

'Fit.'

'Once again.'

'Shit.'

'Good. Now let's try it again . . . ' She stopped abruptly, confused, and put a prim hand over her mouth. Mitchell put his head back and laughed, directing the air stream through his mouth.

That night, in his cell, watching for the regular crepe-soled passage of the gun-rail guard, with the battery-powered recorder turned low, he spoke into the mike, listened to himself, erased, spoke again, listened, until, at last, at first light, he fell asleep exhausted, an hour before the morning wake-up bell racketed through the cellblock, wrenching him loose from a dream in which, speaking to a huge gathering in a cathedral, he suddenly snorted through his nose and blew the entire assemblage into a disarray of shattered limbs and organs.

On Monday morning Morris Laplace waked him early. In the grayed dawn light of the ward, Laplace administered a subcutaneous shot of what Katsouras had informed him was soluble phenobarbital, 0.12 grams.

'Make you calm,' Laplace said. 'I'll give you another shot in about an hour. Make you so you won't be bothered by nothing.'

'I wouldn't be bothered anyway.'

What real need was there for him to sound like a hard case, to impress a pathetic old-timer like Laplace with his toughness. None. No reason, except that it was the way of his world, the thieves' world. Of *any* world?

'You say,' Laplace said. 'But if you was to hear all that crunching noise without being doped, and knowing they was cutting you up – '

'Go peddle your papers, old man.'

'Cons,' Laplace said. 'They're nice people, grateful. You know, some day I'm going to get pissed off and slip somebody an air bubble through the needle. Wham! – an embolism. That'll show them how tough they are.'

Laplace wheeled his gear away. Mitchell dozed, and waked when Laplace returned to give him another shot of phenobarbital. There was no conversation this time. He pillowed his head on his hands and listened to the familiar sounds of the ward awakening from the little death of sleep to the protracted one of daytime...

He was taken up to surgery. Katsouras, dressed again in his pale blue gown, administered a shot, followed by several more – pinpricks – in the area of his ears.

'What's in that needle, Doc?'

'Nupercaine. Local anesthetic.'

'Could do without it,' Mitchell said drowsily. 'That's how tough I am.'

'Maybe,' Katsouras said. 'But *I* couldn't.'

Katsouras went away and Mitchell looked without interest at the ceiling. Presently the ceiling started to move backward, and he realised, lazily, that he was being wheeled into the operating room. Katsouras was talking to the surgical nurse who had attended at his palate operation. Katsouras was holding what seemed to be a cotton stocking. He came over, followed by the nurse. She lifted him up, and Katsouras slipped the stocking over his head and rolled it down over his neck. There were holes in the stocking for his ears; the nurse fished them out.

Katsouras spoke to him. 'We sew the stocking to the skin so that it doesn't move around. Any objection?'

Mitchell felt a dull, blunted, painless series of touches at his right ear; then, after a moment, at his left.

'Almost ready,' Katsouras said, his voice vague, floating. 'But first we infiltrate the skin behind the ears and the mastoid region with epinephrine . . . ' He was doing something around the right ear. 'Listen carefully, so if you ever have to perform an otopasty you'll know how to proceed . . . And now the left ear.'

'What?' Mitchell said.

'It's to improve hemostasis – blood clotting . . . Now we'll let you cook for five minutes, and then we'll operate you.'

The nurse was hovering over the table. She was blocky, solemn, with a faint down on her cheeks and chin, and she regarded him calmly and professionally. She was a nurse to trust, Mitchell thought.

'I trust you, Nurse,' he said. After a while Katsouras returned and said something to the nurse about anesthesia. 'How do you know it's working?'

'We test by sticking you with a knife.'

'When do you do that?'

'I just did it. Do me a favor and shut up so I can go to work. If I need your advice as we go along, I'll be sure to consult you.'

Mitchell felt a sensation at his right ear, as if someone had rubbed a rather insensitive finger over his skin, and it was accompanied by a dull crunching or cracking sound. It wasn't pleasant, but there was no pain. He realised that he was being cut, but it didn't seem to matter much. The touches and rubbings continued, with discernible differences in their kind, and, sometimes, the crunching sounds were louder than usual. On occasion Katsouras would speak crisply to the nurse, and, rarely, she would reply.

110

Sometime later he heard Katsouras mutter, 'Ear one. All snugged down. Now for ear two.'

'Wake me up when you get to ear three,' Mitchell said.

Although he was somewhat hazy about the details of the transition, Mitchell was aware that he had been returned to the ward. Katsouras was standing over his bed, wearing slacks and a boldly colored checked sports jacket.

'You look like a jockey's agent,' Mitchell said. Something white and bulky obtruded on his peripheral vision. He touched the side of his face. 'What's this thing?'

Katsouras said, 'You'll hurt some when the ears wake up. You can have aspirin or codeine. Don't abuse the privilege, the pain won't be all that bad. What you've got around your head is a series of dressings, then a circular compression dressing of sterile gauze, and over all, an elastic bandage. It's to prevent your ears from falling off.'

'Please,' Mitchell said.

'I'll remove the dressings in forty-eight hours, except for the compression dressing. You'll be wearing that at night for approximately three months.'

'You sure you know what you're doing?'

'Patients,' Katsouras said, sighing. 'Ears heal by fibro-cartilagious union, which you can look up in the dictionary when you get a chance. The process takes about three months to completion, and the compression dressing guards against accidental trauma. Convinced?'

'If you say so. I think it's beginning to hurt.'

'So? You're tough, aren't you?'

'I'm tough,' Mitchell said. 'I guess I'm tough.'

Mitchell walked into the doctor's office, but started to back out when he saw Shannon. The prison lieutenant was seated in a chair in a corner, and his eyes flicked quickly to Mitchell, automatically challenging.

'Come on in,' Katsouras said.

'I can come back later.'

'Lieutenant Shannon is observing our program. Sit down.'

Mitchell looked at Shannon, who flicked another glance at him, casually contemptuous.

'You don't mind?' Katsouras said.

Shannon moved slightly. 'Try minding, bum. Just try minding.'

Mitchell shrugged and sat down. 'I don't run the prison.'

'That'll be the day,' Shannon said, 'when a bum runs the prison.' Katsouras started to protest. Shannon cut him off coldly. 'Or when a doctor runs the prison. That'll be the day, too.'

Katsouras remained bland. 'Let's go inside and look at the ears,' he said to Mitchell.

Mitchell got up. Shannon didn't move, and Mitchell had to step carefully over his outstretched legs. The legs pulled back for Katsouras. In the consultation room, Katsouras switched on the overhead lamp. Mitchell shied away from Katsouras' touch at his left ear.

'Still tender,' Katsouras said. 'But beautiful.'

Shannon came into the room. 'Looks like good work, Doc.'

'I dressed the wound, God healed it. Ambrose Paré said that about three hundred years ago. It still goes.'

Mitchell said, 'No false modesty, Doc. Let God do his own bragging.'

'You sonofabitch, don't back-talk the doctor.'

Shannon's voice, sudden, high-pitched and hard, held the force of a blow. But Mitchell knew it was phony. Shannon wasn't stupid, he couldn't mistake banter for disrespect. So he was deliberately provoking a situation.

Katsouras said, 'Don't get excited. He made a little joke, that's all.'

'He's a bum,' Shannon said, 'and bums have to learn to respect their betters.'

Katsouras said mildly, 'Who's to say who his betters are?'

'You do-gooders rupture my butt. He's a bum, and he's in

here to be punished for being a bum. That's justice. But you'd think they were heroes the way you psalm-singers go around kissing their asses. You think he's grateful for what you're doing for him?'

'It's irrelevant,' Katsouras said. 'I wouldn't get out of bed in the morning if I was looking for gratitude – from *anyone.*'

'Don't expect any from *me*,' Shannon said. 'You're not doing *me* any good with all this crap.'

Katsouras finished examining Mitchell. 'You need a score card to tell the scar from the skin fold.'

'Can I give up that headband at night?'

Beneath the crook of Katsouras' elbow Mitchell watched Shannon light a cigarette. He held the match for a moment, and then flipped it, still lit, toward Mitchell. It landed on Mitchell's shoe, went out, and clung. Mitchell dislodged the burnt skeleton with a little kick of his foot.

'Wear it for two or three weeks more and then we'll see,' Katsouras said. He switched out the overhead light. 'How's the speech therapy going?'

'Fine. Erna thinks I'll be finished soon.'

'Get finished,' Shannon said. 'So you can start doing a little work around here for your keep.'

'He hasn't really lost so much time,' Kassouras said. 'A few hours a week for therapy, a few days for postoperative recovery.'

'It upsets the routine.'

'Routine – the holy of holies.'

'Yeah, the holy of holies. Routine is what prison is all about. It's what keeps all these bums from killing each other or humping each other silly or tearing the walls down. We got four thousand animals in here, and without routine you'd have bedlam. Tell me what other way there is.'

'One way – stop thinking of them as animals.'

'Shit.' Shannon spat heavily on the floor and rubbed his

foot over it. 'They're animals. You think this one – ' The
jerk of his head toward Mitchell was contemptuous. 'You
think this bum won't be back inside again?'

'I can't say. But I can hope not.'

'Down deep he's a bum, your knife can't cut that out of
him. A bum is a bum.' He shifted his bright malicious gaze to
Mitchell. 'Am I right, Sedley?'

'I guess you're right, Chief.'

'Why are you calling me chief, Sedley? I'm not a chief.'

Mitchell said nothing.

'I asked you a question, Sedley. Answer.'

Mitchell looked down at his hands crawling across his lap
toward each other, as if joined together they might put up a
stronger resistance to losing control.

'My name is Lieutenant Shannon.' The bright blue eyes
danced. 'Let me hear you say it, bum.'

'What's the point of this?' Katsouras said.

'Say it, bum.'

'Lieutenant Shannon.' Anger had caused him to regress;
he heard the syllables come out in a muffled snort.

'Lieutenant Shannon.' The high voice was a cruel, accur-
ate imitation. 'Now say this, bum – "a bum is a bum and will
always be a bum".'

Katsouras said. 'Forchrissake, Lieutenant!'

'Say it,' Shannon said. 'Say "I'm a bum, and a bum is
always a bum".'

'Lieutenant!'

'Say it, bum!'

'Go fuck yourself!'

Mitchell saw a flash of glee light up Shannon's eyes, and
he knew what was coming when Shannon shot out of his
chair, but he still wasn't quick enough to protect himself.
Shannon's open palm rang against the side of his head. He
bounced off the table, but Katsouras bore him back. He
struggled, cursing in a mindless, muffled rage, but Katsouras

kept him pinned against the table, smothering him with his weight.

His strength spent itself, and he lay quiet. Katsouras shifted some of his weight, cautiously, as if testing his intent, then removed it and let him up. Shannon was gone.

'I used to be a wrestler in college,' Katsouras said cheerfully 'I know how to use my weight for leverage.'

Mitchell put his hand tentatively to his face. The skin seemed on fire. 'Christ, the bastard. The bastard!'

'You're snuffling.' Katsouras gently removed Mitchell's hand from his face and bent close, peering. 'Try it again.'

'The bastard. The *bastard*.'

'That's better. He missed the ear. He was going for it, you know. Such beautiful work, and he might have messed it up.'

'I'd better get back to the library,' Mitchell said.

'Look – don't try anything stupid.'

'Not now. I'm fine now.'

'Don't worry. I'm going to have a talk with the warden.'

'Forget it. He'll back up Shannon and wreck your program.'

'I'm a physician, I don't stand for brutalisation of my patients.' He picked up the phone. 'I'm going to make an appointment with him –'

Mitchell put his hand on the phone. 'I was never a wrestler, but I know a hell of a lot more about the penitentiary and prison politics than you do. You want your program to continue? Hang up.'

Katsouras glared at him, but after a moment, cradled the phone.

She stood up with what was meant to be an air of finality but was curiously tentative. He looked at her – a tall, thin black girl, with an earnest face that only barely suggested the missionary zeal burning inside her.

'Well, that's it. There's nothing more to do.'

115

'I'm graduated?' He tried to keep the pleasure out of his voice, but he could hear it, taste it. 'You're giving me the gate?'

'You speak very well, I'm surprised . . . I mean, that it took so short a time. If you just keep practicing, so that you don't backslide . . . '

She was ill at ease. Her cheeks were darkened by a blush, her bag swung back and forth in agitation. Suddenly, now, Mitchell thought, we have a relationship, now that we're not going to see each other again. No, he corrected himself, now the relationship is *asserting* itself; now that we're no longer a determined teacher and an equally determined student, it's safe to admit that we like each other.

He said, 'You know, Erna, in all this time I never once told you how much I appreciated what you were doing for me.'

Quickly, as if to head off a revelation of feeling, she said, 'You always did say thank you after each session. Not that your manners were all that wonderful.'

'I'm not going to make a scene,' he said, smiling. 'I just want to say that you're a very fine teacher, and that you're going to be a blessing to a lot of people before you hang up your huffer-puffer.'

She looked hunted, and said, 'A teacher is only as good as his pupil.'

He put out his hand. She hesitated, and then took it. Her grip was hard and bony and warm. It occurred to him that it was their first physical contact of any kind. He held on to her hand, and then, in a gesture that astonished him even as he was making it, bent over and gently brushed the skinny knuckles with his lips.

She turned and fled, in a form of terror, then suddenly returned, rummaging in her bag. She pushed something at him. 'Graduation present, remembrance gift . . . ' and she was gone again.

It was a huffer-puffer, neatly, patiently constructed of aluminum worked into the proper two-tiered shape. He placed it in position under his nose, and said, directing the air stream through his mouth, enunciating distinctly, 'Thank you, Erna, thank you very much.'

10

Katsouras had never been in the library before, and his presence seemed somehow to be a violation of the orbit in which they saw each other: office, operating room, hospital ward. He bestowed an obligatory glance on the stacks of books, but he had no interest in them. His manner showed that he had come on a special mission.

'Is it true you're going to be paroled?' He couldn't keep his voice from showing dismay.

'I came up before the board. I don't know whether they'll give it to me or not.'

'They asked me for a deposition.'

'I know. Thanks.'

'How do you think they'll decide?'

'Parole boards are freaks. No way of figuring them. I've been up before them before and been turned down. There's a technique. Maybe I didn't have it before. My sentence only has a year to run, maybe they'll give it to me this time.'

Katsouras picked up a book and looked at the title gloomily. 'It's a hell of a thing to say, but I wish you were staying around a little longer. I should have bum-rapped you on the deposition.'

'You'll find another patient, Doc.'

'I've *got* other patients, but you're my number one project.'

Mitchell said, 'We're talking about getting out of prison, Doc, about becoming a free man.'

'I'm a Greek bastard. I know it.'

'I looked into the mirror the other day. Except that it isn't so easy to find my ears any more, I'm still Johnny Handsome, the ugliest man in town.'

'Oh, the palate is nothing? Jesus, stop overwhelming me with appreciation. How much time before you know the board's decision?'

'A few weeks, maybe a month or more. If I had known how upset you were, I'd have spat in the board's eye.'

'Weeks, maybe more than a month,' Katsouras said reflectively. 'I could do the nose and chin in that time, though it's rushing things. Of course, there's postoperative care –'

'Don't you consult the patient? It sounds like surgical rape.'

'Hell, don't you *want* to get fixed up? Don't you *want* to stay out of prison?'

'So far, palate and ears together, I'm the same man. Don't forget, it's just a *theory* that you can make a few passes with a sharp knife and return me to a state of grace and innocence.'

'Don't twist what I said. All I've ever promised is that cosmetic surgery can give you a sense of confidence in your appearance, a feeling of security about the way you look to other people. The ears were just a beginning. When we get the nose and chin fixed up, you won't recognise yourself. You *will* be a different man.'

'On the outside. On the inside, Caliban.'

'But why not a *handsome* Caliban?'

Mitchell laughed. Katsouras eyed him shrewdly, as if assessing the good nature of his laughter. Satisfied, he smiled.

'I'll expect you in my office tomorrow morning. We'll plan our procedures. Naturally, I'll want your opinion on a few matters of surgical technique.'

The next night, late, long after he had left Katsouras' office, Mitchell lay awake in his cell, trying to pinpoint the precise moment when it had happened. It was a signal, indefinable, sharp thrill which he could only equate for newness and wonder with his first ejaculation, self-induced, in the sweat of a long-ago sleepless midnight. Even the sense of guilt. Above all, the sense of guilt. And it wasn't until dawn, as he strove to separate the ceiling from the amorphous grayness that filled the cell, that he could conclude, weary from debate with himself, that as it was wrong to feel guilt about masturbation, so it was wrong to feel guilt about his first touch of vanity.

He had gone to Katsouras' office and taken his seat in the black leather chair, and waited until Katsouras finished making notes in a folder. When Katsouras closed the folder, he looked up with a frown.

'I realise you feel that I think of you as just a piece of meat.'

'What brings this up?'

'The way I reacted yesterday to the idea of your being paroled.'

Mitchell shrugged. 'We all have our thing. Yours is carving up meat.'

'A surgeon isn't supposed to get too involved with his patients.'

'He might get fond of the meat and start trembling when he carved it.'

'But I don't entirely subscribe to the idea. I'm a friendly Greek, and I think that the mysterious, aloof doctor concept is for the birds. But I learned years ago, at Sing Sing, that you can't engage inmates in personal chatter. They're suspicious, they think you're prying. So I restrain my natural inclination and don't ask any questions.

'You'd get lies for answers, anyway.'

'Would you lie to me?'

'Sure. About anything that mattered. If it didn't matter, I might tell the truth.'

'I used to be curious about how people landed in prison. I

thought it might be useful to help me understand them. But I always got the same answer. Framed. Every last sonofabitch I ever met in Sing Sing was innocent. You too?'

'I was framed.'

'Exactly what I mean. So I don't ask questions, and my patients think I don't care,' Katsouras was upset. 'The hell with it. Let's talk about the operations.'

'Would you really like to know how I got here?'

'At this point? It wouldn't have much pertinence. It would just be curiosity.'

'Then I'll satisfy your curiosity.'

He heard himself volunteer with something like astonishment. He had never told anybody about it, though it had chafed, or worse, throughout the years of his imprisonment. Not the event itself, not the crime; that had represented normal risk in the life of a thief, and he had no bitch about it. But the aftermath . . .

He said, 'The score was a jewelry store, but don't think we were high-class jewel thieves. It was a *credit* jewelry store, in a blue-collar neighborhood. Cheap diamonds, chips, a lot of flashy but low-carat stuff, some gold and platinum settings, watches, semi-precious stones . . . I doubt that the most expensive items in the store could set you back much more than five or six hundred dollars. It was strictly a smash-and-grab operation. There were four of us, and if we could sweep enough stuff fast enough, we might clear a thousand or fifteen hundred each after you discount the fence's percentage.'

'Sounds like a high risk for so little gain,' Katsouras said.

'Whoever said thieves were smart? Anyway, we broke in and started sweeping up the junk, but our lookout spotted a police car coming a few blocks away. He wasn't coming for *us*, as it turned out, just answering some kind of call in the area. But it looked bad to the lookout. He hit his horn, and everybody started piling out of the door for the car. It was a very long, very narrow store, and I happened to be in the

121

back of it, in the repair department, hooking all the repair-watches that looked like gold. The others scrambled out, but by the time I reached the door, it was too late. The cops were practically rubbing bumpers with our car by then, so my friends took off and left me inside the store.'

'So much for honor among thieves,' Katsouras said.

Mitchell smiled. 'They didn't have any other choice, unless they wanted to shoot it out, and that would have been stupid. So they took off, leaving me inside, hunkered down behind a counter to avoid the headlights of the cop car, which were now heading straight in and shining right through the plate-glass show windows. It was tough titty, but nobody's fault. Honor? What kind of honor would there be in all four of us being collared?'

'Then you're not mad at being abandoned?'

'Abandoned? They took off to save their skins, that's all.'

'And left you to be caught.'

'And left me to get away if I could. I almost did. Instead of chasing after our car, the cops decided to stay. I guess they must have caught a glimpse of me, and figured it was a lot easier to take one man in a closed area than to chase three in a fast car. So they ducked out of the cop car and pulled their guns and hollered for me to come out. Actually, I was pretty lucky. Sometimes, in situations like that, cops get silly, and they come in shooting, lots of fire power. Other times they call for you to come out, and when you do, they shoot you down, even if you're unarmed. This particular pair of cops just flattened themselves on either side of the door, with their guns drawn, and yelled for me to come outside.'

'And you did?'

'I went out the *back* door. I don't know how long they stood there hollering for me to come out, but –'

'Then you got away?'

'From the jewelry store, yes. I was in a town I didn't know, so all I could do was keep moving and try to put as much distance between me and the scene as I could. Finally

I found a bus stop, but while I was waiting for a bus to show up, a cop car came along and picked me up on suspicion. Suspicion of nothing. It wasn't until I was in their car that the robbery flash came over their radio. They went racing back to the jewelry store, and one of the cops there said he recognised me, and they arrested me and charged me with robbery.'

'Did he really recognise you?'

'Not a chance. He couldn't have seen anything more than my shadow at the other end of the store, and even that for just a single instant. He lied in his teeth, the sonofabitch.'

'You make him sound like a villain,' Katsouras said mildly. 'Whether he was lying or not, he had the right man, didn't he?'

'He lied about having seen me,' Mitchell said. 'To that degree I actually *was* framed.'

'I don't dig the distinction. You *were* guilty, you *were* robbing the store.'

Thieves and straight people lived by different modes of logic, Mitchell thought, not merely different views on the sanctity of property, what was right and wrong, the inviolability of laws, the merits of the police. In the new vocabulary, he had heard thieves defined as being anti-establishment, but that was nonsense. The thief had a vested interest in the establishment, and would seek to preserve it so that he could separate it from a reasonable amount of its goods and riches.

Amused by his own conceit, he smiled and said, 'We're on different wavelengths, Doc. Anyway, that's the story of my downfall.'

'You pleaded guilty and were sentenced?'

He shook his head. 'I went to trial and was convicted by a jury of my peers, a lousy lawyer, and a man's avarice.'

He could tell from Katsouras' startled expression that he had reveiled himself, shown the anger and bitterness that he had fueled for five years in the solitariness of his mind. Every-

123

body needed a beacon, he thought wryly, and his had been hatred and its malignant dream, revenge.

Katsouras said anxiously, 'Relax. Take it easy. You don't have to talk about it if it bothers you.'

'I want to.' And it was true, or, at least, half true. Quite suddenly he wanted to hear about it himself, as it were, to test and taste what he had never before articulated except in his secret voice. 'I want to.'

'Up to you,' Katsouras said cautiously.

'I was indicted,' He said levelly, 'brought to trial and convicted. I never should have taken a fall. The case was flimsy, and there were two ways to beat it. One was to have a decent lawyer, who would have torn the case to bits. The other was to lay a little grease on the cop who claimed to have made me in the jewelry store.'

Katsouras looked shocked.

'Either way, it would have cost two or three thousand dollars. But I was tapped out. I didn't have a nickel. Jappy Schroeder had the money. But he wouldn't spring for it.'

'I can't believe the part about the cop taking a bribe,' Katsouras said.

Mitchell smiled. 'He actually *came* to me and *offered* the deal. I sent him to see Jappy. Jappy turned him away.'

'I gather that Jappy was one of the people involved in the robbery?'

'Without the cop's testimony, there wouldn't even have been a trial. They would simply have let me go for lack of evidence. But the sonofabitch was so pathologically stingy . . .' He broke off, feeling hatred well up in him like bile.

'You said something about a lawyer . . . ' Katsouras' voice was tentative, he looked distraught.

'Any halfway decent criminal lawyer would have made mincemeat out of the cop's testimony. But Jappy wouldn't shell out. So the court assigned a lawyer, an old jackleg shyster who lived on the bottle, and couldn't concentrate for thirty consecutive seconds. So the state stole it, and I went to the penitentiary.'

Katsouras said, 'Did this Jappy have the money? Did he hold a grudge against you?'

'It was just the money. He's pathological about money, so he sold me out.'

'What I don't understand,' Katsouras said, 'is why *you* didn't give *him* away. In anger. Don't tell me there *is* a code of the underworld?'

'I might have bought myself immunity, or a lighter sentence, by singing, but there was no future in it. I had to go on living in the thief's world.'

Katsouras was making an effort to understand. 'Did he threaten you? Were you afraid he could get at you, even in prison?'

'It takes clout to run something like that. Jappy was a small-time crook, like me. He couldn't have pulled anything off in the penitentiary.'

Katsouras said, shrewdly, 'You've been nursing this thing for five years. When you get out, are you going to even the score?'

'It was a bad scene,' Mitchell said, 'but it's done, it's over with.'

'You're sure? Look, Mitchell, if you have any ideas –'

'No ideas. Tell me about the operations.'

'The operations,' Katsouras said. 'The operations.'

'It's over, Doc.' Mitchell smiled. 'Thieves' honor.'

Katsouras appraised the smile, and seemed satisfied. 'Okay. The operations. Nose and chin. I'll do the nose first, and the chin a few weeks later. It's a rush, but we're fighting time. The nose. Yours is a rare beauty. How many times has it been broken?'

'I stopped counting after three. Once with a sawed-off baseball bat. That was the worst. It busted it all to hell.'

Katsouras nodded in agreement. 'I'll tell you a few things about noses. The nose, before it has been busted all to hell with a baseball bat, is shaped and constructed like a tent, with the dorsum' – he stroked the ridge of his own nose – 'serving as the ridgepole. People are more sensitive about their noses than any other feature, for the obvious reason – it's the largest and the most prominent. Most rhinoplasties, by the way, are performed on women. In men, usually -- except those that have professional reasons for it, like actors, and God knows actors have enough hang-ups of their own – in men we frequently find that there are deep-seated psychological problems that a new nose won't heal. But we do perform them on men. With increasing frequency, in fact.'

'Good. I don't want to break new medical ground.'

'I'm going to rebuild your nose practically from scratch. Create a nose, Incidentally, at no extra charge, I'll fix up a badly deviated septum, so you'll be able to breathe better. Okay. For building material we take some autogenous tissue – '

'Translation, please.'

'Self-binding. Specifically, a rectangle of cancellous iliac bone – cancellous means spongy, the ilium is your hipbone. We cut the iliac bone out of you, shape and smooth it in the form of the letter *L,* and build the new nose around it. All the work is done from the inside, and there are no scars.

'Now. When I get the iliac bone out of you, I take enough to go around for the nose *and* chin. Economy. I don't have to cut you up twice. I just refrigerate the extra bone until it's needed.'

'Will I miss the hipbone?'

'Not at all. Unless my hand slips, there should be no loss of motion or mobility. The hip operation, by the way, is probably more painful than anything else I've done or will be doing to you.'

'I'll bite a bullet.'

'It hurts after the operation, but not for very long. General anesthetic, and I'll do the nose procedure while you're still asleep, so you'll be spared all the unpleasant noises.'

Katsouras adjusted the lamp and reached for his camera. As the lamp flooded Mitchell's face with brightness, he instinctively ducked his head. He was an avoider of light, a seeker of shadows. Not only his face, he thought, but his metier; darkness was the thief's element.

Mitchell shut his eyes, listening to a silence broken only by Katsouras' muted breathing and the click of the shutter. Several times Katsouras tilted his head, his fingers firm in guidance. When the clicks stopped, Mitchell opened his eyes.

Katsouras was back behind the desk. 'Everybody wants a movie actor's nose, but we try to give them one that conforms to the face.'

He pulled a sheet of paper toward him and began to draw noses, frowning with concentration.

'I want a movie actor's nose,' Mitchell said.

'You've got one. A character actor's.'

Mitchell laughed, but it sounded hollow, because he knew that while he didn't necesarily want a movie actor's nose, he did want one that would be attractive. He sat back in his chair, and put his hand to his face, cupping his nose. It was the gesture he had used to conceal his face as a boy. He had eventually discarded it, in defiance of this ugliness. But now, as once in his boyhood, he found himself imagining a handsome face beneath the hand.

Incredibly, the boyhood fantasy had resurrected itself. But could those paper noses Katsouras was drawing represent reality? Could one of those two-dimensional shapes become solid, become flesh, and somehow float magically from the page to his face? His hand slipped lower and created a chin.

'Tell me about the chin, Doc.'

Was it his own voice he heard, made muddy by anxiety, by greed? Yes, he cared about being presentable. He wanted to be looked at by people, not studied; to be ignored – yes, he would settle for being ignored.

127

'The chin? I shape the iliac bone, as I do for the nose . . . '

'The same shape, of course,' Mitchell said. He needed the joke to relieve his tension.

'Smart-ass. There are two techniques. In one, I cut you open under the chin and insert the bone. This leaves a scar, but it falls into the line of the neck creases, so it isn't visible.'

'And the other way?'

'I make a cut in the bottom of your mouth, and drop the bone in. The scar is inside, and naturally doesn't show. Incidentally, the chin procedure will help to rectify the malocclusion of your teeth, though you'll probably need a little additional dental work.'

'Through the mouth,' Mitchell said, trying to make his voice casual. 'If it's all the same to you.'

'Sure. It's all the same to me.'

The morning of the operation he was awakened by a new ward boy, who told him that Morris Laplace had gone home. The prison jargon for being released was, he thought, inappropriate for an old con like Laplace. The penitentiary was his real – and only – home; sooner or later, he would come back to it. When the ward boy left, he diverted himself by trying to remember some of the details of the operation that Katsouras had spelled out for him. After Dr. Wilson put him to sleep, Katsouras would cut out a quantity of hipbone. Then the nose operation would begin. His head would be placed on a soft doughnut-shaped ring, and the vibrissae (the technical term for nostril hairs) would be trimmed with blunt-tipped scissors dipped in petrolatum so that the hairs would stick to it. An ophthalmic ointment would be placed in each eye to prevent irritation. His face would be prepared surgically with aqueous Zephiran (whatever that was) and his nose cleaned out with a cotton-tipped applicator, much as a mother cleaned out an infant's nose . . .

When he was wheeled up to the operating room he was already sedated. He was vaguely aware of the presence of

128

Dr. Wilson and the stocky surgical nurse, but he was back in the ward before he saw Katsouras.

'Good afternoon,' Katsouras said.

An amorphous cloud of whiteness hovered irritatingly in front of him. He tried to brush it away, and realised that it was a dressing on his nose, impinging on his peripheral vision. Breathing was difficult, and his mouth tasted of blood.

'You have one of the finest set of shiners I've ever seen,' Katsouras said cheerfully. 'Ecchymosis.'

I am no stranger to ecchymosis, Mitchell thought, that black-and-blue protest of the body's outrage at the violence done to it. I have worn it often as the badge of a bad, dangerous life . . .

'Do as little talking as you can for a few days,' Katsouras said. 'We have a slight paradox. I'd like you to have complete bed rest for about forty-eight hours, to prevent elevation of arterial and venous pressure in the head. At the same time, you should be on your feet quickly because of the hip, to prevent the possibility of a limp. Can't do both, so we'll serve the interests of the nose. Two days in bed, then up and walking on the third day.'

Mitchell touched the dressing.

'Your nose is bandaged and taped. No splints, to avoid necrosis of the soft tissues. Liquid diet for the rest of today and tomorrow. Cracked-ice compresses to put over your eyes to minimise the swelling. You can change those yourself as needed. You've got gauze sponges under your nostrils. Nursie will replace those as indicated. For pain, aspirin or codeine, dispensed on reasonable request by Nursie. I think you're going to have a nice schnozzola. The hip wound is dressed and won't be touched. We'll remove it in a couple of days. Any questions?'

Mitchell wet his lips. His voice came out as a cracked whisper. 'Just one. Can I suffer in peace?'

9

It was Mitchell's first time on the yard in a week. He moved slowly, mindful of Katsouras' admonition to avoid strenuous physical activity, and was waiting at the gate when the recall bell sounded. As he started inside, a small man pulled at his sleeve. 'You Sedley?'

Mitchell nodded cautiously.

'Your parole came through. You're going home.'

Mitchell's heart lurched. 'How do you know?'

'I'm a clerk. I handled the papers.'

Mitchell looked at him fiercely. 'No mistake?'

The little man shook his head. 'You got a butt?'

His fingers numb, trembling, Mitchell put a pack of cigarettes in the man's hand.

'Lucky bastard,' the man said. 'I'm here for keeps. I killed my business partner and his wife. I didn't have anything against his wife. She screamed, and kept screaming, and in the state I was in, it got on my nerves, so I killed her, too.'

Mitchell was shivering with a strange, unreal excitement that was close to being sexual in its steamy urgency.

'Beautiful,' Katsouras said. 'Look at that bridge. Like a Roman god. Greek gods didn't have any bridges. Take a look at it.'

Mitchell took the mirror and gave himself a fleeting glance. 'It looks like a hip.'

'Careful — you're letting your emotions run away with

you.' Katsouras put the mirror away. 'The nose is still fat. It'll start thinning down, though you'll have *some* swelling for about a year. Breathing rough?'

'A bit. Would irrigation help it?'

'Gee, Doctor, I would never have thought of that myself. No.' He picked up a thin swab and dipped it into a solution. 'I'll clean the rims of your nostrils, but that's all I care to risk now.'

'You're the doctor.'

'Flattery will get you nowhere.' Katsouras tossed the discolored swabs away. 'In a few days I'll clean you up a little inside, and do something to shrink the mucosa. I'll see you every two days for the next few weeks. After that a checkup once a month for three or four months, and that's it.'

I'll be long gone by then, Mitchell thought. It had been several hours since he had heard about his parole, and euphoria had been replaced by uneasiness. What would he do when he got out? How would he adjust to freedom? For many convicts, these questions were academic. They would hit the free world and start stealing again. They would make a score or two, they would party mightily on the proceeds, and then they would take a fall and end up in prison. Which, if the psychologists were to be believed, was exactly where they wanted to be in the first instance. Well, he wasn't about to deny the psychologists. He had seen too many thieves scatter clues like maniacs, everything but leave a calling card complete with telephone number and zip code.

Katsouras had gone to the refrigerator. Now he was seated again, and bouncing a piece of bone in his hand. When he had Mitchell's attention, he held the bone up between his fingers for inspection.

'This is your chin.'

He would have to be told, Mitchell thought. What was the sense of prolonging it?

'The way the nose is healing, I'd like to go ahead with the chin in about three weeks.'

'I won't be here.'

Katsouras almost dropped the piece of iliac bone. 'It came through? Shit.'

'Shit on *you*,' Mitchell said. 'We're talking about my freedom.'

Katsouras showed no disposition to retreat. He said, 'Damnit, I hate to see it screwed up after all this work.'

'I appreciate what you've done. I also know your motives.'

'I'm a thoroughly selfish bastard, I have no genuine concern in the patient, right?' He put the bone on the desk, and said quietly, 'Do you trust me at all?'

'As much as I trust anybody.'

'Jesus, don't go maudlin that way, it's embarrassing. Look.' He touched the bone with his fingernail. 'You need this. Without it you're incomplete, you're a halfway job. You also need those busted eyebrows fixed up –'

'You mean *you* need them fixed up.'

' – not so much because they're a disfigurement, though they are, but because they're the insignia of a violent mode of life. Okay, suppose we forget the eyebrows. But not the chin, for God's sake. Your chin is a *basic* disfigurement, one of the stigmata that led to your anti-social behavior.'

'Assume you're a hundred-percent right, what's the difference? I'll be out of here in a few days.'

'I know that. I'm going to ask you to do something – delay your release for a few weeks. Now tell me I'm demented.'

'You're demented.' Mitchell put his hand over the receding slope that passed for his chin. 'There's probably no way of delaying release even if I asked for it.'

'But if it could be done? If we found some way to arrange it?'

'All I'd have to do is suggest it, and they'd hand me a one-way ticket to the psycho ward.'

'But if I could swing it?'

Mitchell tightened his hand over his chin and said nothing.

The chin operation was performed under local anesthetic and took under two hours, with the bone being inserted through an incision in Mitchell's mouth, just forward of the tongue.

As matters turned out, it hadn't been difficult to arrange for Mitchell to stay beyond the date of his official release, nor was it in any way unprecedented. Katsouras deposed that Mitchell was his patient, in the midst of a treatment it would be medically unsound to terminate, and when Mitchell agreed to it, the delay was granted. But despite Katsouras' pleas, he had refused to stay a moment longer than the absolute minimum essential for postoperative care.

'This is our last meeting,' Katsouras said.

He was behind his desk. After turning the lamp off he had removed his white coat and put on a tweed jacket, as though, Mitchell thought, he were performing some sentimental rite.

'Don't get sloppy,' Mitchell said. 'Life is full of last meetings. They're the only thing that makes it bearable.'

'Don't be so goddamn cynical.' Katsouras' dark eyes were sad, humid. The other side of the Greek coin of euphoria, Mitchell thought. 'I need to be told about life by a convict. You're some expert on how to live.'

'Touché,' Mitchell said. 'That's French for you burn my ass.'

Katsouras sighed. 'Do you know what you're going to do?'

'I've been offered a job. The management of the Munchmore Biscuit Company has a social conscience. It hires a few ex-convicts each year. They're in Amesville. It's a small town near Melton.'

'Don't knock kindness,' Katsouras said. 'What will your job be?'

'Sales manager,' Mitchell said, and smiled at Katsouras'

involuntary tic of surprise. 'I'll be working in the shipping room.'

'Well, it's a place to begin.'

'Sure. Give me a year or two and I'll work my way up to chairman of the board.'

'Smart-ass. What are you equipped to do?'

'Steal. You ever read *Hudibras*? Samuel Butler. He says, "The thief. Once committed beyond a certain point he should not worry himself about not being a thief any more. Thieving is God's message to him. Let him try and be a good thief." '

'I don't read dirty books. I'll want to see your nose another time or two, and the chin, too. Can you get to my office? It's about sixty miles from Melton.'

'I guess so, if I have to.'

'You don't *have* to do *anything*,' Katsouras said. 'I can refer you to a plastic man in Melton, if you prefer.'

'I'll come to your office. The new man might be an even worse doctor than you.'

Katsouras was silent for a moment, then said, 'By the way, I had a chat with our old friend Lieutenant Shannon the other day.'

The change of subject was abrupt. Katsouras was queasy about saying good-bye, and clutching at conversational straws to postpone it. Mitchell grunted.

'He said he's thinking of leaving the prison service and taking a job in a police force somewhere upstate.'

'Somewhere's loss is the penitentiary's gain.'

'I'll be glad to see him go. He's a cruel, crude man.'

'He's a cop. What do you expect?'

'Don't blame all cops because Shannon is a rotten one. I've known some damn good ones, honest and bright and enlightenend.'

'It's only straight people who ever get to know enlightened cops. The kind crooks get to meet are all like Shannon.'

'You know what he said when he told me he was leaving?'

'He said, "I can't make any money in here." '

Katsouras looked startled. 'And accompanied by a big dirty wink. How did you know what he would say?'

'He's a cop on the take. All the way. He takes every place in the prison, even packs – cigarettes – from the poorest cons in the place. No mercy. He's a thief at heart.'

'Does the warden know it?' Katsouras shrugged, and answered himself. 'Oh well . . . *You're* not one of his contributors, I hope.'

'I am.'

'But you haven't *got* anything.'

Mitchell smiled. 'It's standard procedure for rich or powerful prison inmates to get all the new or dirty books before anybody else. They pay off in packs.'

'Do you allow that to go on?'

'I don't. I *didn't,* until Shannon got into the act. Now I dot it, and the packs are paid directly to Mr. Shannon.'

'I guess I've got a lot to learn.' Katsouras sighed, and stared at the desk. Then he looked up moodily at Mitchell and said, 'So you're going out.'

'I'm going out.'

'A different man. I want you to understand that. A differen man.'

'Is that right? Can you tell?'

'You're now an attractive man, Mitchell. Even with those lousy eyebrows. You are an *entirely different-looking man* than you were – I want you to get that through your head. Your face is different. Your voice is different. Your posture is different. Remember when I told you your own mother wouldn't know you? Well, she wouldn't. You want a last look in my mirror?'

'What would you do if I howled with rage?'

Katsouras hesitated. 'Look, I'm not supposed to push you. They tell me it's bad psychology, it makes people defensive. But you're too stupid or stubborn to get it yourself. Or admit it, which comes to the same thing. So I'll tell you one more

135

time. *You are not recognisable as the man who came in here five years ago.* You don't have to hide any more. You're nice-looking, and I wish to hell you'd get that through your head.'

'You're the doctor.'

'So I've heard. Katsouras glanced at his watch. 'I've got another patient.'

'God help him.' Mitchell stood up and put out his hand. 'We haven't shaken hands in five minutes. Shake.'

Their handshake was hard, muscular, brief.

'Thanks for everything, Dr. Katsouras.'

'My pleasure, Mr. Sedley.'

Five of them were being released, and a prison wagon was waiting in the yard to drive them to the bus station in Fredding, where they would disperse. The prison captain shook their hands and mumbled some ritual phrases halfway between congratulatory and cautionary. They were decompressed through four or five compartments separated by bars and steel doors, and then they were out in the sunlight, squinting like moles. They got into the station wagon, taking their seats stiffly, nervously, questioning the plausibility of what was happening. The station wagon began to move, the front gate opened, and they were outside in the free world.

Half aloud, Mitchell said, 'I can do without another sound of clanging steel for the rest of my life.'

As the station wagon sped toward Fredding he looked at his companions. They were silent, inturned, but it wasn't hard to read their minds. They were concentrating with total effort on how to get back into prison. They didn't know it, Mitchell thought, but that was exactly what they were doing.

But you, Mitchell said to himself, *you're different. Aren't you? Well, aren't you?*

12

Before long, he came to regard his employment at the Munchmore plant and his residence in Amesville as a time out of time – an interregnum – in which he was neither what he had been nor what he would become. It was a marching in place. He understood that he was a man in search of his identity, though he balked at putting it in such portentous terms. Yet that was exactly it – except that when he finally found out who he was, he realised that he had rediscovered his old self. It was a marching in place.

Without conviction, almost by default, he decided to go straight when he left Fredding. He worked out a simple-minded formula to enable him to make up his mind: thieving is bad because it leads to prison, and prison is unthinkable. Ergo, don't be a thief. Dr. Katsouras entered the equation, but in a way that was more ironic than anything else. Win this one for the Old Doc! He formulated another practical approach: thieving is a bad habit, and bad habits are injurious. Ergo, give up the habit.

But you couldn't go straight just because you recognised the moral imperative any more than you could quit smoking because it lead to lung cancer, heart disease, and morning phlegm. Knowing the answer was not the whole of the solution. You had to work out the details, and the details were burdensome. There were withdrawal symptoms, nearly irresistible temptations, selfserving rationalisations, and compensatory bad habits like overeating. He put on twenty pounds in his first five weeks in the free world. Temptation was everywhere, and each time you overcame it, you never knew whether, in the long run, the effort required for the victory strengthened your resolution or lowered your store of resistance.

In his first week at the plant he picked out a number of ex-convicts. Munchmore employed about fifty of them throughout the plant, mostly in menial jobs. For Mitchell, they might just as well have worn a stamp on their forehead: the hard, suspicious face, the underlying toughness, the aura of suppressed recklessness and violence. Prison put its imprimatur on a man. On one occasion, in the company lunchroom, two men seated behind him had been chatting, and their use of prison slang had identified them as ex-convicts, sight unseen. Not very bright ones, either. The smart thief avoided underworld slang, because it was a dead giveaway to the police.

A few days later he ran into Morris Laplace, wearing the alpaca coat that was the uniform of Munchmore messengers, pushing a rubber-wheeled cart filled with mail. Although they hadn't been very friendly in prison, Laplace was delighted to see him, and after thirty seconds of conversation, to impress on him that he would only hold his square job until he put together a little working capital, after which he would return to 'the life'.

Then, with a knowing tilt of his head, 'You, too, Johnny?'

'No. I'm straight from here on in.'

Laplace winked. 'Sure. A feller like you. Listen, how's about a beer after work?'

Mitchell begged off, but when he came through the front gate at quitting time Laplace was waiting in his car, a beat-up Oldsmobile that must have been over ten years old. Laplace insisted on driving him home.

'I know you're putting me on about going straight,' Laplace said. 'You're gonna get you a stake and work off your parole time, and then you're gonna pull a job.'

'I'm finished with the life,' Mitchell said.

'A big shot like you? A feller who pulled in the pen like you did?'

In the prison lexicon, the status of the men inside depended on the importance of their crime. A man who pulled a big score, and who had a hundred thousand dollars in his possession, if only for a few minutes before the cops took it away from him, rated high. At the other end of the spectrum, a car thief or lush-roller was held in small regard. A cop-killer was a man of marks; so, in fact, was any murderer, except the killer of a woman or child. Somehow – probably because he thought Mitchell had gotten preferential treatment from Katsouras – Laplace had decided that he had been a convict with high status.

He said, 'I wasn't a big shot. I was a small-time thief.'

Laplace let him off at his boarding house, and winking elaborately, said, 'I know you're going straight and all, but when you get ready to go back to the life, you won't forget your old friend Morris, will you, Johnny?'

'I won't forget you,' Mitchell said. 'And when I send for you, remember to bring along your bedpan. Okay, old-timer?'

He left Laplace in the car, cursing him with shrill venom, and hurried inside.

His parole officer was named Harry Baumer, and he was a good enough joe. He was a couple of years away from retirement age, and he wasn't about to rock any boats, which suited Mitchell well enough. Their meetings were usually brief, and it wasn't until the second or third that Baumer's questions became even the least bit searching.

'You haven't volunteered anything about your job,' Baumer said.

They were sitting in his small office, containing a scarred oak desk, painted-flake file cabinets, two well-used but serviceable chairs. Sunlight fought its way through a window that might never have been washed in the entire twenty-eight years of Baumer's tenure.

'Sure I have,' Mitchell said. 'I told you it was fine.'

'I know. But how come you haven't complained even once?'

'It's my job. What's the sense of complaining?'

'Is it monotonous?'

He thought of the shipping room, littered and noisy; the endlessly repetitious motions; the strain the packages put on arm and back muscles; the exhaustion when deadline pressures forced overtime.

'I guess so,' he said. 'I guess all jobs are monotonous.'

'It depends. Some jobs *aren't*.'

'Stealing,' Mitchell said. 'Stealing isn't monotonous.'

Baumer grinned. 'All I'm trying to say is that you're too bright for that kind of a job.'

'I was too bright for stealing, too.'

'You're a tough customer to argue with,' Baumer said mildly. 'What I'm trying to get at – what do you do to break the monotony?'

'You mean do I consort with bad companions, or get drunk or start fights?' He grinned. 'No. I go home to my room, mostly, and I read.'

'Kind of monastic. Don't you ever make a night of it with the boys?'

'I spend the day with the boys, that's enough.'

'What about, ah, the fair sex?'

'What, ah, about them?'

'You're a nice-looking guy, and there must be a lot of horny chicks in that factory. I just wondered if, you know, you were scoring.'

'Is screwing a violation of parole?'

'Cool it,' Baumer said. 'I'm just trying to pry in a friendly way.'

'You know the answer yourself,' Mitchell said. 'There are

140

plenty of opportunities, but I just don't fool around. I'm not queer, it's just my preference.'

'How about your supervisor – is he satisfied with your work?'

'You'd have to be a cretin not to make out. All day long I bind packages of biscuits with metal tape, stencil the address on the package, and then heft it into one of twenty bins according to geographical location. If you like binding and stenciling, it's a fascinating job. If not, it's just a job.'

'Well, it's a start. Maybe they'll give you a promotion to something more interesting. Or, in time, when you've got your sea legs in the free world, you might find a better job somewhere else. Meanwhile, at least, it's honest work.'

Mitchell grinned. 'It doesn't say too much for honesty.'

The first time a girl looked at him with interest he made a comically self-denigrating gesture: he looked behind him exaggeratedly to see who she really meant. A lot of girls looked at him, or spoke to him invitingly, but it gave him no pleasure. As all through his life he had been rejected because of his face, and his other qualities ignored, so now he was accepted for his face, and his face alone. And as for sex, which steamed out of the discontented, bored factory girls, whose only relief from uninflected dullness was promiscuous balling, he didn't want that either. Sex was necessary, but it could lead to involvement, so it was much simpler and safer to buy it at the cathouse.

If he had allowed it to, his mirror might have given him pleasure, but he used x-ray vision, penetrating the surface layers of skin and flesh to the man beneath. Caliban. Society accepted him at face value now, but the irony was that society misread his bland new face as it had the old. Society, like the girls, cared only for surfaces.

The craving to steal sometimes became acute, and then he would visit the cathouse four, five times a week, thrusting

141

frantically at the professionally accommodating bodies that squirmed beneath him. But it was a diversion for his craving, not a substitute for it. He would perform prodigies of wrapping and binding on the job, but that was no better. It was impossible to turn off his mind as he performed the simple manual motions, or listened to (even attempted to join) the endless sameness of his co-workers' talk (sports and girls and cars), always with the omnipresent cloying smell of sweet dough in his nostrils . . . He walked the streets in a panic late at night, fighting to shut out the voice that promised him that stealing something, anything, as a token, would relieve the pressure, but he knew that it wouldn't, that it was like the cigarette smoker who deluded himself with the fancy that if he could smoke just three cigarettes a day . . .

And yet, one day, he boosted a nineteen-cent pen in a dime store. A monstrous stupidity, and a measure of his desperation. A nineteen-cent pen – but if he had been caught he could have been sent back to the penitentiary to serve out the rest of his term. In the end, some semblance of sanity returned, and in the act of walking out of the store, he veered at the last moment to the checkout counter and paid for the pen. Outside, with the rush of air, he became almost physically sick at the enormity of the risk he had taken.

At this time he had already become aware of the situation on the odd Wednesdays at the Amesville Peoples Bank. He had thought about it on occasion, not seriously, but as a dentist, perhaps, might look at another dentist's handiwork. But now, as he hurried home with the pen in its flimsy bag (and the receipt of purchase), there was a subtle change. Now, as a cigarette smoker does with a simulated cigarette, he made contemplation of the bank a pacifier.

He could not have said at exactly what moment it ceased being fantasy and turned into an exercise leading up to a determination to actually rob the bank. But the precise moment wasn't the conclusive factor, any more than it was

142

to the smoker who suddenly (but not really) went into a store and bought a pack of cigarettes.

Maybe if he had gone back over it painstakingly, he could have isolated the series of emotional steps that led him to where he now stood, but he was certain that most of it would wash out in the admission that he had no taste or vocation for the deadly, unrewarding dullness of the straight life. Once upon a time it might have been different, but now, after twenty years of being a thief, he *was* a thief, and that was the end of it, let the psychological chips fall where they may. Butler: 'Once committed beyond a certain point . . . Thieving is God's message to him . . . '

And so, where he had grown sick with fright at the idea of boosting a cheap pen, he was cool and professional at the thought of robbing the bank. It was one thing to risk your freedom for a nineteen-cent pen, another for a million-dollar score. Still he might never have done it. But when he saw the possibility of getting rich *and* revenging himself on Jappy, it became irresistible.

He knew he was irrevocably committed the day he phoned Dr. Katsouras.

Because prison was the single environment he shared with Katsouras (and because Katsouras had rarely talked about himself), he had been surprised, on his first visit several months before for a checkup, to see a tall dark-haired woman and two boisterous children who looked like half-pint versions of their father sitting on the front porch of the large white house where Katsouras lived and made his office. Katsouras struck him as being somewhat more formal than he remembered him; or perhaps the difference had been in himself, now that he was a free man. But this time, when he arrived by bus from Melton in the morning, their old easy relationship seemed reestablished. They chatted about Mitchell's new life, and Katsouras seemed cautiously pleased. Mitchell played it in a low key, not celebrating the joys of freedom or his job, but complaining about both of them in a mild way, and this struck the right note.

'Stop bitching,' Katsouras said. 'Maybe the quality of life isn't all that much better outside of prison, but at least you can go for a walk a night if you want to.'

'You're an honest man, Doc, and I'm not using that word in the usual pejorative sense. You may make saint some day. Saint Katsouras the Good.'

'I'm glad it's working out decently. And why shouldn't it, after one of the most fantastically successful surgical series in history.'

'Saint Katsouras the Humble.'

'Humility is for the birds, not for good surgeons. Let's take a look at those eyebrows.' He tilted his light and leaned forward in frowning concentration, touching the brows lightly as he examined them. 'What makes you suddenly want to have it done?'

'What kind of a dumb question is that? Didn't you urge me to have it done?'

'I did, and you said no, and now you say yes. Why the change of heart? I'm obliged to ask you that. Motivation is important, I told you that a long time ago, and there are times when we'll decline to perform cosmetic surgery.'

'Oh, my motivation is the best. I want to get a job as an eyebrow model.'

Katsouras turned off the lamp. 'I'm serious.'

Mitchell spread his hands. 'I haven't got any overriding reason for wanting it, except . . . How do I say it? Except that I have a certain feeling of incompleteness. It's not all that vitally important, and if you don't want to do it, okay, it's not going to make me to unhappy that I'll start boosting lamb chops from the supermarket.'

'I'm not the only plastic surgeon in these parts. I could give you the names of three good men in the area, and any one of them would probably do it for you.'

'I'll go to another doctor when I want delicate and subtle

work done. For the crude stuff I like you, you're reliable.'

Katsouras studied him intently, his brown eyes speculative, and for a wild moment Mitchell was sure that Katsouras had seen through him, that he had somehow guessed that he wanted the operation in order to perfect his disguise. But if he held such a notion, or even weighed it, his smile announced a favorable verdict.

'When do you want to get started? There's a fairly long period of hospitalisation. Can you get, say, a couple of weeks off?'

'I'll have to clear it with the personnel department, and my parole officer.'

'It's a lovely operation,' Katsouras said. 'An island flap with a buried vascular pedicle. We use you as your own skin donor – '

Mitchell brought up the subject of payment.

Katsouras waved the idea away with his hand. 'Forget it. If I billed you now, I'd start regretting all the free work I did before. Besides, you couldn't afford my fees.'

'Just tell me how much, and I'll steal it.'

'Smart-ass.'

'Not a penny more or less, your exact fee,' Mitchell said. 'Look, I've got a little money in the bank, and I'd feel better if you let me pay the freight.'

Katsouras shrugged. 'Let's say a hundred dollars.'

'Come on. Doctors get a hundred dollars for telling you to take aspirin over the phone.'

'Doctors adjust their fees to their patient. I get big money for fixing up sagging tits and asses for rich old broads, so I can afford to do other work more cheaply. What you lose on the swings you make up on the roundabouts.'

At Fredding, it had astonished Mitchell that only the most observant of his fellow convicts realised that he was having his face remade. The others, aware that something had changed, simply remarked that he was looking well, and let it go at that. When he returned to work in the Munchmore shipping room, his colleagues seemed totally unaware of his repaired eyebrows. They said he was looking well, and asked if he was feeling okay after his operation (the nature of which he had never described to them), and that was that. When they had first began, months before, Katsouras had predicted exactly such a lack of acuity, or of interest, and it was true.

The previous night Mitchell had turned on all the lights in his room and trained them on the mirror framed over his old-fashioned dresser. Then he inspected himself, peering at his face from every conceivable distance and angle – sometimes so close that his nose touched the glass, again from six feet away side view, threequarter view, smiling, frowning, even, with the help of a hand mirror, at the back of his head. In the end, marveling at it, he conceded that he could fool his own mother, and that if he could do that, he could fool Jappy or anybody else on earth. He would have to watch two things carefully – maintaining his new erect posture and avoiding regression in his speech, but he had done so well with both in the past months that he felt a high degree of confidence.

His hair, which had been black six years ago, had turned gray; he had let it grow long after leaving Fredding, and he combed it low over his forehead, in the new style, so that even his hairline was no longer what it used to be. His eyes, of course, were the same color, but there was nothing distinctive about light hazel eyes. Still . . . And the next day he went to an optometrist, had his eyes refracted, and ordered blue contact lenses.

The conflict between his desire to avenge himself on Jappy for five years in the penitentiary, and the fact that he couldn't even attempt the robbery without Jappy's help, resolved itself pragmatically. Without Jappy, there could be neither robbery nor revenge. With Jappy, the first was viable and the second was at least a distant possibility. It had to be Jappy. Not only because he had no other underworld contacts, but because Jappy had a high degree of competence, caution, and organisational intelligence (plus access to the few additional bodies who could be necessary).

In order to make a half million dollars, he had to allow Jappy to make a half million dollars. On cold balance, assuming you could equate such irreconcilable factors as revenge and money, a half million dollars won hands down. Take the cash, and let the vengeance go. Nevertheless, he gave himself a promissory note: if the slightest opportunity represented itself to double-cross Jappy, he would seize it, whatever the risks.

And on that basis, which seemed to serve his own ends best, he settled the matter.

He took an early-morning flight on a Saturday, dropped the letter into a corner pillar box on Market Street, and was back home the same evening. He hadn't sought Braumer's permission to leave town; there was little chance of being found out unless the plane fell down, and then it wouldn't matter. San Francisco was a long way to travel simply for a postmark, but it was essential; even if he had known someone there who might have mailed the letter for him, he wouldn't have trusted him. He wanted the seams to be tightly joined.

The two letters were simple enough to write, though they made him uncomfortable – not the feigning of his own death but the complexity of his feelings about Jappy. He kept the letter to Jappy short, as, in fact, he did with the letter from his 'friend,' whom he gave the name of Al Ford.

He typed the Ford letter after hours on the shipping-room machine, redoing it several times, less for content than spelling and syntax, feeling alternately that he was over- or underdoing it. The Ford letter read:

Dear Mr. Schroeder — A couple days before he past on, Johnnie asked would I send the inclose letter to you after he past on. I promised I would send it. I was his friend on the ward, though I'm getting better and out of the hospital in one week time.

The last few weeks he was doped up all the time so no pain you'll be glad to hear this and the last few days in a comma and didn't wake up. Cancer in the pancras. But the dope kept him from having no pain.

He was a good pal though I knew him only a short time. And then he past on.

Yours truly, Johnnie's pal,

And he appended a signature, painstakingly inscribing it in a large hand with childishly formed letters.

He wrote the enclosed in his own hand, allowing it to waver from time to time, but not too much, because he had to be sure the handwriting was clearly recognisable as his own.

Jappy: You're probably surprised that I'm writing to you. So am I. But I have nobody else to write to, which must say something about my life. A lousy life.

I'm sick, dying, and the end is in clear sight. I want somebody to know I'm going, I don't know why, but it seems important not to just conk out without a trace. It's pretty funny that the only person I can think of to write to is a sonofabitch.

So, if you can stop laughing long enough, have a drink of that rotgut whiskey of yours to mark my passage.

Johnny Handsome

He heard about Shannon from Laplace, who continued to try to buddy up to him — God knew why, except that he still harbored the illusion that he was a big-time thief — and who had turned out to be impervious to insult, at least beyond the moment it was delivered. So he found himself having to duck away from him in the corridors of the plant, and inventing new excuses for not having a friendly beer.

But on a rainy week night Laplace cornered him. He had gone to the library in Melton, and Laplace had shown up – followed him there, for all he knew, because it didn't seem likely that Laplace was a great reader. He was sitting at a table, reading a current magazine, when Laplace slid into a seat beside him. He continued to read, ignoring Laplace's wheezy whisper, but the mention of Shannon's name caught his attention.

'What about Shannon?'

'Our old friend from the pen – Lieutenant Shannon? He quit the penitentiary eight, nine months ago.'

Mitchell nodded. 'I heard.' He went back to his magazine.

'Working upstate, in charge of detectives. City of Philbin.'

'Where?' Mitchell said. His fingers were gouging the pages of the magazine.

'Philbin.'

Mitchell saw what his fingers were doing to the magazine. He opened his hand, and began to smooth out the wrinkled pages.

'I sure as hell hate to be in any town Shannon was a cop in,' Laplace said, and cackled. 'Couldn't hardly afford it.'

Laplace chatted on in his sly old-man's voice, not minding that Mitchell didn't answer him, perhaps satisfied that he was not being insulted. And Mitchell thought, dully watching his fingers ironing out the damaged pages. With Shannon in town, there's no way I could miss being spotted, being given away. And so it's all over, the whole thing is over before it has begun.

But later, after he had gotten rid of Laplace, while he was walking through the rain from the bus stop, he realised that it didn't have to be over at all; that, providentially, there might be a way to earn half a million dollars and revenge himself on Jappy at the same time. It wouldn't cost him a penny. In fact, Jappy would foot the entire bill.

They met in Woodrow, a town midway between Philbin and Melton. It was near seven, and dark, when Mitchell got off the bus. He walked through the dingy terminal, smelling of frying hamburger and tired bodies, and turned left on Woodrow's main street, empty except for a few people heading for the movie house or the brightly beckoning neon of a few bars and restaurants. Two blocks on, there were no more lights, only the darkened windows of closed stores. He continued at an even, unhurried pace, and soon he heard the car behind him, close to the curb. He didn't turn or stop walking. The car trailed him for another hundred yards, then shot by him and stopped. The door on the curb-side opened.

He got in and the car took off. Shannon's face was underlit, pink, in the faint diffusion of light from the dashboard. He drove with his left hand; his right lay on the seat between them. For all the indication he gave, he might have been alone in the car. His arrogance and contempt were overpowering, but in the circumstances they were phony.

Shannon found a country road and drove along it for ten minutes. Once or twice he slowed down, as if looking for a place to stop, but went on. Finally, on a dark barren portion of the road, he turned off the blacktop into a rutted path that ran obliquely into an overhang of trees. He bulled the car into matted underbrush that concealed them almost completely from the road. He switched the headlights off, rolled down his window, and lit a cigarette. Then, still looking ahead through the windshield, he spoke for the first time.

'What's on your mind?' His voice was hard.

'A million dollars,' Mitchell said.

Shannon puffed a cloud of smoke into a silence. He was a presence in the car, his bulk filling the space behind the wheel. He fixed Mitchell with a cold blue stare. 'If you've got in mind what I think you have, I'm going to pull you out of that seat and beat you to a bleeding pulp.'

Mitchell said nothing. He met Shannon's glare levelly.

'Don't ever forget one thing,' Shannon said. 'I'm a cop.'

'I don't care what you call yourself. You're on the take.'

On the seat between them Shannon's big hand twitched, but it remained where it was. 'I warn you, bum, don't push me.'

His voice was edgy, but Mitchell wasn't concerned. He had gone all the way, in a single sentence, in challenging him, and Sannon had let the gage lie. He said quietly, 'I'll try not to go over the limit. You want me to continue?'

'You haven't said anything yet. Are you going to make your point?'

'Right now,' Mitchell said. 'I know where I can steal a million dollars. I want to offer you half of it.'

Shannon said, 'I never hit an insane man in my life yet, but there's always a first time. I'm going to beat your brains out, buster!'

It was a last twitch of phony pride, and Mitchell was unmoved by it. He waited calmly for it to spend itself.

'Or if you're not insane,' Shannon said, 'Then you've got more pure stupid gall than any bum I ever met. Where did you get the crazy idea you could present a proposition like that to a cop? Are you trying to commit suicide?'

Mitchell said coldly, 'I got the idea about you at Fredding. And I knew there was no mistake about it when you agreed to meet me tonight.'

'You sonofabitch, you realise that with what you told me already, I could send you back to prison for twenty years?'

Mitchell laughed, and for a moment, watching the muscles in Shannon's throat cord, he thought he might have pushed too hard. But the tension didn't last. Still, Shannon had to make a last concession to appearances. Leaning forward, he turned the ignition key and started the engine.

'I'm taking you in, bum. We're driving back to Philbin and I'm going to book you for attempted robbery, attempted bribery of a police officer, violation of parole . . .'

'Sure,' Mitchell said. 'Sure you are, Lieutenant.'

Shannon backed the car out jerkily and headed down the country road, his lights bouncing as he drove with his left wheels on the crown of the blacktop.

'You're going the wrong way,' Mitchell said politely.

Shannon was silent for a moment, hunched over the wheel, then he said quietly, 'What's the proposition?'

They drove through the countryside for more than an hour, over dark silent roads, only rarely meeting another set of headlights. Shannon listened quietly, occasionally interrupting with a question. Whether or not he bought into the deal, Mitchell knew, was now simply a matter of practicality. If he thought it would work, he would buy. There was no more pretense.

His questions were intelligent. 'I have to get it clear in my mind why a guy wants to give away a half million dollars of his own money.'

'I'm not giving away a penny of mine, just Jappy Schroeder's.'

'All this fancywork just because you might have run into me in Philbin?'

'Insurance. I was sure you would know Jappy; in fact, you tell me you do business with him. We'd have been bound to run into each other. Could I take the chance that you *wouldn't* have given me away?'

Shannon nodded. 'Still, there may be a little more to it. You carry a grudge against Jappy Schroeder?'

'Yes. But there's nothing psycho about it, if that's what you mean.'

'That's what I mean.'

'It's a rare combination of business and pleasure. He helps me make a big score, and then I take his cut of the score away from him.'

Shannon said, 'It's more complicated than I like things to be. There's a lot of bad feelings involved in giving an old buddy the business out of revenge.'

152

'The revenge is secondary. What counts is a million dollars. I'd give anybody away for that.'

'Including your friendly neighborhood lieutenant of detectives?'

'We all have to take *some* things on faith. I'm taking a few myself.'

Shannon said, 'Suppose you don't go over? Suppose he makes you as Johnny Handsome?'

'Then you forget the whole thing, and all it cost you is an auto ride and a few gallons of gas. You remember what I used to look like. You think he'll make me?'

Shannon slowed the car, turned, and studied him. 'No. I honestly don't think he'll connect you.'

'Then that's it,' Mitchell said. 'That's the thing.'

Shannon said, 'I'll take you back to the bus station.'

They drove in silence to the center of town. Mitchell said, 'Thanks for the ride, lieutenant.'

Shannon nodded. 'We'll be in touch.' He gunned the motor. 'I wish it wasn't so goddamn complicated. A lot of things have to work if it's going to come off.'

'You don't make half a million dollars simply,' Mitchell said. 'Anyway, *you* can't lose. You don't become involved *unless* everything works.'

'The other thing bothers me. It takes a real cold-ass man to double-cross his own buddies.'

'They're bums,' Mitchell said. 'Why worry about a bunch of bums?'

Shannon nodded thoughtfully. 'Let's keep in touch.'

Mitchell got out of the car and walked toward the bus station a block away. He knew without turning that Shannon was still sitting there and watching him. And thinking. Well, let him think. He wouldn't back out. Police badge or no police badge, a bum was a bum.

Three weeks later Mitchell went to Baumer's office for his last meeting. When it was over, he was no longer on parole;

153

he had paid his debt to society in full.

The next day was his last in the employ of the Munch-more Biscuit Company. He had been very correct in submitting his resignation: he had given the company a full two weeks' notice. He packed his bag the following morning, ate his lunch at a drugstore counter, walked around for a while, and then caught the bus for Philbin.

PART III
REAL WORLD

13

Jappy was so painstaking and methodical that Mitchell was frequently at the point of showing his impatience. But he knew that no perfectable detail would escape Jappy's scrutiny, and that this was Jappy's strength.

They drove to Amesville on a payday, at Jappy's insistence, so he could see the situation at the bank when the Munchmore workers piled in to cash their checks.

'What's the connection?' Mitchell said. 'That all takes place a few hours *after* we hit the bank.'

'You never know,' Jappy said. 'Later, sweating out prison, it don't do any good to wish you had checked up on *everything*. Beforehand is the only time, even if it *don't* seem to have any connection.'

They sat as they had before – Jappy beside Battler, Mitchell in the rear seat alone. They made the long ride virtually in silence, and arrived at the center of town a few minutes past twelve. Traffic, which had been flowing near the town line, slowed down to a bumper-to-bumper crawl. They inched slowly ahead, and it was twelve-thirty by the time they reached the supermarket lot. There was a long line stretching around the bank.

Jappy told Battler to keep going. 'I don't want to make a habit of showing up in the same place. Somebody might notice and remember you. The next time we park here it's to rob the bank.'

They followed the signs to the municipal parking lot two blocks further south and a long block to the right.

Jappy got out. 'I'm going to make a deposit to my savings account.'

'With that mob, you'll be a long time,' Battler said.

'That's the idea. I'll be able to see a lot.' Before walking off he said, 'If you decide to walk around, stay away from the center of town and don't go together.'

Mitchell allowed Jappy a few minutes' headway, and then got out of the car. Battler said he would stay. He walked up to Main Street. To the left, far up the street, the long lines in front of the bank seemed motionless. He turned right and walked through an untidy area of small businesses – an auto body works, a plumber's shop, an upholstery and carpet store – each of them spilling out its detritus toward the street. Then the town again became residential – huge and somewhat run-down old houses, the houses of the first settlers of the town, turreted, verandaed, and bay-windowed, many of them now become tourist homes or antique shops.

He paused at the white bridge leading over the small span of the Ames River, running clear and shallow over the smoothly washed stones of its bed. He leaned on the parapet and thought of the year he had spent living in this town. Had it ended only a few weeks ago? Already it was remote, out of time. He had come and gone, and left no footprint, permitted no human contact. Even at the cathouse, which lay just out of sight around the bend of this same river, he had chosen a different girl each time. He had arrived in town a stranger and left it a stranger.

He stared mindlessly at the water, killing time, and then went back to the parking lot. Battler, sitting monolithically behind the wheel, barely nodded as he got into the car. Mitchell lit a cigarette, and smoked it and two more before Jappy returned and took his place in the front seat. Battler put the car in gear and pulled out of the parking lot.

'Head south, and take the first secondary road to the west

that you come to,' Jappy said. 'I put five hundred in my account.'

'When we clean them out,' Mitchell said, 'we'll make sure to leave them enough to pay you off when you close out your account. Plus interest.'

Battler turned onto Main Street and they headed toward the small white bridge.

'I counted four cops,' Jappy said to Mitchell. Bank dick and three town cops, one inside and two outside. You said there would be only one town cop.'

'The outside ones keep the line orderly. They don't turn up until near noon. In the morning it's like I said – the bank dick and one town cop.'

'Okay. I picked up something. The alarm is connected to police headquarters. It operates on a foot pedal. I don't like that too much.'

Battler said, 'How do you figure the bank dick and the other cop to behave?'

'You never know. I think the bank dick will be a good boy. The town cop – you can never tell what a young cop will do. No sense. Do they have the same cop each time, Mitchell?'

'They rotate them. But you almost always catch one of the young ones.'

'The bank personnel – there's more of them today than last week.'

'They put on extra help for the payday Wednesdays. They're mostly women, aren't they?'

'Three women, two men. Bank tellers usually act sensible in a stickup. But there's that foot-pedal alarm. It's easy to sneak a foot onto it. You can't see down there from the other side of the counter.'

'We have to discourage anybody from thinking brave thoughts,' Mitchell said. 'Go in very tough and mean from the start, and scare the crap out of them. None of this courtesy and good-manners stuff, even though it makes good reading in the next day's papers.'

Jappy nodded in agreement. 'I don't read my press notices, anyway. First thing we tell them is that if anybody moves we'll blow their goddamn head off.'

'And if somebody moves?' Battler said.

'We blow their goddamn head off.'

They had already covered the network of roads in and around Amesville from every conceivable compass point – state highways, county roads, secondary arteries, town roads winding through rural back areas – always with an open road map on which Jappy made notations of such minutiae as unrecorded distances, crossroads, curves, hills, even blind driveways. The car had not been washed in weeks, by design, so that its color was obscured under a heavy layer of grime. Except for the windshield, the windows were streaked and dirty, and had the effect of semi-opaque curtains.

The road they were traveling now wound through rural, sparsely inhabited areas, and joined a secondary county road eight miles farther on, which in turn connected with a state highway. With the inevitable road map open on his lap, Jappy carefully noted each landmark, each bend of the road, checking on his past notations, occasionally entering a new one.

At the state highway, he folded the map away into the glove compartment and directed Battler to return home.

'Okay,' Jappy said. 'Two Wednesdays from today' I'll make another deposit in my account. At nine o'clock in the morning.'

Mitchell said, 'There's nothing to see, for God's sake.'

'Don't try to *guess* what there is to see. Just keep one thing in mind – anybody who thinks it's easy to steal a million dollars will end up in shitsville. You anxious for another stretch in the penitentiary?'

'I would cut my throat first.'

'Mine too,' Jappy said. 'So we don't do any guessing.'

There was a long interval between Jappy's knock on the door at the top of the iron stairway and the buzz that released the lock. Inside, Tully and Sunny were at opposite ends of the room, but their faces were flushed and Sunny's dress was rumpled.

'This is an office, not a goddamn boudoir,' Jappy said. 'Clear out, the both of you.'

'Jesus, you're polite,' Sunny said. 'You're like a goddamn knight of King Arthur's table, you're so friggin' courteous. Not to mention your innuendos that we were messing around.'

'What am I supposed to do?' Tully said. 'I mean, are we working together, or not? You treat me and Bobby like a couple of goddamn *cops*.'

Jappy said wearily, 'When it's time, you'll be told everything. Until then, stop making waves.'

Sunny said, 'If you had any guts you wouldn't let him treat you like a second-class citizen. But you haven't *got* any guts.'

Tully diverted his anger to the girl. 'Flake off, you lousy bitch!'

'Screw your mother!' She picked up her bag and headed for the door. 'If she'll let you.'

Tully shoved her through the door so forcefully that she bounced off the railing. He slammed the door, shutting off her scream of anger.

'Some pair.' Jappy shook his head. 'Okay. Let's get down to business. We still got the two big problems – the alarm and the getaway. As far as I can see right now, the alarm is something we can't control because it's the human factor. Maybe one of the tellers kicks it, maybe not. But I'm going to think some more about it. The getaway is rough. One hundred and sixty-five miles in a car full of stolen money. It's a problem.'

'Change cars,' Battler said. 'We have another car, or even two more, stashed along the road someplace –'

'With nobody in them,' Jappy said. 'We're not hiring anybody else for this trick, and that means the cars will be sitting there with nobody in them. Suppose a kid comes along and heists one of them for a joyride? Suppose one of them don't start? Suppose one of them has a flat tire?'

'If we have enough cars –'

'The more cars you have, the more you increase the chances that one of them might have trouble. Besides, it don't matter *what* car you're in, you're *still* in a car full of money.'

'You know me,' Battler said. 'I can drive anything they have right off the road.'

'You're the best wheelman I ever knew. But no matter how good you are, you can't run through a roadblock short of driving a tank. Nor there won't be hick cops at the checkpoints but smart state troopers with rifles. You can't bluff them out. You can't bluff *anybody* out with a million dollars on the floor of your car.'

In the long quiet that followed, Jappy started to open his desk drawer – the one in which he kept his liquor bottle – but thought better of it, converting his gesture clumsily into a scratching of his leg.

Battler broke the silence. 'Suppose we can't think of something?'

'We'll think of something,' Jappy said. 'But if we can't, I won't rob the bank. I don't care if they *hand* us the money at the bank, and even wrap it up in nice packages. If you can't get away with it, you're better off not having it.'

Mitchell said, 'How long will they keep the roadblocks up after the robbery?'

'Who knows? A few hours, maybe six or eight hours, maybe even a little more. But they'll probably have heavy patrols out for even longer, maybe twenty-four hours.'

'Would you say the heat would be off in forty-eight hours?'

'Long before that. They don't figure on bank robbers to *walk* away with the loot.'

'That's the answer,' Mitchell said.

'Walk?'

'Hang around in Amesville for forty-eight hours.'

They drove to Amesville again the next morning. It was drizzling, and the fields beyond the streaked car windows lay sodden and dispirited. Scarcely anyone spoke, as if, Mitchell thought, their spirits, like the day, were wetted down. At the outskirts of Amesville, Jappy broke the silence.

'Day like this,' he said, 'is lousy for running all over the countryside house-hunting. I'd just as lief let an agent do the work.'

'We discussed that last night,' Mitchell said. 'Didn't we agree that it was bad to establish contact with anybody who might identify us later on?'

'I know, I know. Don't mind me.'

Battler drove directly to the municipal parking lot. Jappy got out and walked up to Main Street. Mitchell and Battler remained in the car. Jappy returned in twenty minutes with a copy of the *Amesville Banner*. He took the town map from the glove compartment and gave it to Mitchell, and then unfolded the paper to the real estate ads.

'We ignore the realtor ads, right? What about the ones with just a phone number?'

'Leave them alone for a moment,' Mitchell said. 'Some of them are blinds for dealers. The kind you want usually say "owner" somewhere in them, or something like "principals only, no agents". You get to recognise which are the right ones after a while.'

Jappy fixed the page with his finger. 'Here's one. "Annual rental, year-old three-bedroom Cape Cod, one acre, landscaped grounds", et cetera, et cetera. "Fashionable Haislip Circle, owner . . . " Where's fashionable Haislip Circle?'

Mitchell read down an alphabetical listing of town streets. 'Haislip Circle – C8'. He ran his finger horizontally along the marginal numbers at the top of the map, and the finger of his left hand along the lettered markings at the left margin of the map, then brought his fingers inward and down until they met. 'It's about a half-mile from the bank, but it's probably a development, which means too many houses too close together, too many nosy neighbors, not enough cover from trees and bushes. Scratch it.'

'Scratch it,' Jappy said. 'How about this one? "Colonial, two-bedroom, sun porch, fireplace . . . owner . . . Old County Road, near State Highway . . . " '

Mitchell tracked the marginal notations. 'Old County Road near State Highway. Got it.' He pursed his lips. 'Worth looking at, but it's a little far out. About six miles, I would judge.'

'Scratch it,' Jappy said. 'We agreed a top of six or seven minutes' riding time, no more. A top of three miles. Correct?'

'Correct.'

' "Two acres, stream, four bedrooms, large attic . . . " No good. Unfurnished.' Jappy's finger walked down the page. ' "Three bedrooms, two baths, game room . . . " Doesn't say anything about the garage. Cranford Road.'

Mitchell checked the map. 'About two miles. It's a possible.'

Before they were finished with the paper's listings, they had four possibilities. The first one they drove to was well situated but it had only a small one-car garage. Mitchell felt that the second house, the one on Cranford Road, was too pretentious. Jappy said it didn't matter and marked it heavily with a star. One of the houses was too close to town, and was eliminated. The last of the four, on Brainerd Street, was a slightly run-down Colonial, two and a half miles out, set well back from the road on a countrified street. They drove by it slowly.

'Good,' Jappy said. 'Now we have this one and the one on Cranford Road. Enough?'

'Enough,' Mitchell said.

'Home now?' Battler said. They were his first words in an hour.

'No,' Jappy said. 'Turn around and head back toward town. Mitchell, you know where police headquarters is?'

Mitchell directed Battler to the municipal parking lot. Beyond it, running to the east, the road split in two, skirted a large grassy plot the size of a couple of football fields, and then ran windingly up to Main Street.

'Straight ahead, on the right,' Mitchell said. 'That's police headquarters.'

It was a two-storied wooden building, with a fenced-in parking lot, standing squarely at the edge of the road. It had the appearance of a remodeled farmhouse.

'That little thing?' Battler said.

'It's bigger inside than you'd think. And it has a big basement with cells and offices. It used to be the town library until a few years ago when they built a new brick building and turned this one over to the cops. They're supposed to be planning a new headquarters right now, but it's taking longer than they thought.'

'They don't have to hurry for *me*,' Jappy said. 'Go past it slow and steady, Battler.'

The car passed within ten feet of the entrance, double doors that stood ajar and gave a view into an entry and, beyond it, a portion of the station itself, with a glimpse of a hatless figure in blue sitting at a raised desk.

The car moved on toward Main Street. Battler said, 'Now what?'

'Now home,' Jappy said. 'We'll come back for another look in a few days.'

'You like to look at police stations?' Battler said.

'I like to look at that one, because it's made out of such nice wood.'

'What's the difference what it's made of?'

'Wood burns good. *Old* wood burns *very* good. We're going to fire-bomb the bejesus out of it.'

Sunny was in Jappy's chair, and Jappy sat on the edge of the desk, reading off the telephone numbers to her. Mitchell stood at the window and idly watched two boys bowling by themselves on contiguous alleys. He heard Sunny, her voice surprisingly well modulated, giving a false name, explaining that she had just moved in from another state, and on behalf of her family, who would follow later, wanted to rent a house. Both parties were in, and she made appointments to see the houses the following day, an hour apart.

Jappy, checking the notes he had made in the margins of the newspaper, said, 'When you see the houses, don't commit yourself. Say you'll be back. If one house is as good as the other, we'll rent the cheaper one. Jesus, these are crazy prices, you have to be independently wealthy.'

'Why bother?' Mitchell said. 'It's a few lousy dollars either way.'

'So far, it's all *my* few lousy dollars.'

'After the score, put in a chit and you'll get reimbursed. But the interest you pick up at the Amesville Peoples has to go into the pot.'

'Bullshit. That's my personal money, and – ' He looked at Mitchell's innocently earnest face. 'Everybody here is a comedian.'

14

At four o'clock the late sun burned through the lacy curtains, struck across the bed, vanished, and reappeared climbing up the front of the old bureau, a huge mahogany piece shaped in soft feminine curves, its finish veined by thousands of delicate cracks.

Mitchell was stretched full-length on the bed. How many weeks had it been since that first twilight walk down Philbin Street to the point a half-hour ago when Jappy, like some general commending his troops to the good will of the god of war, had declared that their preparations were over? It was in the middle of a dry run – the thirtieth, the fortieth? – and Jappy had said unexpectedly, 'That's it. If we don't know it by now, we'll never know it. Tomorrow we're gonna rob a bank.'

If it didn't come off, Mitchell reflected, it wouldn't be through any oversight of Jappy's. He was a man who passionately wanted to stay alive and free, and who believed that the outcome of any action was determined ninety percent before the event. Mitchell had worried that he might be overdoing it, and like an overtrained fighter, leaving the fight in the gym.

'Look,' Jappy had said. 'The whole actual robbery is going to take about two minutes, and the getaway about two or three more. Four minutes altogether. Five. But that's long enough to crowd in about a thousand mistakes, and any single one of them could put you under the ground or behind the bars. All you can do – except for luck, good or bad, which you can't do anything about anyway – all you can do is try to eliminate the mistakes. That's what I try to do, that's *all* I try to do.'

It wasn't until three weeks before that Jappy had finally filled in Tully and Bobby on the specific details of the robbery. He had driven them over the various roads that had pertinence to the operation, and shown them the bank and the police station. He sent them into the bank separately (Bobby to ask questions about buying savings bonds, Tully to make inquiries about mortgage loans), and told them exactly what to look for, what to observe carefully and what not to, and how to relate what they saw in terms of the diagram he had made of the bank, and which they had been studying for several days.

A day later he had driven down alone with Bobby and they had studied the police headquarters, and Bobby had been told exactly where to stop the car, and where to stand when he threw the fire bombs, and what to do afterwards.

Finally, before they left for home, Jappy went to the bank and made a deposit in his savings account. What had this last visit accomplished? Nothing. No, that wasn't quite true. Jappy had brought back two observations: first, that the bank dick, the Dutchman, was left-handed, a detail to remember if he went for his gun; and second, that at several spots in the bank the glare of the sun could strike you blind. So now they knew about watching the Dutchman's left hand, and where not to stand to avoid being dazzled by the sun.

'Suppose it's a rainy day?' he said, needling Jappy, and Jappy had answered, 'If it's a rainy day, I wasted some time telling you about the sun. If not, you learned something that might save your life.' And Jappy was right, of course. Jappy played the percentages.

Jappy watched over the rehearsals with the meticulous eye for detail of a theatrical director. Frequently he stood off to the side and observed, interrupting the action to make a point: 'No, Tully, stand further over that way, so you don't have to shift your eyes to watch both cops,' or, 'Mitchell, don't look behind to see what's happening. Concentrate on the money, nothing else.' Sometimes he would listen to suggestions, and his judgments were always carefully reasoned.

He had held a debate with himself on the subject of disarming the cops. 'You got them lying on their faces, and they can't do much from that position. When you take a gun away from a cop, you embarrass him and take away, like, his manhood, so maybe he puts up a fight. Also, when you take his gun you're too close to him, and he can grab you, and it's hard to give you help because you're in the line of fire. But when we're on the way out, they may try to pull their guns. That's when we disarm them.'

He was indefatigable and infinitely patient, no matter how many times they performed even the simplest action. 'We have to be in and out fast, and that doesn't mean speed but smoothness. The timing has to be perfect and the teamwork has to be perfect – like a football team. If everybody does what he's supposed to do, and does it perfect, you move the ball. If you don't move the ball, you're either dead or in jail – and as far as I'm concerned one is as bad as the other.'

The office above the bowling alleys had become a scale replica of the bank, with furniture pushed around to represent the vault, the tellers' windows, the president's private office, the tables holding bank forms and pens . . . And always Jappy's tireless voice: 'You get the two cops to lay down here, the people in the bank get shoved up against this wall, the tellers go there, Tully, you're covering the cops from here, Mitchell, you move straight on this line to the vault, Bobby, the second you come in you head for the vault this way, so you don't get between Tully and the cops . . . '

In the occasional rest periods, they flopped in their chairs, sullen, hardly speaking. Even then Jappy never let up.

'We have to get it all down so perfect that you can do it in your sleep.'

'I *do* it in my sleep,' Mitchell said.

And so it had gone, day after day, with all of them becoming tense, feisty, worn. For Mitchell, the physical tiredness was a hazard – he had to be doubly on guard to avoid slouching or regressing to nasility in his speech. The only break in the routine had been unexpected and unwelcome. One afternoon, without warning, Shannon had appeared, announcing himself with his hard, demanding cop's knock at the door.

Jappy said, 'Relax. Nobody knows anything. Cool it.'

Mitchell said, 'The furniture. Push it back in place?'

'No time.'

He pressed the buzzer, and Shannon came in. He shut the door, and his sharp blue eyes flashed around the room.

'Hello, Jappy.' He looked the room over again. 'Something different here. You moved the furniture around.'

'I get tired of it in the same place, so I moved it around.'

'It looks crummy this way.'

'If I knew that's how you felt, I wouldn't have changed it.'

'You got lousy taste, Jappy. In friends, especially. Good afternoon, bums.'

Jappy said, 'What's on your mind, Lieutenant?'

'Why do I need something on my mind? Can't I just drop around for a social visit to my favorite set of bums?'

'If you say so, Lieutenant.'

'I say so,' Shannon said mildly. 'By the way, I was by here two, three days ago. You were out.'

Jappy nodded. 'If you were here and I wasn't in, then I was out. It figures.'

'It figures. All of these nice gentlemen were out, too. Were they all with you on some, like, enterprise, Jappy?'

'I don't know where they were. We got the honor system here. Nobody has to check out where he is with anybody else.'

'Honor among bums,' Shannon said. 'I like that sentiment.' His gaze moved on, settled on Mitchell. 'Mr. Smith, right? John Smith? Are you enjoying your stay in our fair city?'

'It's not so bad,' Mitchell said, 'considering it's the blowhole of the universe.'

'I'm glad to hear that. I would hate to think you didn't like our city and might want to leave it.'

'I'm thinking of settling down and spending my retirement years here.' His voice was light, but just under the surface of his calmness he was raging. The bastard! The bastard – to risk so much for the sake of meaningless showboating.

Shannon started to respond, then turned to Tully. Mitchell's heartbeat slowed, but its tick seemed hollow.

'Well, here's Anatole,' Shannon said, smiling. 'How are you, Anatole?'

'Shit,' Tully said.

'Shit,' Shannon said. 'How do you like that for a witty answer?'

'Shit,' Tully said, and spat on the floor.

'Don't spit on the goddamn floor, you slob,' Jappy yelled.

'Bobby?' Shannon turned, jovial. 'You look pretty in your wig, Bobby. Maybe you should drop in downtown some day for a new picture? The old one is all skin on top and doesn't do you justice.'

'I must have had a very close haircut when they shot that picture,' Bobby said. 'Crew cut.'

'Besides, you were framed.'

Bobby said in surprise, 'Certainly I was framed.'

'Battler? How is the old punchy Battler today? Are the bells ringing upstairs, Battler?'

In all, Shannon hadn't spent more than fifteen minutes in the room, but he had left them quivering with anger. When the door shut behind him, Tully burst out, 'What the hell was that bastard doing here? You think he's tumbled to something?'

'No,' Jappy said. 'If he had something in mind, *anything*, we'd have been quoted a price. He was just here because he's a plain sonofabitch at heart. He's what you call a sadist.'

'Well, I don't like it,' Tully said. 'He gives me the crawls.'

Jappy said to Mitchell, 'You gave him a couple of funny cracks.'

Mitchell shrugged. 'He's just a cop.' It was the truth. Shannon was a cop, and couldn't help behaving like one even when he was planning to steal a million dollars.

Three days before, in a car bearing out-of-state plates, Sunny had driven to Amesville to take possession of the rented house on Brainerd Street. The following day, according to Jappy's precise instructions, she had driven to Melton and shopped for enough food for her own needs for three days, and for all of them for two additional days. She was under instructions to show herself sparingly outside the house, and not at all in town. 'I can't stand three days without a man,' Sunny had complained. 'If I don't get it at night, I can't go to sleep,' and Jappy had told her, 'Well, for the next three nights you'll have to make it with a banana.'

This morning Jappy had checked out their equipment, making them stand inspection like garrison soldiers. He had had them break down their guns and had even looked over their ammunition. He had tested their masks for fit and for possible tears, and gone over the canvas government-surplus barracks bags to make sure there were no holes in them and that the drawstrings worked. He gave the Chrysler a final inspection even though Battler had all but taken it apart and put it together again.

At their final rehearsal, a few hours ago, he had still been able to find faults, but time had run out. Reluctantly, he dismissed them with instructions to rest, and report at the alleys at four-thirty in the morning ready for work.

And so, Mitchell thought, shifting his position on the bed, and so, at last, it had all come together. He knew that he should have profound feelings about it — anxiety or fear or anticipation, but all he felt was exhaustion. He was worked out, drained. He should take some aspirin, try to sleep . . .

Shannon came a few minutes before midnight, and they talked for twenty minutes. When Shannon left he tried again to sleep, but it was useless. At three o'clock he got up stiffly in the chill of the room, and shaved and showered slowly. Then, even more slowly, he dressed, and swallowed some more aspirins, and at last it was time to go and rob the bank.

15

The imbecile grin perched on his knee appeared to broaden each time the car jounced. Except for the wide-mouthed grin, the mask was austere, drawn, tapering at the chin, almost, Mitchell thought, a formalised death mask. He had a sudden vision of himself lying dead on the floor of the bank, grinning frozenly at the hilarious joke of death . . .

He made an abrupt movement, almost a shiver, to throw off the image, and Tully, sitting beside him, turned a pale face toward him in inquiry. In the front seat, Battler's head and shoulders and Jappy's were as unmoving as cardboard cutouts.

He picked up the mask and examined it. Jappy had bought six of the masks a number of years back at a close-out sale, for no better reason than that they were an irresistible bargain, and stowed them away against a time when they might be needed. Conspicuous though they were, they would be untraceable back to Jappy's purchase. They were constructed of a soft plastic material that held tightly to the face without revealing its contours. The masks, together with the white cotton gloves and the identical dark business suits, constituted an excellent disguise. Another example of Jappy's genius for details. He was a thoughtful, well-organised man, and he deserved to be a successful thief, but he had never been very lucky.

And his luck was still running bad. No, it wasn't a matter of luck this time but of his own character. If he wasn't so miserly, if he hadn't let Johnny Handsome go to prison rather than spend a few thousand dollars . . .

Under Battler's handling, the car moved at a steady forty-five miles an hour, and, as so often seemed to be the case with a very good driver, the ride was extraordinarily smooth, as if the road, rewarding competence, had obligingly planed itself free of bumps.

Three or four miles ahead of them, Bobby was proceeding at the same pace – or, at least, was supposed to be. On one occasion he had come into view on a long curve, which meant that his pace had lagged. They had not seen him a second time, so he had either adjusted his speed, or more likely, Battler had made a subtle correction of his own. Bobby's car was a well-kept Buick that he had boosted at the railroad station in the early morning. It obviously belonged to a commuter who had remained away overnight, so that by the time the theft of the car was reported, they would long since have abandoned it. That, too, was one of Jappy's intelligent touches.

Tully, wearing his mask, was making comical sounds of menace, clawing at the air with his hands.

Jappy faced around. 'Take that thing off, you stupid clown.'

Behind the grin, Tully's voice was incongruously petulant. 'Christ, a little fun, you're all acting like you're going to a funeral.'

'Take it off. You want somebody in a passing car to spot it?'

Tully peeled the mask off. He was scared, and trying to cover it with bravado. As for himself, Mitchell thought, he felt nerveless but detached, except for a tiny shadow of anxiety in a corner of his mind. It had risen with Shannon's arrival the night before. Not that there was anything to justify it. For once Shannon was neither sarcastic nor menacing. In fact, he had been uncharacteristically nervous. It was understandable. Like all of them, he was a petty thief

175

making his first venture into the big time; and, possibly, he was enough of a cop to be uneasy at the commission of a crime, which he doubtless differentiated in his mind from graft or corruption, both permissible to a cop by ancient tradition.

Shannon and he had to trust each other, as, in partnership, all thieves had to trust other thieves. But he would have felt more at ease if Shannon had not been a cop. Maybe, he thought with a smile, it was because he hadn't worked with cops before, and had no way to measure their trustworthiness, as he had – more or less – a thief's.

He had told Shannon that they would be lying low for two and a half days after the robbery.

'You have a hideout someplace? Whereabouts?'

'Someplace,' Mitchell said.

Shannon shrugged. 'Your business, I guess. Let's talk about picking up the money.'

Mitchell nodded. 'We'll be leaving the hideout about eleven at night, and getting back home after the alleys are closed.'

He described the dead area beneath the floor of the alleys, behind the automatic pin-setting mechanism. For reasons of space, the money would be distributed among three or four alleys. Afterwards the gang would disperse. Mitchell would return to the hotel. Shannon would pick him up there and they would drive back to the alleys. Shannon would climb the iron stairs, with Mitchell remaining below, and force Jappy to admit him.

'And if he won't?'

'You're a cop, aren't you? Bust his door down.'

Shannon would put his gun on Jappy, and make him turn over the keys to the alleys. Shannon would toss them down to Mitchell, who would remove the money, transfer it to four valises, and stow it in the trunk of Shannon's car. Then they would leave, taking Jappy with them. They would drive back to the hotel, where Mitchell would transfer his half of the money to a rented car and drive off. A half-hour later he would kick Jappy out of the car in the middle of nowhere. Meanwhile, Shannon would put his two valises in the hideaway he had already chosen.

'You'll catch an airplane for someplace?' Shannon said.

'Maybe.'

'And if you're caught?'

'You're worried I'll blow the whistle on you? How can I? *Nobody* can, without admitting he robbed a bank. And even if anybody did, you could laugh it off – as long as your money doesn't turn up.'

'Don't worry about that. Nobody will find it.'

'Want to tell me where you're going to put it?'

Shannon grinned and picked up his hat. 'What do I say – good luck?'

'Suit yourself,' Mitchell said.

At seven-thirty Jappy broke out a Thermos bottle and passed around paper cups of coffee and sweet buns. Battler kept looking into the back of the car nervously.

'Try not to get it dirty with crumbs.'

Battler's fastidiousness, in the context of their being on their way to rob a bank, didn't affect Mitchell as being humorous. Like Battler's his own mind was at a remove from the work at hand. The bank robbery was only a way station; there was more to come later. He had woven a devious plot, and there were many places where it could fail. Beginning with the robbery, he reminded himself. If that went wrong, everything did. Yet he wasn't able to concentrate on it fully. Like Battler, he was worrying about crumbs.

'You sleeping, ferchrissake?'

He realised that he had closed his eyes. Jappy, twisted in his seat, was staring at him in annoyance.

Tully said, 'He's trying to show us how cool he is. But I'll bet he's shitting his pants.'

Mitchell was silent, sipping at his lukewarm coffee.

Jappy said, 'It wouldn't hurt to go over the whole thing one last time.'

'Christ,' Tully said. 'It's coming out of my ears *now*.'

'In a thing like this,' Jappy said stubbornly, 'you can't be too perfect. Also, it'll make the trip less boring.'

'Listen,' Battler said, 'everybody put your empty cups in the paper bag.'

The sun came higher, bringing with it warmth, or the illusion of warmth. The number of cars on the road had multiplied. Most contained three or four men, car pools of blue-collar workers. The white-collar people, in somewhat newer cars, would not join the morning go-to-work parade for another half-hour. It was America on the road, Mitchell thought, driving bleary-eyed to its daily destination of quiet desperation, never questioning its tropistic straight-world response to each new sun.

Jappy turned. 'I'm reminding everybody again. About shooting. Don't do it unless you have to, and if you have to, don't hesitate. Shoot to kill.'

Tully said, 'Why? If we just wound somebody, the law ain't so tough.'

'Look who knows about the law. Listen to me – I want whoever has to be shot stopped cold. You never know if one shot does it. So keep shooting.'

Battler said, 'Exactly five minutes to the pull-off.'

'Bobby may be there already,' Jappy said. 'I don't want him sitting around too long. Pick it up a little.'

Battler said, 'We're right on schedule. On the button.'

'I know,' Jappy said, sighing. 'But move it up a little *ahead* of schedule.'

It was impossible to tell whether or not Battler increased his speed. Nothing changed in the solid, immovable set of his shoulders. Through the windows, farmland slipped by, stretching flat back from the road almost to the horizon. In the near distance, cattle stood motionless.

'Two minutes,' Battler said. 'I'll hit it right on the nose.'

The meeting place was the remains of a gas station that had gone out of business and been mindlessly vandalised. Except for the central building, which had resisted being leveled, only the concrete islands for the gas pumps had not been destroyed. The building itself was gutted inside. Battler slid off the highway and gunned the car around to the back of the garage structure across cracked pavement. There, hidden from the road, Bobby's car was pulled up beside a rubble of rusting metal and fire-scarred tires. Battler drew in alongside him.

'You're a couple of minutes late,' Bobby said.

Battler shook his head. 'On time. To the second.'

Jappy got out and went around to the passenger's side of Bobby's car and opened the door. He lifted a square of canvas, and Mitchell watched him examine what lay beneath it: five beer bottles filled with a mixture of gasoline and benzine, each with a cloth wick sticking out. He saw Jappy nod his head, and then put the canvas back in place over the fire bombs. Jappy shut the car door securely and came around to the driver's window.

'Let's see your watch, Bobby.'

'We already synchronised before we left,' Bobby said.

'Let's see it.'

Bobby put his arm on the window ledge. Jappy placed his own arm parallel to Bobby's so that the rims of both watches touched. He bent low to study their dials.

'Twenty-one jewels,' Bobby said. 'It could stay synchronised for a month.'

'He only boosts the very best,' Tully said.

'Boost! I bought it downtown, two hundred and fifty skins, *cash*.'

Jappy said, 'Stop yakking and start concentrating on the job.'

179

'Nothing to worry about,' Bobby said.

'Better *start* worrying. Like me. Worry – you know what I mean?' He looked at his watch. Get moving. You got exactly twelve minutes and fifty seconds.'

'Check.'

'I got just one more thing to say to you – don't miss.'

'Don't worry,' Bobby said, and moved off. He turned the corner of the garage building, and a moment later they heard his motor roar as he gunned his way back onto the highway.

Jappy got back into the car. 'Go head,' he said to Battler.

Battler eased the Chrysler over the rubble and rounded the garage building to the highway. He drove smoothly, unhurriedly, and no one spoke until they reached the outskirts of Amesville.

Jappy said, 'Two minutes, and we go. Any last questions?'

'Christ, no,' Tully said.

'Mitchell?'

'Let's rob the bank,' Mitchell said.

Traffic on Amesville's main street was sparse, and it flowed without interruption. Stores were opening up along the street, but business would be slow until the noontime invasion of employees from the biscuit plant. When the bank came in view, a couple of blocks ahead, they were forty-five seconds from zero hour.

Jappy looked up from his wristwatch and turned around, his lips forming a silent *whoosh*. Bobby had released his first fire bomb. Mitchell formed pictures in his mind: Bobby getting out of his car squarely in front of the police station and taking a step or two toward the wooden structure. The wick of the first bomb would already be lit. Calmly, methodically, just before throwing it, he would light the wick of the second from it, then send the first bomb sailing end-over-end through the open door. He would already be lighting the third bomb from the burning wick of the second. Bomb two would go crashing through the window, and if bomb one had brought someone running to the window, the bottle might hit him, or at least spray him, sending him reeling back screaming as the flames ate his flesh. The old wood of the building would already be catching, but Bobby would be thorough – a fourth bomb, even a fifth . . .

If it was done now, they could play carillons on their foot-pedal alarms for all the good it would do them. The cops would be too busy saving themselves from the fire to hear them, in the unlikely event that the wires had failed to fuse in the intense heat. And if Bobby had failed? Well, in that case it was tough titty. They were committed.

There were two cars in the parking stalls provided for customers in front of the bank. But more people than just the occupants of the two cars would be inside; more than likely there would be a few merchants who had walked from their stores to lay in a supply of bills and coins for the day's operations. Except for the yellow bulbs of the bank's central overhead chandelier, nothing could be seen of the interior through the bright sun-struck windows.

Battler flipped his directional signal for a left turn, and glided in, stopping broadside to the bank entrance. Mitchell lowered his head and slipped on his mask. When he looked up, Jappy and Tully were already masked. Jappy nodded, and they flung the doors open and piled out, carrying their weapons at the ready. Behind them they heard Battler pull away for his place in the supermarket parking lot. They aligned themselves at the entrance, and went into the bank shoulder-to-shoulder, chillingly alike in their prim black suits, white gloves, and demented grins.

16

That something as ridiculous as a dog – less than twelve inches of fluff and soprano indignation – threw Tully into a panic didn't surprise Mitchell. Accidents were by their nature unpredictable. He even took a sour satisfaction from the fact that Tully lost his cool; it justified the misgivings he had felt about him from the start. Of course, the young cop had also lost his cool, but he couldn't be held accountable to them for his actions. Neither could the dog.

Up to then, everything had gone smoothly, and none of them had seemed to be any more ruffled than during one of the numerous dry runs. With Jappy slightly in the lead, the ugly twelve-gauge sawed-off held menacingly forward, they had charged into the bank, their bodies taut and threatening – Jappy had even rehearsed them in their stance – their feet making a scuffling sound on the imitation-marble vinyl floor. They stopped, and Jappy announced the ground rules.

'Nobody move.' His voice was harsh, vibrant, and very loud, designed to terrorise. 'I said *nobody*, or you'll get your goddamn guts spilled over the floor.' He swung the muzzle of the sawed-off toward the tellers. 'Stay away from that alarm pedal, you bitches!' Just in case Bobby had failed to knock out the police station.

Listening to Jappy, Mitchell was struck with the thought that he might have lifted his speech word for word from a late-night movie on television. And yet, how many ways were there of saying it? And maybe it was all the more effective for being so banal. Nobody moved a step, although almost everyone made an involuntary jerk or shudder, and an old man put his hand over his heart as if to repress some wild leap of the organ against his rib cage.

There were twelve people in the bank: three tellers (two of them housewifely women), the town cop and the bank cop, the president of the bank, his assistant, and four customers: the old man, who was wearing a worn, once-elegant tweed jacket; a man in a butcher's apron discolored with brown bloodstains; a tall, thin man with a goatee whom Mitchell placed, after a moment, as a pharmacist; and two women, a stout middle-aged one holding a toy poodle at the end of a thin length of chain leash, and a woman with frizzy white hair and a roll-collar sweater who might have been selected by a casting director for the role of farmer's wife.

He took in these details in his first glance, and was already moving in a quick gliding walk toward the rear of the bank, past the blur of pale frightened faces that lined his way. They were not his business. Jappy would see to it that they were controlled, intimidated. Tully was covering the two cops, who represented the only threat. He heard Tully's voice, high-pitched and almost hysterical with urgency, demanding that the cops lie down on the floor.

It was a critical moment. If the cops obeyed, fine. If not, there would be trouble. But the schedule didn't allow him to wait for the outcome. He glanced at them as he went by. They were close to each other – they had probably been chatting – which made them a compact target. The Dutchman looked stunned and wary. The young cop was beginning to get angry, his face reddening, and Mitchell knew that at best he would be slow to obey. If he was *too* slow, Tully might panic and shoot. The Dutchman would help, he'd try to get the young cop to lie down.

'Down on that friggin' floor . . . ' The hysteria in Tully's voice was a form of violence. 'Lie down, you sonofabitches . . . '

Two more strides brought Mitchell to the vault, its massive door open at a ninety-degree angle, almost but not quite concealing Neville, the bank president, and his assistant. Like the customers, they were frozen in terror, but sooner or later Neville might think of slamming the vault door shut. To discourage him, if that was his intent, Mitchell said in a hard ringing voice, 'Step back from that door or I'll shoot you both down.'

There was no flicker of resistance. In fact, whether out of fear or intelligence, or somewhat of both, they did more than he asked for. As they moved away from the vault they raised their hands over their heads, straining for height, their jackets and vests hiking up to show white shirts.

Thanks for small things, Mitchell thought, and said. 'If they start coming down I'll shoot them off at the wrists.'

Outside, there was a sudden wail of sirens and a clangor of bells, furious and insistent, filling the bank with sound. Bobby had done his job, Mitchell thought, unless the engines were hell-bent on extinguishing a kitchen-stove fire somewhere. He threw down the bundle of barracks bags, pinned it with his foot, and tugged away the canvas strap that bound them together, meanwhile making a thrusting motion of his gun at Neville and the assistant.

He took a look behind him. Both cops were on the floor, face down – the town cop a long slim line, the Dutchman a sack of rumpled blue, the end result of fifty years of starchy food and too much beer. Tully stood above them, the nickel gleam of his revolver pointed down. The customers were huddled together in a tight knot beside the tellers' counters, covered by Jappy's shotgun. The bank door opened and a man came in, stopping abruptly, turning pale. Jappy waved him in with the shotgun, and the man moved tremblingly to join the group at the tellers' windows.

The door opened again and Bobby came in, his mask a hideous grin. Mitchell shook the barracks bags loose and stepped into the vault entrance. The money was stacked to his left, on the steel floor, piles of bills like building bricks, neatly bound. The outermost edge of the stack was a foot inside the vault door. He menaced Neville and the assistant with his gun, then dropped it in his pocket and bent to the money. When he faced about with the first armful of bills, Bobby was ready, holding the mouth of a bag open. He dumped the bills and turned back into the vault.

Unloading the new batch, he whispered, 'Did it go up?'

The smiling mask nodded. 'Beautiful. It caught like paper, and burned up very good.'

As he bent for another pile of bills, the bank suddenly echoed with a frenzied high-pitched yapping, joined in a moment by the voice of the dog's owner, hysterically urging the dog to keep quiet. Waiting while Bobby pinched a barracks bag shut and shook out another, Mitchell saw the little dog turn itself upside down in fury. It fell heavily on its back, and then, as it righted itself, pulled backward against the leash. The collar slipped off its head and it was free. It paused, as if in surprise at the unexpected freedom, then, screeching shrilly, launched itself toward Tully, a furiously skittering ball of fluff.

He deposited his load of bills into Bobby's bag, and was gathering a fresh armful when he heard Tully's boom of rage. Turning, he saw the dog make a speedy rush at Tully's stamping feet, retreat, dancing on its hind legs, then dash in again with its tiny white teeth bared. Tully danced an antic jig that was part evasion, part attempt to stomp the dog. He caught a blurred glimpse of Jappy, and wondered if, behind the cheerful mask, Jappy was as imperturbable as usual. He doubted it.

Bobby was shaking the bag impatiently. He was already bending into the vault when he heard the shot, and he turned back in time to see the dog's body leaping in the air before it fell and lay still. The dog's owner screamed. Tully fired twice more, the force of the slugs shoving the fluffy body across the floor toward its screaming owner as patches of hair and pink flesh flew from it. Jappy was shouting. As Mitchell turned away, the shotgun went off, booming through the bank. The next shots were Tully's revolver. Mitchell counted two, very close together, then a third. He fought the instinct to turn, and instead methodically filled his arms with stacks of bills. He dumped his bills into the barracks bag. Neville and the assistant were dead-white, and their upstretched hands were shaking. The smell of cordite was heavy in the air.

Bobby said, 'Jappy shot one of the cops. Tully shot them too.'

He looked. The young town cop was lying on his side, jack-knifed, his abdomen a bloody mess. He wasn't moving. The Dutchman was trying for his gun, which lay a foot beyond his reaching fingers. He seemed to have been hit several times. Jappy was watching him, the shotgun pointing downward almost negligently. Then he said something to Tully, who held his revolver down and at full-arm's-length, and fired twice. The Dutchman's body twitched each time, then lay still.

Jappy turned to the huddle beside the tellers' counters and said in a loud clear voice, 'Anybody makes a wrong move, he gets the same thing.'

Smart Jappy, Mitchell thought. The shooting was unwelcome, but it had happened, and he was getting extra milage out of it. Tully was staring at the torn bodies of the cops and the rivulets of blood crawling in random patterns along the floor.

Bobby said, 'After Tully shot the dog the town cop went for his gun. Jappy blasted him. Then Tully popped the Dutchman a few times.'

Mitchell returned to the vault. He worked quickly but smoothly, rhythmically, picking up the bills, cradling them, dumping them into the open bags. Pick up, cradle, turn, dump, turn back, single step into vault, pick up bills . . . And the vault floor was bare, empty.

'That's it,' he said to Bobby. 'Close it up.'

'My God,' Neville said. 'My God, sir . . .'

Mitchell ignored him. He bent over and gripped two of the barrack bags by their cords, as Bobby was doing. 'Ready,' he said to Bobby.

Bobby led the way, dragging the bags behind him, and Mitchell followed in his path. Bobby hesitated before a puddle of blood, then plowed through it. One of his bags left a red smear. Mitchell followed directly behind him.

As they went by, Jappy and Tully shifted slightly to cover their exit. They cleared the front door and began to run, dragging the bags behind them, past Bobby's abandoned Buick, across the service road to the Chrysler. The rear door of the car flew open. They tossed the bags in, then followed. Mitchell pulled the door shut and looked through the window. Jappy and Tully were backing out of the bank, their guns still pointed inward. They turned at the same time and ran for the car. Battler pushed the front door open. Tully got in first, then Jappy, who pulled the door shut after him. The car was already moving. It bumped over the berm and swung into the street.

Mitchell looked at his wristwatch. Two minutes and forty-five seconds, portal to portal.

Across the street, in front of a hardware store, a small group of people was watching. They looked frightened, but not too frightened to be fascinated spectators. As the Chrysler shot by they shrank back, and a display tipped over, scattering green spidery leaf rakes among them.

On the road to the house on Brainerd Street they met only one car. Later, if someone questioned the driver, he would say that they were going hell-bent for the state highway. It was a perfectly logical assumption.

17

The driveway was littered with leaves, and it occurred to Mitchell that it would have helped appearances if Sunny had raked it clean. He was getting like Jappy – a demon for details.

Battler swung the Chrysler into the driveway and through the open garage door. He drew up beside Sunny's red hard-top, pulled the emergency brake up, and jumped out of the car. A moment later the garage darkened as the double door came down on the cement floor with a thud.

Jappy said, 'Everybody grab a bag.'

Mitchell lifted his feet and tossed the barracks bags out of the car. Single file, each of them carrying a bag, they passed through a metal-lined door into the basement. The rough cement floor was covered with a layer of fluffy dust that made a blurry record of their footprints. Jappy led them up a wooden stairway, the treads springy under their feet, through another opening into a passageway between the kitchen and living room.

Sunny was waiting for them. She let out a squeal of delight when she saw the barrack bags and threw her arms around Tully. He tried to push her off, but she clung to him as they all followed Jappy into the living room. Music, turned low, was coming from a radio sitting on the shelf of an empty bookcase.

'Get the local station,' Jappy said to Sunny.

'Orders,' Sunny said. 'The first thing out of your mouth,

orders.' But she went to the radio. She turned the volume up, and a burst of raucous hard rock filled the room. 'The local station.'

Mitchell took in the room. It was adequately furnished, but lacked any touch of grace or warmth. The furniture was serviceable but dowdy, the lamps modern in the fashion of twenty-five years ago.

Jappy said to Sunny, 'Leave it on. It happened only a few minutes ago, the radio station don't even know about it yet. Make it a little softer.'

Sunny wiggled. 'That's real groovy music.'

'Don't touch it,' Jappy said. The radio had suddenly gone silent. It hummed mindlessly for a long moment, and then a voice came on, a young man's voice, quavering with excitement. 'We interrupt our program . . . ' He paused, and they cauld hear him gulping air. 'The Amesville Peoples Bank has just been robbed.' Silence. 'By an armed gang. Let me repeat. The Amesville Peoples Bank has just been robbed by an armed gang . . . ' A pause, and the sound of whispering; he was being fed information right beside the mike. 'That is all we have at the present time – the bank has been robbed. We will resume our regularly scheduled program, but will interrupt as soon as we have more information.'

The music picked up. Sunny burst into laughter. 'Can I have the next dance?'

Jappy motioned to her to turn the volume down. 'Get some coffee going.' Sunny, making a face, went out to the kitchen. 'Everybody sit down,' Jappy said. 'Unwind. The robbery is over. We scored. Everybody take a seat.'

Tully kicked one of the bags. 'What about opening them up and taking a look at the loot?'

Jappy said, 'It's just money inside. Don't you know what money looks like?'

'Not a million,' Tully said. 'I don't know what a million looks like.'

189

'It's like a thousand, except a lot more.'

'Jee-sus,' Tully said jubilantly. 'A million! And it was easy. Easy!'

'It wasn't easy,' Jappy said wearily. 'Go sit down.'

Mitchell took a seat on a faded beige sofa between Battler and Bobby. He said to Jappy, 'There didn't have to be any shooting.'

Tully bristled. 'If that fucking little dog had attacked *you* – '

'The dog pulled a gun on you?'

'He was trying to bite me. What am I supposed to do – get chewed up by a dog?'

Jappy said, 'It wasn't his fault – not entirely, anyway.'

'What do you mean *entirely*? Not my fault, *period*. We rehearsed this thing for weeks, but there wasn't anything about a dog in a single goddam one of those rehearsals.'

Battler gave a short grunting laugh, and Tully joined in uncertainly.

'The dog was really going for him,' Jappy said. 'Maybe he could have just kicked him, I don't know. But the dog was taking his attention away from the cops, and he had to do something. Maybe shooting was the right thing.'

'I sure did do something – I blew the guts out of that stinking mutt.'

Jappy said, 'The young cop panicked, and went for his gun. I had to hit him. Then the Dutchman started to go for *his* gun . . . ' He shook his head. 'That surprised me. I thought he had more sense.'

'Did we kill them?' Tully said. His voice wavered between pride and anxiety. 'You think they're dead?'

'I didn't take their pulse,' Jappy said. He spoke to Mitchell. 'You think it would have been better if we let *them* shoot *us*?'

'I don't like to make cops any madder than I have to. They chase bank robbers out of duty, but they'll go after cop-killers on their own time if they have to.'

Jappy shrugged. 'If they didn't go for their guns, they wouldn't have gotten shot. Embarrassed, but not shot.'

The music on the radio stopped. Bobby reached over and turned up the volume. The announcer's young voice was breathless and grainy. 'We interrupt to bring you more news about the bank robbery.' He paused, as if to calm himself, then continued: 'Here are all of the facts we have been able to gather at this time. Shortly after nine o-clock this morning six armed men wearing masks –'

'Six, ferchrissake,' Tully said.

' . . . at gunpoint, while others cleaned out the vault. There were a number of shots fired, and it is believed that at least two people were wounded. Nobody yet knows the exact amount that was stolen, but it was believed to be in the area of one million dollars. *One* million *dollars!*'

'What about the robbers?' Jappy said. 'Did they get away?'

'The robbers are believed to have escaped, though an intensive search is already in progress to apprehend –'

'Thanks,' Jappy said.

' . . . State police already on the scene . . . ' The announcer gasped audibly, then said hoarsely, 'Just been handed a bulletin. The Amesville police headquarters was burned to the ground earlier today by a flash fire of unknown origin . . . ' His professional voice deserted him, and he said in awe, 'This is a disastrous day for Amesville, ladies and gentlemen, a very disastrous day.'

'They haven't connected it up yet,' Jappy said. 'The state cops will get things straight, but it'll take a little while.'

' . . . all the information we have at this time on the twin tragedies that have struck Amesville on this Wednesday morning. Incredulous and amazing. As soon as bulletins arrive we'll put them right on the air. Sports director Marve Holman is on the scene at this very moment, and as soon as he's able to get through to us, we'll bring you up to date.' He paused for breath. 'What an incredulous series of events, ladies and gentlemen . . . '

'Coffee.' Sunny was carrying a tray with cups and saucers and a dish of buns. 'Coffee to celebrate the bank trick – wow!'

Sports director Marve Holman – whose voice was as young as the announcer's but more disciplined – arrived at the studio and was put on the air to give his 'eyewitness' account.

'A band of heavily armed men, wearing grinning masks and dressed alike in black or navy-blue suits, burst into the Amesville Peoples Bank shortly after nine. Menacing the bank staff as well as several customers with a bristling array of armament, the gang proceeded to clean out the vault, taking the vast sum of money earmarked for cashing pay checks of employees of the Munchmore Biscuit Company, believed to total approximately one million dollars.'

'Tell him we'll give him the exact amount as soon as we count it,' Tully said.

'Although the attitude of the robbers was highly menacing, no actual violence occurred until just before they ran out, when, without warning, they opened fire with a fusillade of shots, cutting down two policemen. No word on their condition is presently available, but they are doubtless serious, since witnesses testified to large amounts of blood that literally covered the floor of the bank. "Like a red lake" was the way one eyewitness put it.

'The robbers made their getaway in a brown or gray sedan with state license plates. A car believed to be the robbers' was seen by Mrs. Louise Vance of Redingote Road, and was speeding toward the state highway. I have been personally informed by Captain William Hamilton of the state police that cordons have been hastily set up at strategic points, and a thorough search of all cars is taking place.'

He paused and cleared his throat. 'Excuse me . . . Due to the fire at Amesville police headquarters, there was some delay in executing speedy police action, according to Captain

Hamilton. Captain Hamilton described the roadblocks as a statewide network, and said that state and local police officers have been mobilised in unprecedented numbers in an all-out effort to apprehend the criminals in what he described as a cold- blooded and heinous crime.'

'Heinous,' Jappy said. 'I thought it was a beautiful crime, myself.'

'We will keep you informed of further developments. I see that Terry Storm, your regular announcer, has some additional details.'

'Thanks, Marve. Marve is now returning to the bank, scene of the robbery, and will be back later on. I have a report on the fire at police headquarters. It has been described by Chief Montrose as having originated from the hurling of fire bombs from a passing car, and the possibility that it is the work of outside agitators is being investigated. The bombs were thrown through the doorway of headquarters, igniting the old wooden structure, which burned furiously. Three policemen, including Chief Montrose, have been rushed to the Melton Hospital suffering with burns. The headquarters building was described by Fire Chief Ed Lohman as leveled to the ground and a total loss.'

Bobby said, 'They still don't connect it up with the bank job.'

'They will,' Jappy said, 'as soon as some brains arrive on the scene.'

' . . . town is in a state of shock. I – One moment, please.' The mike cut out for almost thirty seconds, and when the announcer returned his voice was almost shrill with excitement. 'I have just been handed two bulletins. The first is a report emanating from Melton General.' Pause. 'Both Officer Sam Hendry of the Amesville police and Edwin Mueller, security officer at the Amesville Peoples Bank, have been declared D.O.A. That's dead on arrival, which means that both men have died of gunshot wounds inflicted by the marauders.' A sound of rustling paper. 'The second bulletin:

A report from the capital states that Governor Foxman has been apprised of the tragedy here, and has expressed his feeling of shock and sorrow. A source close to the governor's mansion indicates that the governor is weighing the sending in of a Guard unit to aid the maintaining of order . . . I have just been handed another bulletin. Colonel Carl Wilmetz, commandant of the state police, is reported on his way to Amesville to take personal charge of the investigation . . . *Another* bulletin. A report has come in that the killers' car has been spotted speeding south on Highway 34, with police units in close pursuit . . . '

Jappy got up and switched off the radio.

Tully protested. 'Come on, just at the best part. I want to find out if they capture the killers' car.'

Battler said, 'You believe that about bringing in soldiers?'

Jappy shook his head. 'No point to it. The police force is knocked out, so maybe they'll leave a few troopers here for a day or two. What do they need soldiers for?'

Tully broke into sudden gleeful laughter. Sunny, her eyes sparkling, jumped into his lap. She mussed his hair. His hand covered her breast. They squirmed for a comfortable position, and kissed.

'Break it up,' Jappy said. 'You want to do any loving, go on upstairs.'

'That's for me,' Tully said. He pushed Sunny from his lap and got to his feet. Standing behind her, his hands clasped over her belly, he pushed her toward the door in a series of erotic bumps. At the threshold, he turned. 'You just going to leave the money lying around like that? You ain't going to hide it?'

'Where?' Jappy said. 'In the cookie jar?'

Sunny pulled Tully out of the room. Their laughter, secret and excited, floated back down the stairs. Then a door slammed.

'It's a way to pass the time,' Jappy said, shrugging.

194

'Nothing to do now but wait. Anybody want to nap or something, go ahead.'

Battler said, 'How about some cards? Bobby? Mitchell? Shoot a little poker?'

Mitchell shook his head. 'I'll find a room and get some shut-eye.'

Jappy said, 'Get these undertaker suits off and into your own clothes. We'll make a bundle of them, with the masks, and get rid of them later. The gloves stay on, for as long as we stay in the house.'

'Even on the terlet?' Bobby said.

The bedroom was small, minimally furnished. The beds were neatly made. Mitchell lay down facing the window. The branch of a tree bisected it; the twigs were dry, withered. He rolled over on his back and stretched his limbs. He was exhausted, but stiff with tension. Bobby lay on the second bed, already asleep, snoring, his hands cupped protectively over his head. Bobby was a great sleeper. In the old days, Mitchell remembered, the joke was that the only way to wake him was to shoot off a gun next to his ear.

He shut his eyes and lay still, but sleep refused to come. Instead, the events of the morning replayed themselves in quick, flashing impressions. The entry into the bank, shoulder-to-shoulder. The ambivalence of the expressions on the faces of several of the bank employees and customers – blood-draining fear mingled with fascination, even secret delight, that their drab lives were suddenly made privileged. The stiff but yielding dignity of the bank president. The solid bricklike piles of money.

His mind stripped the bricks into thin leaves, flimsy green rectangles. He thought of his eventual share of the loot – half a million dollars – and, like Tully, couldn't imagine what it looked like. What would he do with it – something sensible? Or would he piss it away mindlessly, the way most thieves would? Jappy was the only thief he had ever known who

195

understood the value of money. Jappy would know how to invest his money, diversify it: so much in tax-free municipal bonds, so much in a chain of bowling alleys, so much in common stock. But Jappy wouldn't have any of the money in the end, his solace would have to come from the interest his money was drawing in the Amesville Peoples Bank. Shannon? If Shannon was smart he would lie low, continue on his job for another two or three years, then pull up stakes.

Jappy. Jappy ending up empty-handed, crazed with the pain of his deprivation. How many times that bitter, vengeful thought had recurred in his dreams. Yet now that it was at hand, in his grasp, he was unable to work up any excitement about it. Maybe he had exhausted his passion by thinking about it too much. Maybe he was still too tightly locked in to his imposture, which, he reminded himself, would have to continue for another forty-eight hours . . .

Katsouras. Before he started doing anything foolish with his money, he would try to do something for Doc Katsouras. Earmark twenty-five thousand, fifty thousand, for Katsouras, and get it to him anonymously. He could use it to finance his rehabilitation programs . . . stupid, ridiculous, impossible. Stolen money. It would be rubbing Doc's nose in his own failure. And Katsouras was a failure. His knife had skimmed the surface, it had never reached down to the core. He had proceeded on the theory that anti-social behavior was skin-deep. He was wrong. Samuel Butler, a scribbler, knew better: *The thief . . . Thieving is God's message to him . . .*

Almost with surprise, he felt himself slide off into sleep. He tried to hold it off, long enough to wrap up his thoughts neatly, but he had lost hold, and he slipped smoothly and pleasantly off the edge of consciousness.

Sunny came to his bed, laughing, eager, and opened wide to him. But when he tried to enter, Johnny Handsome was already there, positioned between her thighs, and their bodies were rising and falling, rising and falling. As she responded to the final thrusts, her face transfigured, she touched him crudely, contemptuously, and Johnny Handsome, burying himself deep in a final triumphant spasm, made her cry out in joy...

He woke, then slept again dreamlessly, and came awake rested, refreshed. On the other bed Bobby still snored in peaceful unbroken rhythm, his worn face a pitiful disclaimer to the tumble of rich black hair. He found a bathroom at the end of the hall, and sloshed cold water on his face until it glowed, smooth and ruddy in the mirror, the face of a fortunate stranger, a borrowed face. He went back to the room and put on his shoes. He started to slip into his gun harness, considered its weight, and tossed it on the bed, on top of the black suit and the grinning mask. Thus, he thought, I discard my guilt. The clothes, the mask, the gun are criminal; I myself am innocent.

As he started down the stairs he heard laughter from one of the rooms, creating a quick vivid image of Tully and Sunny on the bed, their bodies intertwined, the flesh young and rosy and eager. He remembered his dream, and grimaced. Downstairs, he went through the connecting hall to the living room. Battler was asleep on the sofa, his belt loosened, his white-gloved hands clenched in loose fists. His face was impassive, closed up. It was his professional fighter's face. Even in a dream it would not give pain away to an opponent.

He went back through the hallway, past the door that led down to the basement, and entered the kitchen. It was a very large room, what the real estate dealers called a country kitchen. The windows were long and narrow, set high on the far wall. Jappy was seated at an enormous round wooden table covered with a checked plastic cloth. The radio had been placed in the center of the table, and it droned steadily. Jappy's feet were propped against the rim of the table. The barracks bags were piled beside his chair. His hand made a reflexive movement toward his shotgun, standing on its butt beside him, propped against a kitchen cabinet, but turned into a gesture indicating the radio. Mitchell sat down.

The same announcer was still speaking, his voice weary but no longer amateur; he had won his brevet in the course of the long morning.

'. . . that the fire-bombing of police headquarters was tied in to the robbery of the bank. From his hospital bed, Amesville Police Chief Montrose has issued the following statement: "They timed it perfectly, not only knocking out the bank's alarm system, and dealing a severe blow to the effectiveness of the police department, but also creating a diversion. Nevertheless, we have not completely ruled out the possibility that the fire-bombing was the work of hippies or radicals. But at this time we are subscribing to the theory of state officers and others to the effect that it was the work of the bank gang. We'll get those murderers if it's the last thing we do," said Chief Montrose, unquote.'

Jappy grunted. 'There's a small-time cop for you. He's lying on his ass in a hospital, he don't have the slightest idea what happened or what's going on, but *he's* going to get us.'

'. . . statement from the Town Council. It was pointed out by Joseph J. Rankin, the minority leader, that the fire-bombing further points up the need for a modern police headquarters, and that this terrible tragedy would not have occurred if the Council majority had not delayed and hampered efforts to begin construction of the new all-brick fireproofed building . . .'

'The politicians,' Jappy said. 'Right in there pitching.' He kicked one of the money bags. 'Maybe we can show our appreciation by making a contribution to the building fund.'

'. . . we now go back by remote to Marve Holman at temporary police headquarters in Town Hall. Come in, Marve . . .'

The new voice faded in, '. . . Special Agent Krantz, of the Federal Bureau of Investigation, who is at this moment in conference with the First Selectman. When he emerges we will attempt to secure a statement. Meanwhile, I have an important bulletin from Captain Hamilton, state police. I quote: "It is now the belief of the division that the gang has succeeded in evading our cordons. However, our vigil will continue to be maintained around the clock until every avenue is exhausted . . . " '

'Bullshit,' Jappy said. 'They haven't got enough cops for around the clock. Besides, they're convinced we got away long before they could set up the roadblocks.'

' . . . "a thirteen-state alarm. These men are killers, cold-blooded fiendish killers, and the entire resources of this state have been marshaled in the effort to apprehend them. From the speed and ruthless precision with which this gang struck, it's clear that they are highly professional bank robbers. We are presently making an exhaustive study of M.O.'s – modus operandi – and we are hopeful that this will lead us to the criminals' identification and ultimate capture. The F.B.I. has entered the case and is cooperating fully." '

'See,' Jappy said with soft vindictivness. 'It pays to be a small-timer. We haven't *got* any M.O. Right, Mitchell?'

For an instant Mitchell thought he had caught a note of abrasiveness in Jappy's voice. But he was smiling, relaxed. Mitchell looked across the table neutrally at Jappy and shrugged.

'I'm just beginning to feel it,' Jappy said. 'The money. A million. I'm a millionaire.'

'I hate to spoil your fun, Jappy, but *we* have a million, it's not all yours.'

'Is that right? How much *is* my share?'

And now there was no mistaking it – an overtone of sharpness, of challenge. He said carefully, 'Exactly? You're better at numbers that I am, *you* figure it.'

'No. I want *you* to say it. Tell me what I'm taking out of

this job. If you can't tell me exactly, give it to me in round numbers. Okay, Mitchell?'

Mitchell's hand moved from his lap toward his left side, but he aborted the gesture before it was fairly started: he wasn't wearing his harness, he had left his gun on the bed.

'I noticed that myself,' Jappy said, 'when you came in. You're not wearing your piece.'

Mitchell got up, knocking over his chair, but he knew even as he moved that it was hopeless. Jappy had the shotgun in his hand.

'Pick up the chair,' Jappy said. 'Pick it up and sit down on it, or I'll blow you to pieces. Both barrels at one time. They're both loaded again. Pick up your chair and sit down.'

Mitchell righted the chair and sat down. In as level a voice as he could muster, he said, 'Okay, you've scared the crap out of me, Jappy. What's the idea?'

'Put your hands on the top of your head, and I'll tell you, Johnny.'

He lifted his hands to his head. 'Who?'

'Johnny Handsome – right?' Jappy smiled. 'I've been on to you for quite a while. Surprised, Johnny?'

'No. I'm not surprised.' The evenness of his voice pleased him. Not that it mattered; he was finished. 'You've been telegraphing it ever since I came into the room.'

18

And so, Mitchell thought, he had been betrayed by Kat-souras, not knowingly, but out of vanity – claiming more for the perfection of his surgery than was justified.

He looked across the table at Jappy, or, rather, at the gun. Jappy's left palm cradled the barrel, and the index finger of his right hand rested in a slight curl on the forward trigger. His hands were steady, and Mitchell took some small comfort in that; if he was killed, it would not be by accident. The radio continued to babble, and it reminded Mitchell that he had a voice of his own. He said, 'Yes, I'm Johnny Handsome. But does it make any difference?'

'Oh, yes.' Jappy's manner was almost jovial. 'It makes a big difference.'

'Look. When I first showed up, if I had told you I was Johnny Handsome, you would have tossed me out.'

'Right,' Jappy said agreeably.

'Right. And then there wouldn't have been any bank job, and you wouldn't have your feet resting on a million dollars.'

'You feel I ought to be grateful to you? Okay, I'm grateful.'

Mitchell lifted his gaze from the shotgun to Jappy's face.

'Okay, I made some wild threats. I was pissed off when you let me take a fall, but it was all talk, and it was six years ago.'

'Sure,' Jappy said. 'All talk.'

His affability was an impenetrable roadblock, Mitchell

thought. He let a moment go by, and then said, 'How did you tumble, Jappy? Somebody at Fredding told you I got plastic surgery?'

'Why should I tell you?' Jappy smiled. 'But what's the difference? Yes, it was somebody at Fredding.'

'When did you find out?'

Jappy's smile broadened. 'A long time ago.'

'Bullshit. You bought me – right down the line.'

'I conned you,' Jappy said. 'I'm a good actor.'

'Maybe *you* are, but not any of the others. They're not smart enough to put on a performance. They would have tipped it.'

Jappy nodded. 'I knew that. So I didn't tell them. They *still* don't know who you are.'

Yes, Mitchell thought, Jappy had pulled it off. Each of them had been playing the same game, running the same bluff, but in the showdown Jappy's hand was stronger. It was Jappy's pot. He was tapped out, the game was over. The smart player knew when he was beaten. Why demean himself by pleading for his life? No. No! It wasn't demeaning to try to survive. If it was, then everybody demeaned himself every day of his life.

He said, 'Look, Jappy, I'm Johnny Handsome, but I made you a million dollars. I popped off six years ago, but I haven't done anything to hurt you.'

'You *used* me,' Jappy said, and there was a hint of passion in his voice. 'When you came back here in disguise you were *using* me.'

Disguise. Mitchell tasted the word. Yes, Jappy had inadvertently hit on something. He wasn't a different Johnny with a different face, but the same Johnny wearing a disguise. Jappy knew more than Katsouras did. Katsouras was just a make-up artist, a provider of disguises.

'The boys will be waking up in a little while,' Jappy said, 'and then we'll get all settled. It'll be quite a little surprise for them.'

202

'What are you going to do with me, Jappy?'

'Kill you.'

It hadn't been an idle question. The answer was something that Mitchell had needed to hear, to stoke up his resolve. Nothing was left now but a desperation move, and it would have to be very soon. As bad as the odds against him were now, they would be impossible when the others joined them. He assessed his meager chances swiftly. The huge table between him and Jappy was an insurmountable obstacle. He would be dead before he got half-way around it. But he might be able to surprise Jappy by diving across the table, hoping that the impetus would carry him into Jappy before he could readjust the tilt of he gun downward and fire. It was a rotten chance, but it was the *only* one.

He gathered himself together, tensing for the spring, but a sudden squeaking sound behind him broke his concentration. He turned around instinctively. The cellar door was open, and Shannon was standing in the passageway.

Hope leaped up in him like a delirium and then died in the instant of its birth. Shannon might have heard about the robbery on the radio and put two and two together, but he wouldn't have known where to come. He had never told Shannon where their hideaway was located. And now, in this moment, he understood everything, and knew how completely and hopelessly he was doomed.

Shannon produced a police positive and weighed it tenderly in his hand. Then, smiling, he said to Jappy, 'Put that cannon away, you'll blow down a wall if you let it go. I can handle him with this little thing.' He turned his smile toward Mitchell. 'Can't I, sweetheart?'

19

Jappy was at some pains to make it clear that he hadn't blown his cool, that neither caprice nor cruelty was influencing his imposition of the death sentence.

'If it was just finding out you were Johnny Handsome, like you said, I'd boot you out on your ass and let it go at that. But you tried to pull a vicious double-cross, you tried to screw me out of every penny of the score. That's the reason why I'm going to waste you.' He paused, and then said coldly, 'You miserable sonofabitch.'

They were seated around the kitchen table, and the homeliness of the setting, taken with the conversational tone of their voices, gave the appearance of a casual get-together of friends or family. Jappy had laid the shotgun across his lap, but he kept his hand on it. Shannon sat with his revolver zeroed in on Mitchell's chest, the safety off, the gun braced on his left wrist in a fixed emplacement. His light eyes wore a lazy expression of mingled amusement and contempt, but Mitchell knew that he would not be taken by surprise.

'I'll put you out quick,' Jappy said, 'even though you deserve to have a slow death. I'm giving up the satisfaction of making you suffer before wasting you.'

'Well,' Mitchell said, 'satisfaction isn't everything.'

Jappy said to Shannon, 'What's it like out there?'

'Official cars all over the place. On the way here I ran into a few roadblocks, but they're loosening up already, they're running people through pretty quick. By now they're convinced you escaped, and they're mostly going through the motions. But they're goddamn mad because those two cops were killed. Did you have to shoot them?'

'We didn't shoot them just for fun. It happened, it was bad luck.'

Shannon said, 'I'm a police officer, you know, and don't forget it. I don't like to see cops get killed.'

'Apologise to him, Jappy,' Mitchell said. 'He rates an apology for his delicate feelings.'

They ignored him. He was already written off, Mitchell thought, already a corpse, and you didn't use up breath talking to the dead. He wondered what dying would be like. A flash of pain, of dread realisation, and then no anguish, no frustrations, no destroying angers . . . Well, he would have one mourner, anyway, when the news reached Katsouras. Or would Katsouras rage at his corpse for treachery?

Shannon's pale blue eyes were watching him shrewdly. 'Thinking it over, Johnny? Wishing you had done it different? Or not at all?'

'I made only one mistake, Lieutenant – failing to guess that a man with your sense of honor, a guardian of the public morals, would pull a double-cross.'

'When you cross a double-crosser you're not crossing *anybody.* It cancels out, bum.'

Mitchell said, 'With all due respect for your strong moral convictions, Lieutenant, I still don't know why you turned against me. Why bother?'

'You really can't figure it yourself?' Shannon's voice was playful. 'I just looked around for better odds. The weak part of your deal was that it would leave four very angry guys. Even though they weren't in any position to squeal, assuming they were in their right minds, there was always the outside possibility that one of them would blow his stack and decide he didn't give a shit what happened to him, as long as he could put the boots to *me.* Human nature is funny. Or suppose one of them got collared for another

205

job a few months from now, and decided either that he had nothing to lose by singing, or that he could make a bargain for leniency. Or suppose one of them plain flipped and came after me with a gun. So I almost blew the whole deal, until I figured out a simple way to beat it.'

He fumbled a cigarette from a pack with his left hand and snapped a lighter under it. The revolver didn't move, its round black eye never wavered from Mitchell's chest.

'Like I say, simple. If I went along with you and got Schroeder's cut, it figured that if I went along with Shroeder I would get your cut. The exact same money either way. But working with you, I had to worry about four enemies. With Schroeder, only one. You. Better odds. And if we got rid of that one, it reduced the odds to perfect. Nothing to worry about. *Zero* worry. So I got in touch with Mr. Schroeder. At first he wanted to call the whole thing off, but when I told him I wouldn't *let* him do that, he changed his mind. He even graciously agreed to match your offer and give me fifty percent of the take.'

'Yeah,' Jappy said. 'Gracious. I still have to break the news to my esteemed colleagues that their share will be a little less than they expected.'

Mitchell said, 'The others still don't know about me *or* Shannon?'

'They don't know *any* of it yet. I *had* to keep them in the dark. If I told them about you, they would have blown it, and I needed you for the job. Also, it was a kick that way – have you take the risk of robbing the bank and then get screwed once we scored. You appreciate the irony?'

'Mr. Schroeder wouldn't believe me at first,' Shannon said. 'Because it made him look stupid.'

'I wasn't stupid. I just didn't make you as Johnny Handsome. You fooled me *that* way, all right.'

'But once he started to believe it,' Shannon said, 'he believed it very good.'

'And nor could I tell them about Shannon,' Jappy said.

'It would have made them very nervous to know they were working with a cop. After all, they never worked with a cop before. Neither did I.'

'Well,' Mitchell said, 'maybe you'll learn to like it. Maybe you and Lieutenant Shannon can form a permanent partnership, and every time you make a score he can come around and collect fifty percent of it. Just because he's a nice guy.'

'Make jokes,' Jappy said placidly. 'Make all of them you can, because you're running out of time.'

Straining, Mitchell heard the distant sound of a toilet flushing. Someone would probably be coming downstairs soon. Or Battler would be waking. The others didn't yet know about him and Shannon . . . A forlorn, unshaped hope formed in his mind.

As though he had been following his thoughts, Jappy said, 'Let's get the rest in here and get them straightened out on everything.'

'Not that I can tell you how to to your job,' Mitchell said, dampening down his urgency, forcing himself to speak slowly, 'but did you consider that if you kill me now, you're going to have to spend another two days with me?'

'That's okay,' Shannon said. 'Dead, you're good company.'

'Decomposition,' Mitchell said. 'Inside of a few hours I'll be stinking so bad you won't be able to stay in the house.'

'You can't stink any worse than you do now,' Jappy said.

Shannon said, 'Wait a minute. He's right. I've walked in a few times on stiffs that started to decompose. You can't live with it. No *way*.'

Mitchell carefully let out his held breath. Listening hard, he thought he heard the squeak of an unoiled door hinge somewhere above.

'I guess it's a problem,' Jappy said. 'But I hate the idea of keeping him under guard for two days, it's risky . . . Wait. Those stiffs you were talking about – weren't they in small closed-in rooms or apartments? Suppose we just open up the windows?'

Shannon shook his head. 'You can't get rid of it all that way. Besides, you let the stink outside and everybody in the neighborhood starts to smell it. It's real powerful.'

'Two days,' Jappy said. 'Even if he's tied up, it means keeping a guard on him around the clock. It's dangerous.'

'You should have thought about this before you decided to kill me,' Mitchell said. 'Bad planning, Jappy.'

Shannon said, 'I tell you, you can't live with the stink.'

Mitchell heard footsteps above, moving through the hallway. It seemed impossible that neither Shannon nor Jappy was aware of it. But he was closer to the stairway than they were, and they were preoccupied with the problem he had raised. But in a matter of seconds . . .

'Look,' he said, trying to pitch his voice loud enough to cover the footsteps without raising their suspicions, 'I've changed my mind. I might as well get it right away. Dying is one thing . . . ' He paused for a breath, and heard the footsteps begin to descend. He went on quickly: 'Sitting around and waiting for it is something else. I'm not that brave.'

'You changed your mind awful goddamn fast,' Jappy said. 'Who told us about the decomposition?'

He plunged on, not even listening for the footsteps now. 'I told you about the decomposition because I wanted to stall. Now I think it's easier to go fast. So I'll tell you what to do. Send out for a couple of hundred pounds of ice cubes, pack them around –'

Tully appeared in the doorway.

'Shannon! Cop!' Mitchell shouted. 'Shoot him!'

He flung himself off his chair to the left, and heard Jappy scream, 'No! Kill Mitchell!'

A gun boomed, and he knew that Shannon had fired. Falling behind the table, he felt a tearing pain in the right side of his chest, high, just below the shoulder. As he hit the floor, twisting, he caught a glimpse of Tully tugging at the gun in his holster. In the next moment he heard a rush of feet and the hoarse sleep-thickened sound of Battler's voice.

He dove under the table, and on his hands and knees, scrambled for Jappy's legs at the far end, antic in rage as he screamed incoherently at Tully. He moved awkwardly, like a crab, desperate with haste, his head thumping the table. There were more shots, a half dozen of them, impinging on each other, filling the room with a hideous stuttering racket. He heard someone scream and someone else grunt. He thumped his head a last time, and then flung himself forward, his fingers reaching for Jappy's ankles. At his touch, Jappy began to back-pedal frantically in a strange high-kicking dance. One of his ankles shook loose. Mitchell clung grimly to the other, but Jappy, bracing himself on his free leg, kicked free of his grasp. Mitchell fell forward, his chin cracking the floor smartly. He lunged forward again, aware that Jappy was backing away, lowering the angle of the shotgun. Something crashed into Jappy and cut him down. It was Shannon, falling heavily, his weight catching Jappy across the knees and thighs, like a tackle taking out a charging guard.

The three of them were intertwined, a huddle of unwilling bodies, limbs threshing in blind terror. Shannon's face came forward and touched his own. He jerked away from its wetness, and realised that he had taken some of Shannon's blood, that a part of Shannon's jaw had been shot away. Shannon's pale eye was staring furiously into his own, and he felt something poke into his ribs. He reached instinctively to grab it, and so he was holding the barrel in his hand when Shannon fired. The slug hit him with the force of a heavy kick. He gasped, but clung to the gun, and when he jerked at it reflexively, it came away, free of Shannon's grip. Shannon fell forward on his bloody face.

Jappy was still entangled, still struggling to bring the shotgun around to bear, but he had no purchase, so that the gun waved around erratically. Mitchell clubbed at Jappy's moving hand with the butt of Shannon's revolver, and heard it strike bone glancingly. But Jappy held tight to the shotgun. Grunting, Jappy pulled up to a sitting position and humped himself backward across the floor, frantically trying to give himself shooting room. Mitchell reversed Shannon's revolver and fired at Jappy point-blank. The revolver jumped upward, and Jappy's face disappeared in a flash of bright red. He fell over backward, a dead weight.

Mitchell took the shotgun from Jappy's inert fingers and swung toward the kitchen doorway, the sharpness of the movement pulling a gasp of pain from him. Between the legs of the table he saw Tully and Battler lying on the floor. Tully was still, his eyes open in a sightless stare. Battler was half reclining, supporting himself on his elbow, his body jerking convulsively as he vomited blood in a terrible red eruption.

A movement behind him caught Mitchell's attention. Shannon was trying to rise. He was bent forward, his forehead braced against the floor, his jaw awash with blood. With his head as a fulcrum, he was trying to lever himself to his knees.

A stirring in the doorway flashed in a corner of Mitchell's vision. Bobby was standing there, his automatic in his hand, his dark face bewildered, his eyes fuzzy with the deep sleep that a noisy gun battle had barely waked him from.

Mitchell rolled onto his stomach, feeling blood flow from his wounds with the jolt. He pointed the shotgun at Bobby's middle. 'Put your gun up, Bobby.' His voice was low, congested, so that he could not be sure that Bobby had heard him.

'Jesus Christ,' Bobby said. 'Jesus God Almighty.'

'It's all right,' Mitchell said. 'Just take it easy, just put your gun up.'

Bobby seemed aware of him for the first time. His eyes widened, but there was no sentience in them, and he couldn't have known what he was doing beyond reflex, when he began to fire. His first shot struck Mitchell in the stomach and the second went wild. Just before the third, Mitchell, almost indifferent to the new searing shock of being hit, pulled the forward trigger of the shotgun. The roar was deafening, a physical force. He saw Bobby jump back against the wall, propelled by the impact of the slugs. He bounced back, his hands clawing at his body, and then doubled up and fell like a sack, leaving traces of himself on the wall, bits of skin and clothing and flesh . . .

Mitchell lowered his head for a second in weariness and pain, then turned. Shannon had at last made it to his hands and knees, and he was moving straight toward Mitchell, white bone showing through the redness of his shattered jaw. Mitchell watched him without feeling. He felt on the verge of blacking out. But he had to hold on, he had to deal with Shannon. Slowly, cumbersomely, he brought the shotgun around toward Shannon. It was very heavy, his hands were trembling, and the stock and barrel were slippery with his own blood. He dragged the gun upward, and then it was a race in slow motion to determine whether Shannon would reach him before he could find the trigger with his numbed finger, or before drowsiness overcame him.

Shannon extended his hand toward the short barrel. There was a booming roar, and as Mitchell started to fall away from the sound, from the kitchen, in a sick whirling fade, he saw Shannon's head disintegrate in a brilliant flowing flash of red.

The last sound he heard was silence.

20

He had wet the bed. It surrounded him, warm, moist, pungent, a sanctuary, until the moment of discovery, his mother screaming and cursing as she flailed away at his dodging head. If he managed to catch most of the wild stinging slaps on his hand and arms, there was never any escape from the lash of that hate-filled voice. Urine, a cocoon, bathing his middle and legs, and the acrid smell . . . The acrid smell, pinching his nostrils, but blended now with something sweeter.

He opened his eyes.

'I thought you were dead.'

He placed himself back in the kitchen of the house on Brainerd Street. Not urine but blood. Not pee-smell but the sharpness of cordite mixed with the sweetness of blood. He was soaked with blood, lying in it, the floor was awash with it. Not all his own. His foot was resting against the softness of flesh, a thigh. Jappy's. No, Shannon's. Shannon had been in front of him, facing him, and he had blown Shannon's head off. Jappy would be off to his right, somewhere. He turned his head and saw Jappy's body in its own private pool of blood; some of it had found a crack in the linoleum and sent off a thin seeking tributary.

His gut was a grinding center of fire. It was using up his breath. It couldn't be borne. It would destroy him; not the wound but the pain. Another wound, in the side, where Shannon had shot him. It was not bad, he must have pushed the barrel away from him by instinct, and the bullet had clipped him and gone on its way. A third wound – the first, actually – below his shoulder. He became aware of his blood seeping away. Not flowing but seeping, slowly. Maybe he was bled out, not enough pressure to cause a flow. Like the beer at the bottom of a barrel, not enough pressure, so you had to tilt the barrel. Must be careful not to tilt himself . . .

Someone had spoken, from some far distance above him.

He was very weak, played out. He wanted to sleep. His eyes shut. When he opened them again he knew that he had blacked out. But he felt rested, stronger. If only the pain wasn't so bad. Without the pain he would be able to function. He was parched, his lips were puffed, cracked. His thirst was enormous. Dehydrated. He had to have water. But he remembered something about not drinking water with a stomach wound. Why? Would it run out the holes? But if he could suck on something, a saturated rag, it would relieve his thirst. He wouldn't have to swallow any of it, just moisten his lips . . .

'When you shut your eyes you look dead. You fooled me. I thought you died again.'

Sunny's voice. He found her. She was seated on a straight wooden chair, he legs wedged into the rungs, as if in refuge against a rising tide of blood on the floor. From this angle she was distorted – her head remote, the line from her waist to her knee impossibly long. Her back was very straight, as if she had set it resolutely to deny the existence of anything behind her, especially the far wall with its gruesome remnants of Bobby – the blood drying now in long wavering vertical streamers, dark viscous splotches where flesh or entrails had clung before surrendering to gravity and falling, bits of skin, hair . . . Bobby's body had tumbled onto Tully's; they lay there together, stacked, like sides of bloody meat. Bobby's head was hidden; he couldn't tell if his hairpiece had remained in place. Battler? Battler had been alive.

As if reading his mind, she said, 'They're all dead.' Her

213

voice was uninflected, bleak. She was old; her youth had run its course in minutes, seconds. 'All dead.'

His idea had worked. Tully had fired at Shannon, and Shannon had fired back. Battler and Shannon had fired. They had all killed each other. Congratulations.

He raised himself slightly on his elbow. It was easier to manage than he had thought, except for the pain. He sought out Sunny's face. It was blank, and her eyes were leeched of expression; not even dazed, merely empty. Out of it. Zonked out.

He said, 'What time is it?' She gave no indication that she had heard him. He tried wetting his stiff parched lips, and said slowly and distinctly, 'I asked you what time it is.'

She studied her wristwatch with infinite care. 'Two-thirty.'

He heard the radio. It still sat in the center of the table; it had survived everything. A muted jazz tune came out of it. He said, 'Why aren't they talking about the bank?' His voice sounded strange, somebody else's voice.

'I changed the station.' The blankness of her eyes yielded to puzzlement. 'You're talking funny.' He understood. He had regressed, let the air stream come through his nose. She said, 'Everybody is dead, quite dead. Like they say, quite dead.'

He noticed something odd about Shannon. His eyes were intact in the ruin of his face, but they were askew, on a different plane from each other, shot out of line.

He said, 'I'm sorry about Tully. I didn't shoot him.'

'Who?'

She was wigged out, totally out of it. He looked at Jappy, sprawled among the barracks bags. Their rough canvas pores had soaked up some of his blood. Would it please Jappy to know that so vital a part of him had merged with the money? Blood money. Have to wash it before using. Never mind – there was so much of it you could afford to throw away the stained bills. He smiled.

'What's so funny?'

Her voice came to him from a far distance, and he wondered if he had passed out again. The smell in the kitchen was nauseating him.

He said, 'It stinks in here. Open a window.' She nodded, but didn't move, 'Open a window, Sunny, I'm feeling sick.'

'Open it yourself.'

He said, 'We have to get out of here. The air is rotten.' He lost the train of his thought in a fog of pain. It cleared. 'The money. Let's get to a doctor so I can get fixed up. No problem with paying for it. I can pay well, you know, I can pay royally for medical services.'

'I'm not getting out of this chair. I'm not going to ruin my shoes.'

She had slipped away again; her eyes were empty. But he needed her help. He could move, he could get up, he was sure of that much, and the bleeding seemed to have slowed to a trickle. But he couldn't manhandle the money bags, he couldn't drive a car. Sunny had to help him.

'Sunny, listen to me. One thing at a time. First, get up from that chair – '

'I won't get my feet wet and ruin my shoes.'

'I'll buy you some new shoes. A dozen pairs. Thirty dollars a pair.'

'I've been paying up to forty and fifty. Thirty-dollar shoes don't make me cream, you know.'

He made a dry wordless sound. He couldn't push his voice past the parched stiffness of his lips. He paused, gathering his resources for the effort, and tried again. It worked. 'Find a cloth. Wet it and give it to me.'

'What for?'

'Thirsty. Do it. Then we'll leave.'

'You're dead, you can't leave.'

But she got off the chair, her face wearing an expression of finicky disgust. She put her feet down carefully, and on her toes, like an arthritic dancer on point, teetered over to

215

the sink. She found a dishcloth and held it under the faucet. She turned, the cloth dripping water.

'Bring it to me.'

She came hesitantly, still on her toes, her calf muscles taut, and stood above him. He raised his arm. The white glove was dyed red. Sunny gasped, and released the cloth and fled back to her chair. The cloth caught on his fingertips. He put it to his lips, wiping them lightly, feeling the cracked flesh catch in the threads of the cloth. Then he put the cloth in his mouth and sucked it, gently squeezing the water out, letting a little of it trickle down his throat.

'Sunny. Sunny?' He waited for her to focus on him. 'You see those bags? Take a look at them.' But she wouldn't, or couldn't, make the effort. He went on: 'They're full of money. A million dollars. Half of it is yours. Half a million. You'll never have to turn a trick again in your whole life.'

'I like to turn tricks.'

He paused, and sucked on the wet cloth. 'Have you ever been to Brazil, Sunny?'

'What?'

Her eyes were still fixed on him, but they were no longer focused. He tried to put more force in his voice, to bring her back. 'Brazil. South America. A paradise. It's where all the very best high-class crooks go – stockbrokers, politicians. No extradition. You and me – and a million dollars.'

'You and me? You and me *what*?'

'We'll go there together, maybe stay together . . . '

'You bastard, you never once gave me a serious look from the time you first saw me.'

'I wanted to. But Tully and you . . . so I didn't – '

'Don't hustle me. I'm no child.'

He sucked on the wet cloth again. 'Okay. But we still have to get away from here. We robbed a bank, we killed two cops – '

'*You* robbed a bank, *you* killed two cops.'

216

He shook his head. 'You're in it as deeply as I am. Accessory. You rented the house . . .'

Her eyes were wandering, moving in a slow aimless arc.

He said sharply, 'Listen to me, Sunny. Pay attention. In about one minute I'm going to get up. I can make it. But then I'm going to need your help. We'll take the barracks bags and throw them down the basement steps, and then take them out to your car. And then you'll drive me to that doctor I know. He'll fix me up. He has a vested interest in me, so he can't refuse.'

'He'll turn you over to the cops. Bullet wounds. That's the law, you know.'

'One thing at a time. First I want you to pull yourself together. Then, when I stand up –'

Her eyes came into focus. 'You're hustling again.'

'No. We can't stay here. You've got to help me.'

She tilted her head and looked at him with curiosity. 'Okay. I'll help you.'

Pain ignited in his middle and she drifted off. He drew his knees up, folding into himself, writhing, as he had seen crushed insects or animals do, and for the first time he wondered if he was dying. He drove his teeth into the dishcloth and bit through it, feeling his teeth meet and grind together. He lowered himself to the floor, gasping. The pain increased, piled up around him and buried him.

He came awake feeling rested. The pain had retreated to a distance. How long had he been out? No more than a minute. He stretched his legs and the pain returned at great speed. The cloth was still between his teeth. He bunched it together thickly and bit down on it. He lifted himself out of his blood and onto his elbow, and sighted in on Sunny sitting on her chair.

He said, 'Help me get up.'

She shook her head. 'I don't want to.'

217

He spoke to her patiently. 'I know what's best, Sunny. For both of us. What I want you to do —'

'It doesn't matter what you want. I phoned the cops.'

Still patient, and as to a child, he said, 'You couldn't have done that, Sunny.'

'I did, you know.' Oddly, she seemed to be trying to match his patience. 'When you were passed out.'

'I was only out a few seconds.'

'About ten minutes. They have an emergency police head-quarters set up in City Hall. I called them up.'

While he was thinking of what to say to her — how to convince her that she hadn't phoned the police, hadn't even left her chair — he knew suddenly that she was telling the simple truth.

'Why did you do that, Sunny?'

'I don't know why I did it.'

She was telling the truth. She didn't know. For a very brief instant he thought of killing her, but her death — her life — was irrelevant. He said gently, 'Sunny, go into the other room.'

Something warm and sweet welled up in his throat. He turned his head and coughed up a splatter of bright blood into the cloth. He wiped his lips clean before turning back to her.

'I told you to go away.'

She didn't say anything, but her image began to waver, blur, and then she disappeared. When he could focus clearly again, when the pain withdrew, he saw that she was no longer on the chair. He found her; she was moving toward the door, past the bodies of Battler and Tully and Bobby, not looking at them, perhaps not even aware of them, picking her way daintily, on her toes, seeking a path through the little lakes of blood. She stopped in the doorway, on dry land, and inspected her shoes.

He felt around for Shannon's .38, and closed his hand on it. Leaning on the revolver, using it for leverage, he began

218

the infinitely slow, rocking process of turning himself so that he faced head-on to the kitchen entrance. It took a long time, and the pain was very bad and did funny things to his breathing. Then it eased, and he wondered if he had blacked out again. He let himself down gingerly on his stomach. He lay still for a moment, with blood leaking from his mouth into the cloth. He rested for a moment, then bent his left arm at the elbow and slowly brought the revolver forward so that the heavy barrel nested in the crook of his elbow, held firm by the meeting of his bicep and forearm. He aimed it at the doorway, then lowered his cheek to the butt and sighted through it.

Sunny was in the sights.

He said, 'I told you to go out.' But his voice was a whisper, and she couldn't have heard him.

She said, 'They'll kill you if you do that.' She was looking at him appraisingly. 'You're handsomer than Tully. You know that?'

He nodded and said, 'I'll be the best-looking man in the whole cemetery.'

She wavered in the doorway, and when his vision steadied again, she was gone. But her final words lingered, and he regretted his wisecrack. He should have told her that his new face had never meant anything to him, that it had never been *his* face, and it still wasn't. Katsouras would never have understood that. Katsouras thought he had given him a face, but it was only a mask. Because his understanding was faulty, Katsouras had failed. And he had failed Katsouras. Everyone failed everyone else, and that was why it was a stinking world.

Sirens faded into his awareness, their screams reaching a crescendo, then dying in a roar of gunned motors and squealing tires. He heard the metallic slam of doors and shouting voices.

He pushed at his pain, trying to dislodge it by an exercise of will, and sighted on the doorway. That was his world now, that rectangular arch and a few feet of scuffed linoleum beneath it. That was what his world had shrunk down to.

His lids fluttered shut. He forced them open. Voices were whispering loudly in the living room. He heard a shuffle of heavy feet. Sunny's voice. More whispering. Total silence, ripped open by the sudden violence of a shout half hysterical with rage and fear.

'Throw your gun out! Throw your fucking gun out and walk on out with your hands on your head! Throw your gun out, you sonofabitch, or we'll blow your fucking head off! Throw your gun out, you bastard . . .'

He braced the revolver securely in the crook of his elbow. He nestled his cheek against the cool smoothness of the barrel.

He waited.

Taking Of Pelham One Two Three

JOHN GODEY

'The plot is simple. Four men hijack a tube train and demand a million dollar ransom. It is a thrill a minute trip, beautifully capturing the feel of all the people involved and of the city itself. I recommend it to the last line'   *Daily Mirror*

'An ingenious idea for a novel — all those characters, all those motives, all that nail-biting. A really exciting, tough thriller'   *Evening Standard*

'Impressive tour de force, well written and planned'
The Observer

The Man With The Black Worry Beads

GEORGE N. RUMANES

GREECE 1941

Across the Mediterranean Rommel is driving his way along the North African coast. Armies may stop him. But his most pressing need is for supplies. The supplies are aboard a fleet of ships docked in the port of Piraeus, close to Athens.

The man to prevent those ships leaving harbour is Petros Zervas – a young Greek saboteur with blue eyes, a sharp knife, a cunning mind and a hatred of Nazis for nationalist reasons. He is the man with the black worry beads.

Almost the first time anyone saw his name it was tattooed onto the belly of a local whore. The first time Major Cunningham of British Intelligence saw his face, he was stealing ammunition from a German arms dump. The first time Trudi Richter – mistress to the German Commandant – heard his voice, he had broken into her apartment and had a knife at her throat.

PACKED WITH ACTION, WITH MEMORABLE CHARACTERS, WITH A MASS OF DETAIL AND INCIDENT *THE MAN WITH THE BLACK WORRY BEADS* IS TRULY THE SORT OF BOOK THAT IT IS HARD TO PUT DOWN ONCE TAKEN UP

Green Dolphin Country

ELIZABETH GOODGE

Marianne · · ·

There was nothing in her immediate ancestry
to account for her headstrong nature or her
passionate hunger for life. Her mother had borne
her in passive rebellion to a man she did not love.
The fierce storm that raged on the night of her
birth seemed to have lent some of its own wildness
to the newborn baby.

And now Marianne, clever but awkward, was
sixteen years old. She day-dreamed restlessly
about the greater world beyond her quiet Channel
Island home. She wanted to discover an exciting
world that was forbidden to a well brought-up
Victorian girl. But most of all, she wanted William
her childhood sweetheart for herself. And
Marguerite, her pretty little sister, wanted him too.

'Breath-taking . . . a long vista of undulating story,
with here and there peaks of volcanic excitement'
Daily Telegraph

GENERAL FICTION FROM CORONET

JOHN GODEY

☐ 18772 7   The Taking of Pelham One
Two Three   40p

GEORGE N. RUMANES

☐ 18808 1   The Man with the Black
Worry Beads   40p

ELIZABETH GOUDGE

☐ 15105 6   Green Dolphin Country   75p
☐ 15104 8   The Scent of Water   40p

ROBERT LITTELL

☐ 18827 8   The Defection of A. J. Lewinter   40p

ANNE EDWARDS

☐ 18814 6   Haunted Summer   40p

ROBERT MARASCO

☐ 18989 4   Burnt Offerings   45p

TAYLOR CALDWELL

☐ 18800 6   Your Sins and Mine   40p
☐ 18801 4   To Look and Pass   35p

All these books are available at your bookshop or newsagent, or can be ordered direct from the publisher. Just tick the titles you want and fill in the form below.

CORONET BOOKS, P.O. Box 11, Falmouth, Cornwall.

Please send cheque or postal order. No currency, and allow the following for postage and packing:

1 book—10p, 2 books—15p, 3 books—20p, 4–5 books—25p, 6–9 books—4p per copy, 10–15 books—2½p per copy, 16–30 books —2p per copy, over 30 books free within the U.K.

Overseas – please allow 10p for the first book and 5p per copy for each additional book.

Name ....

Address ....

....

....